sons of darkness,
sons of light

JOHN A. WILLIAMS

sons of darkness,
sons of light

A Novel of Some Probability

with a new foreword by RICHARD YARBOROUGH

Northeastern University Press : BOSTON

Northeastern University Press

Library of Congress Cataloging-in-Publication Data

Williams, John Alfred, 1925–
    Sons of darkness, sons of light : a novel of some
  probability ; foreword by Richard Yarborough /
  John A. Williams.
        p.   cm.—(Northeastern library of Black literature)
    ISBN 1-55553-396-5 (alk. paper)
    1. Afro-Americans—New York (State)—New York—
  Fiction.   I. Title.   II. Series.
  PS3573.I4495S66   1999
  813'.54—dc21   99-15203

Printed and bound by Edwards Brothers, Inc., Lillington,
North Carolina. The paper is Glatfelter Offset, an acid-free
sheet.

MANUFACTURED IN THE UNITED STATES OF AMERICA
03   02   01   00   99   5   4   3   2   1

To Harry Sions

After they have withdrawn from the slain towards the encampment, they shall all together sing the hymn of return. In the morning they shall launder their garments, wash themselves of the blood of the guilty cadavers, and return to the place where they had stood, where they had arrayed the line before the falling of the enemy's slain.

COLUMN XIV SECTION XXI
*The Scroll of the War of the Sons of Light
Against the Sons of Darkness*

foreword

The conquests of England, every single one of them bloody, are part
of what Americans have in mind when they speak of England's glory.
In the United States, violence and heroism have been made
synonymous except when it comes to blacks.

—James Baldwin, *The Fire Next Time*

To speak of themes such as the burden of empathy, the struggle for communication across racial, ethnic, gender, and gen-
erational lines, and the search for moral coherence as one
describes a novel that posits the near inevitability of interra-
cial warfare in the United States may seem paradoxical. However, this is precisely what confronts the reader of John A.
Williams's *Sons of Darkness, Sons of Light*. Published at the
height of the Black Arts movement and fueled by rage and
hope in equal measure, *Sons* is a fascinating novel written by
one of our most distinguished, if unjustly neglected, contemporary authors. Both deserve greater appreciation.

When *Sons of Darkness, Sons of Light* appeared in 1969,

the United States was in the midst of a remarkable and traumatic era. The Vietnam War showed no signs of slackening; and as the number of American casualties grew, domestic protest against U.S. involvement in Southeast Asia reached fever pitch, particularly on college campuses. With the assassinations of the Reverend Martin Luther King, Jr., and Robert F. Kennedy, 1968 seemed especially marked by tragedy and death. To many, these murders signified the passing of the last best chance for unifying a nation increasingly torn by violent confrontation and ideological extremism.

King's death in particular constituted the final straw for many African Americans, and violence erupted in 125 cities in the wake of his shooting in Memphis. Although perhaps unprecedented in terms of intensity and the sheer number of locales involved, these civil disturbances represented but the latest in a series of outbreaks in black communities dating back to the Watts uprising in Los Angeles in 1965. Each subsequent year brought apprehension that the country was in for another "long, hot summer" as, to paraphrase King, blacks' "legitimate discontent" increasingly found outlet in violence and confrontational politics. The Kerner Commission's report in 1968 that the United States was moving toward two nations—"one white, one black, separate and unequal"—simply confirmed what so many African Americans saw played out in their everyday lives, despite the dramatic progress that had been made as a result of the Civil Rights movement. The same anger and militancy that the medal-winning black sprinters Tommie Smith and John Carlos displayed to widespread condemnation in their protest at the 1968 Olympics also drove African American citizens to take to the streets in frustration with a country that was tiring of claims on its conscience. The assault by the Chicago police force on the protesters at the

Democratic National Convention, the shutting down of Resurrection City, which had been constructed in the nation's capital as part of the Poor People's March on Washington, and the election of Richard Nixon on a Republican platform advocating a return to "law and order" all appeared to mark the end of society's willingness to address directly issues of social justice.

The political radicalism among African Americans in the last years of the 1960s is evident in the literature of the period, with the rise of black cultural nationalism and of what the critics Hoyt Fuller and Addison Gayle termed the "Black Aesthetic." Many African American writers viewed their art as a potentially efficacious weapon in the broader black liberation struggle, and they turned their backs on white expectations and mainstream literary conventions as they sought new languages and forms for their new militant spirit. In 1968 and 1969 alone, the following works appeared: *Black Pride* by Don L. Lee, *Cities Burning* by Dudley Randall, *Homecoming* by Sonia Sanchez, *Bloodline* by Ernest Gaines, *Howard Street* by Nathan Heard, *Riot* by Gwendolyn Brooks, *Black Magic Poetry* by Amiri Baraka, *Die Nigger Die!* by H. Rap Brown, *Soul on Ice* by Eldridge Cleaver, *This Child's Gonna Live* by Sarah Wright, *Hue and Cry* by James Alan McPherson, *All-Night Visitors* by Clarence Major, *The Life and Loves of Mr. Jiveass Nigger* by Cecil Brown, *Once* by Alice Walker, *My Main Mother* by Barry Beckham, *Yellow Back Radio Broke-Down* by Ishmael Reed, and *The Chosen Place, the Timeless People* by Paule Marshall. At the heart of this unprecedented outpouring of black literature was John A. Williams, who was acknowledged, even then, to stand at the front rank of American novelists of his generation, regardless of race.

Born in Jackson, Mississippi, in 1925 and raised in Syracuse, New York, Williams did not achieve literary celebrity easily or early in life. After a stint in the navy, which he joined in 1943 (and where he began writing), he returned to Syracuse, completed high school, and got married. In 1950 he graduated from Syracuse University with a degree in Journalism and English, and he immediately entered graduate school there. The fifties for Williams were marked by a struggle to find meaningful labor as he worked in a foundry, a supermarket, and then the Onandaga County welfare office. With the dissolution of his marriage, he moved to Los Angeles in 1954, only to return east two years later, this time to New York City. For the remainder of the decade, he held jobs with a number of publishers as he sought futilely to sell his own fiction.

Williams's luck finally turned in 1960, when Ace Books issued a paperback edition of his first novel, *The Angry Ones*. Since then, and despite occasionally mixed reviews and uneven sales, Williams has established himself as among the most prolific authors of our time. He has produced more than ten novels and several works of nonfiction, including biographies of Martin Luther King, Jr., *The King God Didn't Save* (1970), and Richard Wright, *The Most Native of Sons* (1970). He has edited such influential collections as *The Angry Black* (1962), *Yardbird I* (1979), and *Amistad I* and *II* (1970, 1971; with Charles F. Harris); and in 1998 he published a collection of poetry, entitled *Safari West*. In addition, since 1968 he has held teaching positions at a number of major colleges, most recently Rutgers University.

Without question, the release in 1967 of *The Man Who Cried I Am* marked the zenith of Williams's literary career in terms of critical attention. Although the novel was immediately lauded as among the most uncompromising and important books of the year, the glowing notices unfortunately did not translate into income. Williams recalled his approach to his next novel, *Sons of Darkness, Sons of Light*, this way:

> I sat down and wrote it comparatively quickly compared to the other books. This was a reaction to my continued poverty after *The Man Who Cried I Am* came along. It looked as if finally, I'd be able to make a little money and help both the boys [his two sons] who were in college at that time. The critical acclaim was good, but I was just as poor as I had always been. . . . So, I sat down and wrote this book.[1]

Indeed, Williams has on several occasions expressed some displeasure with *Sons*, describing it as a "potboiler" in an interview: "I just feel that it came too easily. It was one of those novels that I don't like very much, that I call a 'straight ahead' novel. You start at A and wind up at Z and then you get off the train."[2] The author's own reservations about the text duly noted, *Sons* stands as a fascinating achievement of an audacious and fertile imagination, and it manifests a key stage in Williams's political and literary development. He said at one point:

> I'm not sorry I did it [*Sons*]. In the process of working it out I came to see pretty much the kind of things that would have to happen for any revolution to become a success and also the things that couldn't happen.[3]

In addition, to the extent that it is very much a novel of its time, *Sons* dramatizes a moment in American cultural history the complexity of which we have yet to appreciate fully. Finally, Williams's skills are such that even a novel that he

ranks among his lesser works remains a rich and fruitful text
that rewards serious analysis and multiple readings.

As a first step to gauging the significance of *Sons of Darkness, Sons of Light,* one must keep in mind that it is but one
in a number of militant revolutionary fantasies that constitute
a small but important strain in the African American fictive
tradition. Other notable examples include Martin Delany's
Blake, Sutton Griggs's *Imperium in Imperio,* Arna Bontemps's
Black Thunder, George Schuyler's *Black Empire,* and Sam
Greenlee's *The Spook Who Sat by the Door.* Given the extent
to which so much black political thought in the late 1960s
focused on attempts to envision radically new social possibili-
ties, it is hardly surprising that fiction set in the near-future
(1973 in *Sons*) would appeal to Williams. This format allowed
him not only to comment directly upon the state of contempo-
raneous race relations but also to present his speculations with
the immediacy of the next day's headlines. When he subtitled
Sons "A Novel of Some Probability," he was issuing an ex-
plicit warning that the cataclysmic events of the book might
not be as far away as some of his readers would like to think.

The opening gambit in the violent racial drama in *Sons*
is, for Williams, an all-too-common occurrence: the shooting
death of a black youth by a white police officer. What is un-
common here, however, is the response to this event on the
part of the protagonist, Eugene Browning, a political science
professor who is now second-in-command at a civil rights organization called the Institute for Racial Justice. Like a number of Williams's heroes, Browning has reached the point of
philosophical and emotional exhaustion in the face of unyield-
ing racism and futile political strategies. He thinks bitterly
early in the novel:

You could work in a famous and vigorous civil rights organization . . . ; you could work with all your heart and what was left of your soul, but you also had to know, finally, that none of that was going to do any good; that you had to obtain your goals by almost the same means *Chuck* [the white man] obtained his, remained the only obvious conclusion, and Chuck did not get his with Freedom Now or Love Your Brother marches.

Later, Browning explains the shift in his attitude this way:

Intelligence doesn't have anything to do with how much a man can take. It can help him to rationalize away the use of violence, thinking about his own skin, but that same intelligence will tell him, finally, that he's got no choice but to be as tough as the next guy or tougher.

To put it more directly, Browning determines, "It would always be open season on blacks until blacks opened the season on whites." Having reached this conclusion, he hires the Mafia to kill the white policeman responsible for the shooting. In one of many ironies that pepper the novel, Browning pays for this service using funds that he has solicited on behalf of the Institute for Racial Justice, a group dedicated to nonviolence.

This apparently straightforward act of cold-blooded, premeditated retaliation spawns the complex plot twists that may have led Williams to term the book a potboiler. However, the real strength of the novel lies not in the intricate interweaving of numerous lines of action but rather in the subjectivity that Williams permits the book's large cast of characters and the humanity with which he invests them.

To anyone exposed to Williams's thematic concerns in *The Man Who Cried I Am,* aspects of *Sons* will strike familiar chords. Among them is Williams's fascination with the dilemma of the black male intellectual caught between a commitment to self-control and rational analysis on the one hand and, on the other, the insistent provocations of a world that seems to have whittled his choices down to either violence or humiliating self-abnegation. However, whereas *The Man Who Cried I Am* focuses primarily upon the experiences of a single character, Max Reddick, *Sons* is more diffuse in perspective, incorporating a remarkable range of points of view. Eugene Browning is clearly the protagonist of the book, but Williams offers us several alternative centers of consciousness, including Browning's wife, Valerie; Mantini, the Mafia elder who supervises the murder; Itzhak Hod, the Israeli hit man whom the Mafia hire; and even John Carrigan, the white policeman responsible for the death of the Harlem teenager. Although some of these figures are more effectively presented than others, their sheer diversity usefully complicates our reading of the novel. Indeed, Williams's commitment to these multiple voices reflects his vision of race relations in the United States as multiethnic long before "cultural diversity" became an all-too-easily-invoked catchphrase.

What Williams so potently renders here and elsewhere in his fiction is the complexity of individual human beings whose choices and behaviors constitute any historical moment. Much of his work, in fact, is driven by his obsession both with historical process writ large and with the unanticipated impact of such process on the messy, chaotic lives of real men and women. For Williams, the personal is the political and vice versa; and his maturity, insight, and suspicion of easy answers keep this novel from toppling over into reductive melodrama.

Williams's approach consistently highlights relationship and human interaction. Accordingly, among the most intriguing aspects of *Sons* is the series of encounters that Browning has with members of the black bourgeoisie as he travels the country seeking funds for his organization. This "odyssey of disillusionment through the world of the black business and professional elites, big-time entertainers, star athletes, and socialites,"[4] as one critic puts it, is a conceptual tour de force that few other writers could carry off. Williams's humanistic perspective on his material is manifested as well in the crucial place that Browning's rocky marriage comes to occupy in the book. As odd as it might seem, this novel about armed revolt is, again like much of Williams's work, centrally concerned with love, connection, and family and the difficulty of holding onto those things in a world full of betrayal, shallowness, racism, manipulation, and violence. That *Sons* ends with a physical act of love that occurs at some remove from the conflict sweeping through urban America reinforces this sense of Williams's thematic priorities.

In an interview conducted in 1971, Williams describes his view of the role of the African American writer this way:

> I think the black writer has two functions of equal importance. One is that given this time and its processes, he really has to deal with and for his people. He has to become an educator, a teacher, a storyteller, a satirist, any vehicle that will help make his people aware of their positions. At the same time, he's also bound to become an expert in his craft: writing a novel, writing poetry, what have you.[5]

Although nowhere near the monumental achievement of *The Man Who Cried I Am*, *Sons* effectively manifests the dual commitment to which Williams alludes here. The critical response to *Sons* was, with rare exception, tepid; reviewers complained about the bitter despair informing the novel, the ambitious plotting, and the thinness of certain characterizations. As Williams himself has conceded, the book is hardly without flaws, particularly when contrasted with the more widely acknowledged achievements represented by *The Man Who Cried I Am* and *Captain Blackman*, the novels released just before and after *Sons*. Nonetheless, with its bold envisioning of social possibility, its honesty, its unsparingly critical perspective on human motivation, and its acceptance of human frailty, *Sons of Darkness, Sons of Light* is a book of no inconsequential force and one that still speaks powerfully to us today.

RICHARD YARBOROUGH

Notes

1. Earl A. Cash, *John A. Williams: The Evolution of a Black Writer* (New York: Third Press, 1975), 138.

2. John O'Brien, *Interviews with Black Writers* (New York: Liveright, 1973), 235.

3. Ibid., 242.

4. Sigmund Ro, *Rage and Celebration: Essays on Contemporary Afro-American Writing* (Atlantic Highlands, N.J.: Humanities Press, 1984), 101.

5. Cash, *Williams*, 147.

sons of darkness,
sons of light

one

Eugene Browning woke and groaned softly. This was to be the day. He looked around the room taking in the familiar objects; his robe and his wife's robe on the chair; the long twin chest of drawers, Val's cosmetics on the top; the mirror, a narrow, fashionable but not very utilitarian rectangle of silver; the van Gogh prints of Postman Roulin and the drawbridge at Arles. . . .

He had once met a couple who told of driving around Arles in search of the drawbridge, only to discover that it had been destroyed in 1935 because it was so old. Nineteen thirty-five was Ethiopia, was China, and there had been 1936 and Spain. A political scientist, like a historian, had an ear for dates, dates when great mistakes had been made, the ones you snapped your fingers over when they were charted out and found to be true moments when history could have been changed; true forks in true roads.

Browning's eye caught the Nigerian original painted in bright tempera. Why was it that Ibadan didn't have the same appeal as Arles? A Nigerian friend had given him the painting. The colors were even more brilliant than those in the van Goghs.

It's hot already, Browning thought. New York City in the summer. It was also sticky and he could feel the humidity banging dully in his sinuses. His armpits were already sopping wet.

His wife Val lay curled on her side facing him. Her sculptured lips were slightly open and above them the faintest of black down lay smoothly. Her long black lashes were made prominent by the brick-brown of her skin. He glanced up at her hair; she wore the "African Look," but preferred to call it the "Natural Look." Browning smiled to himself. Africa was the last place Val would ever wish to visit.

"Hey," he whispered. Maybe it would make him feel better, put a soft edge on this all-important day. He put a hand on her hip and worked her gown up. His fingers slid along the smooth, soft flesh.

"Uh-uh," she said, removing his hand.

He put his hand back. "C'mon, will you?"

"Uh-uh." She turned away from him.

"Oh, hell," he said.

She turned toward him, her eyes wide. "Oh, Gene, I'm sorry, dear —"

"To hell with it, just to hell with it," Browning said, making the sheet snap as he jumped from the bed and stomped into the bathroom, slamming the door after him.

Valerie Browning got up. It was going to be another one of those mornings; it was going to be all wrong again, like everything else these days. She glanced bitterly at the bathroom door. He knows if he wants his breakfast on time I have to get in there first, she thought.

She rushed through the apartment calling the girls and

pulling up the shades. She peered outside. This weather wasn't going to help anything either. She put up the coffee, the dry cereal and the milk and placed the bread in the toaster. The cold eggs in her hand made her think of her husband, and of her eldest daughter Nora. That damned girl, Valerie thought to herself. Kids just don't try to take it easy on their parents; anything goes. Coming in here with that white boy again last night. I didn't tell her *not* to, but she *knows* I don't like that sort of thing. People don't fool me one bit. I know they think she's a little whore already. Damn these kids and damn it all. She brushed away the biting tears that had come to her eyes. She hoped, by God, that Chris wouldn't give her trouble like that when she was eighteen, but if Nora set the example, what else could you expect?

And Gene. What on earth was happening to that man? Two years back in New York and the last twelve months had been one holy terror. They should get out and go back to some small college again and let these crazy New Yorkers be! He was tired all the time, and nervous and brooding. And the place was filled with the most predatory women, black and white, who didn't give a damn what a man had at home. Sure, she was all for civil rights, but she thought twice about it when it was wrecking the family. Long meetings every night, men *and* women calling about this or that. Valerie hated it; she wished they'd never left Weston, but then she had been as happy as Gene for the chance to become directly and actively involved (it looked so simple then) in the Movement and get out of Weston, a small northern Pennsylvania college.

Dressing, Browning knew that his wife was annoyed with him and disturbed about Nora and that Chance boy. Not that he didn't have some reservations himself, but he had explained to her last night that what really mattered was the boy's being a good kid. Black people could not start behaving like white people. Nora had met the Chance boy's folks. Said they were nice, or at least no aftertaste. None of this meant she was marrying the boy; she wasn't marrying anyone until she finished Hunter and *then* he'd have to see. Break her hipbones first, Browning had told his wife. But Val remained sullen. She didn't like that kind of thing.

Browning touched his wife on the shoulder when he went into the kitchen. Then he looked, as he looked every morning, at the Harlem rooftops that stretched eastward from the foot of Morningside Heights all the way to the Harlem River. The view was a gray, black, and brown checkerboard of roofs, broken now and again by sleek-looking high-risers and soot-streaked buildings. Here and there, almost as anachronisms, he could see dots of green that were trees. Way over, almost obscured by the morning's heat haze, was the Triboro Bridge.

"Where are the girls?" Browning asked when he sat down at the table.

"They're coming. Are you going to talk to Nora about that white boy?"

"You mean the Chance boy? We went through that; I don't want to hear about it this morning." He tried to snap his paper, but it crumpled hopelessly.

"Gene, listen: if anything happens to that girl, it'll be your fault!"

He continued to read for a moment. She was in a bad mood. Cool. But he said, finally, "Damn it, Val. I don't see a thing in the world wrong with what's going on. They take the same classes; they feel the same way about a lot of things, I gather, and that's rare in this world —"

He broke off when he realized that she was staring at him; she was misinterpreting his last words, twisting them into herself.

"Yes," she said, "I suppose it is."

Browning reached over and turned on the radio.

The President was giving a graduation address in the Midwest and was expected to mention the joint maneuvers of the United States and island Chinese forces on Formosa as well as the increasing patrol activity by both U.S. and mainland Chinese on the borders of China.

Locally, a plane chartered to fly to Europe with one hundred people had broken down before takeoff, leaving the passengers stranded.

High school students were to demonstrate at the school where three days ago a white cop had shot and killed a Negro student.

It was going to be in the upper 90's today.

Val was speaking. "We have got to get out of this city for a while, Gene. There's real madness here in the summer."

He glanced at her. It wasn't eight yet and she was leaning against the stove, whipped. And she would have to pull most of the day at the agency where she was in charge of child placement. "A good, *long* vacation," she said, almost pleading.

Browning stared down at the table thinking, Can't you understand, woman! There are things I have to do, must do! There isn't time for a vacation, at least *my* vacation. But he couldn't tell her that.

"It's all the meetings, Gene," she said. "Nights and weekends. It's just too much. This year has been sheer, holy hell."

He understood then that she meant it was too much for

her, not him, and he was suddenly saddened. He turned. Nora stood at his elbow.

"Morning," she said quietly, sitting down.

Browning smiled. "How goes it, baby?"

Her eyes closed with an understanding smile. "All right." The smile vanished as she looked toward her mother.

"Where's Chris?" Valerie asked.

"She's coming."

"Almost finished with the first year," Browning said to Nora. "You're doin' good, kid."

Nora smiled again. "Better next year," she said.

"Maybe then you won't have boys on the brain so much," Valerie said.

Nora's lips tightened. She exchanged glances with her father.

"I was a boy once," Browning said lightly, "and you liked me."

"That was different." Valerie shouted, "Chris, c'mon now."

"What was different about it?"

Valerie sat down heavily. "You *know* what was different."

Browning supposed that beside color she was talking about The Pill. They didn't know if Nora was taking it, but hadn't ruled that out. Browning didn't much like the idea of his daughter shacked up with some college junior, black or white, or anyone else for that matter, but what was he going to do? Life went on. You could talk until you got blue in the face, but when that urge came falling down, what was one to do but go along with it?

Chris came in and glanced briefly at each face. "Morning. Is it safe to come in here?"

Browning suppressed a smile. Chris was the tough, no-nonsense one.

"Sit down and hush and eat," Valerie said.

"That's what I hope I can do," Chris said.

My women, Browning thought, looking at each of them. Lovely, like sisters, except that the girls wore their hair long. The noses with their soft flaring of the nostrils, and the lips were almost identical. Nora's facial bones were rather like her mother's, while Chris's were more like his, round, less angular. He rose. "I've got to hit it," he said. "See you girls. I'm going to be late, Val."

Valerie stopped eating. "Again?" Browning noticed that her lips were pressed together like Nora's had been moments ago. "Okay," she said.

And Browning thought, One day I hope you understand. We've been married for almost twenty years and you still won't understand. You won't think back to our dreams as a point of reference, all those things we talked about in so many places and at so many different times. About a good world. I look and listen and you've become, night by night, deed by deed, just like the others. You don't dream any more and perhaps you never did. I understand women are like that, but I wanted to believe you weren't. I've been troubled for a year and all you can think of is that it's the job. Damn, Val.

Browning climbed slowly out of the subway, paused for breath and glanced eastward toward the ancient, cable-stitched Brooklyn Bridge. Ahead of him, a thick slab of glass, concrete and steel, was the Chase Manhattan Building. Impressive, respectable, but there was the enemy: wherever there was money and in too many places where there wasn't. And the Woolworth Building, the five-and-dime empire in which once the boy met the girl and lived happily ever after (the legend used to go that way). Down here at City Hall Park was the perfect merging: political power and big business. And just a few blocks away, Wall Street.

Browning walked south toward his office. Once he had loved this city, loved every piece of grit that ever flew into his eyes; he delighted in the Canarsie, Bronx and Harlem accents. He loved the way New Yorkers moved, how lovely their women were, the excitement and, yes, the positive sense of power. But just last year it had all become malevolent to him. A Canarsie accent became the accent of people who hated you because you were not what they were; Bronx accents made him cautious, and Harlem accents plunged him into sadness. New York had changed him so suddenly and completely that he knew he would never be the same. Now New York and all that it had meant was an affront to his intelligence, and more, an insult to his spirit.

Well, that was because last year he had faced up to it. How could he not have known the truth about America and Americans, teaching political science as he had? My God, you started lying with the Pilgrims and you kept right on lying. Year after year those rows of mostly white faces stared blankly back at you. They'd already absorbed their history by the time he got them, and their history told them that the black man standing before them was supposed to know nothing about it. He had been a victim of both accident and design, and he helped the system to function because he, a victim of the lie, abetted it by his presence in that place.

Take this morning. This morning, the director of the Institute for Racial Justice, Bill Barton, his boss, would have a meeting about the cop who killed the kid. Everyone in the meeting would discuss the ramifications of Sergeant Carrigan's act with an eye toward summer rioting in the old style. The telephone would ring constantly and the newsmen would barge in asking the same stupid questions and Barton would give them the same stupid answers. They would all play their roles. The television people would come in, puffing off the elevators, carrying their Arriflexes, Auricons and Eclairs, fixing the Lowell lights or adjusting the Sun Guns as they hopped along the halls trailing their microphones.

What was there to say? The facts were these: Sergeant Carrigan, Detective First Grade, twice decorated for disarming and taking into custody adult hoodlums, had shot a sixteen-year-old Negro boy five times in the chest, killing him. Carrigan said the youth had been about to attack him with a knife, but no knife had been found. Everyone knew in some part of his mind that for Carrigan, that day, it had been open season on Negroes and if it hadn't been the boy, it might have been one of those old black ladies with bad feet that you see waiting for the Fifth Avenue bus to take them back uptown after a day's work in the kitchens and nurseries of the monied. Who in the hell was kidding whom?

You could work in a famous and vigorous civil rights organization in charge of the college program as the number-two man; you could work with all your heart and what was left of your soul, but you also had to know, finally, that none of that was going to do any good; that you had to obtain your goals by almost the same means *Chuck* obtained his, remained the only obvious conclusion, and Chuck did not get his with Freedom Now or Love Your Brother marches. That was the truth, all done with lies, white and black.

As soon as Browning walked into his office, which was filled with the velvety hum of small rubber-bladed fans, his secretary greeted him. "Bill wants to see you right away, Gene. Before the meeting."

Browning nodded when Sam Tate came in. He was a dark nervous man with a pocked face. Tate sucked his teeth. "That goddamn cop started *this* summer rolling, didn't he, baby?" Tate edged closer to Browning's desk. "I took a quick walk around uptown this morning and people are already in the street talking about it. Lots of cops up there, too. With the riot helmets. I mean more than usual." Tate now paced before Browning's desk. "Yeah, yeah, it's going to be a bitch out there before this one blows over."

The eagerness in Tate's voice irritated Browning. "Sure, just like the last one." When it's over, black and white would be on the street together sweeping up the glass, getting ready to go back into business. In New York, as in no other place, black and white needed each other. The rich couldn't get along without the poor. Who, after all, built all those great castles in Europe? The pyramids in Egypt? The skyscrapers?

Marvin Dunbar, the labor organizer, filled the doorway with his crude, bulky form. His face was marked with scars and one of his eyes was half-closed. Dunbar looked like he had just crashed a line of scabs; his scars and the eye were souvenirs from the labor-troubled thirties. There were rumors that he had fought in the Spanish Civil War with the Lincoln Battalion. Here then was a man of dream and conviction, but why, Browning wondered, doesn't he think like me *now*.

"This time tomorrow," Dunbar said, "New York City

will be a wreck. These New York Negroes finally have had it. They are going to rip the I-beams out of this town. Imagine the insolence of that Irish bastard. If Negroes don't understand now how white America thinks of them, and do something about it, we can forget this. It'll be back to the cotton patch. It's awful to say, but this may be just what we need." Dunbar left the doorway and Tate hastened after him.

Now Browning was aware that every telephone in the place seemed to be ringing. He rose and went to Barton's office. Barton had been a basketball player, college and two years with the Globies, and he still had that athlete's cool. He had moved around a little, Urban League, Fellowship of Reconciliation, the N double A, before coming to IRJ. "Close the door," he said, "and sit down." Barton's long legs were draped over his desk. Already there was a sheen of perspiration on his equine face, and the tips of his brush moustache gleamed with it. Barton's slender fingers drummed softly on the desktop. He stopped and picked up a sheet of paper.

"Look, Gene, you've been working pretty hard and I get worried when it goes too rough around here. I want you to take a change of pace for a couple of weeks." Barton passed over the paper and then some carbon copies. "There is a list of some cats who might give us a nice piece of change. Talk to them. You've got to meet them sooner or later. Whenever I get out there, all they want to hear is Goose Tatum. Tell you something: don't accept pledges. I mean, if you can help it. Take whatever cash they've got on hand or get them to write out a check for what they've got in the bank and they'll tell you it's damn little and they'd rather send you something bigger a little later. Take the check. No laters. You've been holed up in those colleges, let me tell you something about your folks. It's now or never; forget about later . . ."

Browning's heart was leaping and skidding. This was a bit too perfect. A good omen. He was moving in the right direction and things were breaking just fine.

". . . and we're going to need that money this summer because of that stupid cop. Meetings, materials . . . we're sure to go way over the budget. I just know it. You work in a place like this and every damned civil rights emergency becomes a financial disaster. Yeah, we'll probably have to put up bail money, too. Fund raising tells me to forget the summer, so our last mailing was in May and it pulled one and a half percent. Trouble may be leaning this way. So go out and get us some money, Gene."

Browning half smiled. That stupid cop, he thought, and sure, because of him you want to be right here answering questions, being interviewed and getting on television.

"Mr. Barton," his secretary said, opening the door with a crash, "there're newspaper people here and a few from television. Can you come out?"

"In a minute, Amanda. And set the meeting back forty-five minutes will you, and make sure and tell the staff." The secretary withdrew and closed the door again. Barton took out a handkerchief and carefully wiped his face and moustache. "Get yourself some money from disbursing. Tell Val I'm sorry."

Browning was nodding absently. He knew that if the ruckus with the cop and the dead kid was over when he came back from his trip, Barton would take off three weeks leaving him in charge. If he got a vacation at all it would be toward the dog end of summer. Poor Val. For himself, he hadn't counted on one. He stood. "Okay if I leave now, as soon as I get straightened out?"

"The sooner the better. And listen. If this thing starts to break out all over, let me know."

Barton stood up, towering over Browning. They shook hands. "Get the bread, Gene," Barton said wearily. "We've got to start getting it from our own. The liberals have had it."

Browning plunged through the door and into the hallway where the newsmen surged forward with notebooks, pencils, wires, microphones, cameras and lights.

"Hey, you! Where's Bill Barton? He coming out? Who are you?"

"Hey, buddy, make a statement about the cop, what do you say?"

"Gimme some light, Steve. More, more!"

"Get his name! Get his name!"

"Hey, what's your name?"

A hot blinding light came on and a frond of mikes were thrust almost in Browning's mouth. He shook his head vigorously and jerked his thumb toward Barton's door. Barton had had time to smooth his clothes and to wipe his face again. Bulling his way through the newsmen, Browning turned once and saw Barton standing easily outside his door, smiling and holding his hands in a calming gesture.

There were still people in the world who ran from cameras and would not allow their pictures to be taken for fear that part of their spirits would be sucked away from them. Perhaps, Browning thought, returning to his own office and closing the door, they were right. The cameras were still doing that to the Movement, the cameras and the microphones.

two

Browning stepped inside the cool bar and sighed with relief. He had walked all the way from Lower Manhattan to the Village and he was sweating. He did not go to bars very often, but he imagined that if he did, he would prefer them in the early afternoon like this when there were few people around and the bartenders read the papers or listened to the radio.

The unfamiliar bartender approached and Browning, startled, said, "A beer. Any kind. Where's Vig?"

The bartender looked more keenly at Browning. "Who?"

"Pete Vigianni."

"Pete Vigianni," the bartender murmured, placing the beer on the bar.

"I'm an old friend of his," Browning said, almost desperately. "He used to be the super of a small house up on Eighty-third Street. His wife's name was Barbara. I lived there for a while —"

"Vig don't work here no more," the bartender said, and Browning was heartened that he had pronounced the name so familiarly. Then he was disappointed. "But you can find him at the Cool Life Bar. There." The bartender was gesturing across the street. Browning almost sagged with relief. "Would he be there now?"

The barman glanced at his watch. "Maybe hanging around. He don't go on until three."

"Thanks." Browning got up from his stool, his beer untouched, pushed out a tip and left.

He walked quickly across the street and had almost entered the bar when someone spoke to him. "Hey, kid, what's new? Long time no see."

"Vig!" Browning stared at him. My God! It was going to be all right after all. "Listen, I want to talk to you."

Vig laughed. His dark blond hair gleamed in the sun. He, too, was getting older. The Village clothes couldn't conceal the slight paunch or the puffing face. "You want to talk? I thought you were just cooling through looking for nice young things. Okay, I'll buy you a beer."

Browning had had that room in the building and taught three days a week at Columbia and took classes. Each Friday noon he took the bus to Albany where his family lived, mostly on Val's salary from a private social service agency, while he picked up his doctorate.

Vig lived on the first floor with his wife and was doing old man's work. He used to stop in and they would have coffee and he would borrow books. Vig didn't go out much. Sometimes at night he sat on the outside railing smoking in the dark, watching each car that passed with keen interest. They had many conversations, but Browning realized that in spite of them he knew almost nothing about Vig. Vig, on the other hand, knew a great deal about Browning and his family, Browning and his dreams. Then one day there was a new superintendent, an old man who was bent and wrinkled.

Browning had not thought of Vig much after that. There was the doctorate to get, and when he got that, the years started to pile up behind him, a stint in Ohio, one in California, South Dakota, and finally, Weston. At Weston, and perhaps it was because of the times, he became deeply involved in the campus civil rights activities. Asked to help organize campus branches of the Institute for Racial Justice in the East on a no-pay basis, Browning did so well that Bill Barton asked him to come to New York. The University at Weston, shaken and irritated by Browning's activities, readily agreed to give him a leave of absence.

Once he was back in New York, Browning gave a great deal of thought to his future. It took a long time to relocate in the city, but he wanted it to be right. After all, he wasn't a kid any more. If it didn't work out, he could return to a college in the city. He'd had enough of the sticks. Thus it was on a late summer afternoon, when he had been looking for a place near the Village, that he ran into Vig.

"What happened to you?" Browning had asked. "One day you were in the house and the next day you were gone." They drank beer then also.

Vig had given him a patient smile. "I had to lay low for a while, Gene. Nothing like a super's job to give you anonymity. My wife?" Vig had laughed. "C'mon, kid. You hide out, you want to be comfortable, right?"

"I don't get it, Vig, What in the hell do you do?"

He had smoothed a shock of hair. "What can I tell

you," he said quietly. "I do a little of this and a little of that. I get by, you know?"

It had leaped flaming into Browning's mind then, and remained there.

Now, two years later, they were back in a bar, across the street from the old one. Vig selected a table near the window. "This all right, kid?" He turned to the bar. "Hey, Nick, fling over a couple of Buds, will you? The real cold ones in the back." He turned to Browning. "You don't look so good, Gene. You working too hard? What are you doing now?"

"You remember the last time I saw you, I was looking for a place for the family and just starting to work in civil rights? Well, I've been on it for two years."

The beer came and Vig said, "Don't you ever come to the Village?"

"Not very often."

"Drink up, Gene. It's on the house. Pay you back for some of that coffee I used to drink. Tell me what's bugging you. Can't have a buddy who let me borrow books looking beat the way you do. It's bad business, especially if you're sitting in a window." Vig glanced down and saw Browning's fingers tremble. "You need some bread, Gene?"

"No." Browning watched Vig turn up his bottle. He stared at the strong, hair-covered forearm. "Vig," Browning said, "how much is a hit?" The words blew through his clenched teeth, shaking and almost inaudible. The bottle in Vig's hand jerked and he carefully lowered it.

"What did you say, kid?" Vig's hand was pressed to his hair again. "A hit?" he said softly, mockingly.

"I asked you," Browning said stubbornly, "how much is a hit?"

Vig bounced against the back of his chair and stared at him. "Man, are you crazy?"

"No, Vig. I asked you a question."

Vig's voice was cold. "I heard you ask it. You must be putting me on. You ask me like that, what does that make me?"

"You told me you did some of this and some of that. Vig, I need help! I need a hit, man! And my asking doesn't make you anything but Vig to me. Did you stop to think, as long as we're talking in square terms, what asking makes me?"

"Let's walk to the park. We'll talk there."

They walked unspeaking to the east side of Washington Square Park, and when they were seated Vig said, "You're having trouble with your wife."

"No."

"C'mon, kid. We all have trouble with the broads. It's nothing to be drug about. Maybe you got a girlfriend. You're not much man if you can't handle both."

"Vig, it's nothing like that."

Vig clapped a hand to his head and then thumped the briefcase Browning had laid across his knees. "I got it. Your wife's got a boyfriend!"

"No."

"Goddamn it, Gene, then get into it."

"Remember those books I used to lend you?"

"Sure, I remember."

"It's about those books; it's about me and my people. Look at me."

"Kid, I been looking at you all afternoon. What do you want from me?"

"I'm black, Vig, you see that?"

"Okay, big deal. So, like I say, what's that got to do with me?"

"I'm getting older and I haven't made any waves, I haven't made anything better. It's getting late. The place is going to pot in a thousand ways. I don't want it to go to pot. I could like the place. The way it's going now, the next time I see you, you'll be at my throat or I'll be at yours —"

"It's bad, Gene, but it's not that bad."

"How do you stop it from getting that bad?"

"You're putting me on again, Gene." Vig glanced up at the sky. "That outfit you belong to, they don't go for nothing like this, do they?"

Browning said hastily, "No, it's not them. It's me. How much would it cost to hit Carrigan?"

Vig put his face in his hands while Browning watched. Through his hands Vig asked, "You aren't kidding, are you, man?"

Browning leaned forward. "Something basic, Vig. Something happens to Carrigan, then what?"

Still speaking through his hands, Vig said, "He's one man, and a cop at that."

Browning replied, "He's a start."

Vig stood suddenly. "This is all crazy, kid. I'm not in that business. A couple of girls, a little junk, a piece of a bar, running errands, but nothing more. You're talking about a big thing here. I mean I just can't do you any good."

"Okay, okay," Browning persisted, "what *would* it cost?"

Vig was walking away, saying, "You knock me out, man, you really knock me out."

"Vig," Browning called after him, but Vig didn't stop.

Browning watched him. Browning had been so sure. Hell, it had been a foolish thing to do. How could it not be when you had to go to *them* even to have that kind of thing done? All right, then. Sooner or later, the kids would get hold of the idea, but they wouldn't be cool about it. They wouldn't be professional, and it would be too goddamned bad for everyone with a black skin.

The outspoken leaders went at it wrong. They used democratic principles, but Chuck had given all he intended to give; the rest would have to be taken. Browning thought he had the answer, but now he was both relieved and irritated. He was relieved because what he was willing to do could not now be done. He was irritated because his was the only answer and he could not put it into action. One didn't go about shouting from the podiums. The years proved that didn't work. Secrecy, apparent noninvolvement, selected acts. That was the answer, the only answer, a wee bit of Mao. Now Vig had told him no. It would be left up to the wild kids, the ones who tipped their hand by walking into state legislatures with loaded guns; the ones running the streets with Molotov cocktails slopping in their pockets. Now what was going to happen?

He had planned it so beautifully, all except where the money was coming from, but Barton dropped that right into his lap. There was the problem of how to handle the checks, but now . . .

Carrigan would have been first, just to shake up New York and to get the news around the world. People would put two and two together. If they missed the point with Carrigan there was that construction worker who had dynamited a classroom at Alabama State College, killing three coeds. One of them had been Leonard Trotman's sister and her death had made him a super-militant with a vengeance. Browning recalled the killer's photo. He was a lean-faced man with thin hair. He had had a fatuous grin on his face. They *all* smiled and smirked because somewhere, sometime, they got patted on the back and their friends cried, "Y' did good, Chuck!"

They all went free or did their little bit of time, for that was the exchange rate still. *Maybe* a little time in exchange for a dead nigger; when the scales balanced things would be different, and white people appeared to have no intention of balancing any scale any time. Browning wanted people to know that if they were willing to take black lives the way they had been, then they also ought to know that they had to forfeit their own. Once everyone understood that, things would improve.

It would always be open season on blacks until blacks opened the season on whites. But how to begin again?

"Daddy, what are you doing home? I thought you told Mother you'd be late."

Nora, hearing him at the door, had come out of her room, still holding the pen with which she'd been writing an essay.

"The boss is sending me on a trip, honey, so I came home to rest before getting ready for it."

Nora's face fell. Her father's presence served as a buffer between herself and her mother. "How long will you be gone?"

"Couple of weeks, but I'm not leaving until sometime tomorrow." Browning looked at her troubled face. "Honey, why don't you make some iced tea while I shower and we can sit down and talk, all right? You got time?"

She took his briefcase and carried it to his room. "All right. You get fresh and I'll have your tea by the time you're out."

When Browning returned to the kitchen, a new flow of perspiration already on his body, Nora placed a glass of tea and a sandwich before him. "You want to talk about Woody, don't you, Daddy?"

Browning shrugged. "Woody, you and your mother, I guess."

"He's nice, he's really nice, Dad, and we haven't done anything to be ashamed of."

"Ashamed on whose terms, yours, mine or your mother's?"

"Mother's terms; I think they're like very basic. We haven't done anything on her terms to be ashamed of."

Browning touched his daughter on the head. "I know it, baby." He thought then, fleetingly, of a coed he'd made love to when he was in South Dakota. He'd been thirty and she was nineteen. Even during the act she called him Mr. Browning, and she had not been ashamed. "And as for your mother, you must know that her concern is for you."

"I know that, Daddy, but here we are in a time when everyone seems to be working to make things right between different kinds of people, and Mother's talking like a white man from Mississippi."

Browning laughed. "You and Chris are her babies and as far as she's concerned, the white man by his historical record doesn't deserve you. It's a reverse thing, you know, with some emotion and some truth, as she sees it."

"But you've got to make exceptions."

"I know that, baby, I know that. It's not like you and the boy were going to run off and get married, is it?"

When Nora's eyes fell, Browning's stomach plunged. "Is it?" he repeated.

She shook her head. "But Daddy, you ought to know that we thought of it. Europe —"

"Oh, God," Browning groaned.

"But, we aren't. We only talked about it."

Browning nodded. He knew that when kids started talking about marriage so young, it was mostly because their underwear was filled with steam.

"The thing is," Nora said, "I want something in my own right, like a college education and a career, like Mother. And I promised you, remember?"

"I remember, honey."

"So we really aren't going to do anything, Daddy."

Except, Browning thought, except — And maybe that's better, maybe not. Who's to say?

"Nora," he said, "I'm going to hold you to that promise. As for your mother, she *is* your mother, and you'll have to go partway with her. There's no choice. And I'll try and see that she's fair."

She kissed him and returned to her room.

In the kitchen's silence, Browning was thinking back to the first time he made love to Val. It was in a closet in her parents' home and they stood up breathing the smell of musty clothes about them. Val had been eighteen.

Browning found himself tired and drained. He placed his glass and plate in the sink and walked through the apartment to Nora's room. "Honey," he said, looking down at her and the essay she was writing. "I have to ask you something. I don't want to, but I have to. Are you taking The Pill?"

She stared at him and he could see her eyes shifting

from one side of his face to the other. "I understand, Daddy. It's all right. I'm not taking The Pill now, but I may in the future."

Browning smiled. "Of course. That makes sense, some kind of sense." He withdrew and went to his own room. He stopped before the print of the drawbridge at Arles and imagined Woody Chance and his daughter, young and laughing, driving through Arles.

He sat down in the soft chair and took from his brief-case the list of the names of people he would see on his trip, along with copies of letters Barton had already sent to them. Browning went to sleep while reading the first letter. He did not wake until Valerie kissed him and shook him gently.

With a glance Browning saw that the sky was now graying with the coming of night. Val sat on the bed, smoking and watching him. "You must've had a very rough day."

"Oh, it's this damned heat," he said, gathering the papers and replacing them in the case. "How was your day?"

"Nothing special. Nora tells me you've got to take a trip."

Browning rubbed his eyes. "Yeah, to raise some money, and so Barton can have the spotlight all to himself."

"But what about vacation?"

"Get the place in Sag Harbor. I won't get any time off until after this mess and after Barton takes his own vaca-tion. But I can get to Sag weekends. Can't be helped, baby. I'm sorry."

"It's always something," she said.

"C'mere," he said.

Valerie smiled and joined him in the chair. "What?" she asked, and then he pulled her close and kissed her, slid his mouth around on hers until her lips opened. His hand went up under her skirt and her garter belt fell away under his fingers. His hand rested on her flesh; the other was pressed against her breast. She made a sound in his ear and he whispered, "Where are the kids?" She whispered back, "Sitting at the table waiting for you to join them for dinner."

"Oh," he said and started to release her, but she pressed back.

"How long will you leave me like this?"

"Only until after dinner," he said.

"Hurry," she said, fixing her stocking and leaving the room.

When Browning arrived in the kitchen, Nora was smiling at the wine and the wineglasses. "Wow, Daddy. Mother went to wake you up and when she came back, zoop! Out came the wine." She grinned. Valerie blushed. Chris looked at everyone trying to understand what was funny. At fifteen, Browning reflected, you're almost there, but not quite. Dinner was one of the most pleasant they'd had in weeks.

Later, his wife sleeping quietly by his side, Browning read, and sometimes listened to the faint sounds of a television program his daughters were watching. When the phone rang he called out, "I'm awake if it's for me." But he was sure it was Woody Chance calling his daughter. So he was surprised when Nora poked her head into the room. "It's for you, Daddy. A man. He didn't give his name."

Browning waited a moment until she had left, then he pulled on his robe. Beneath it he was naked. He walked to the telephone stand. "Hello," he said. He didn't recognize the voice, but that didn't bother him. He was always getting calls from people he didn't know. It was the message that jolted him.

"Mr. Browning? Eugene Browning?"

"Yes, who is this, please?"

The caller ignored the question and continued talking. "If you are Eugene Browning, listen carefully. Tomorrow afternoon at two o'clock you will start walking clockwise around the Central Park Reservoir. Keep walking until you are stopped. Keep walking. Is that clear?"

"Yes," Browning said.

The caller rang off and Browning hung up very slowly. It had worked after all. It was on again. He would have to take a later flight tomorrow. He could arrange that in the morning.

He slipped naked back under the sheet and drew his wife to him again. The last time, he knew, had been for her. It had always been that way before he went on a trip, as if she wanted it to be so good that no matter how many other women he looked at while he was away, the memory of her would keep him faithful. This time was for him. Quietly, so they could hear any approaching footsteps or the telephone, they made love.

three

Browning had never walked around the cinder path of the Reservoir. He found it pleasant with the wind coming off the water. Behind the heat haze he saw the gray-blue outlines of the buildings of the city all around him.

There was a lower path and on it Browning saw couples walking arm in arm and men jogging. He could tell the real runners from the exercisers. The real runners never shortened their crisp little strides, and their elbows were held close to their bodies with their fists swinging halfway across their chests. Their shoulders were held steady, although relaxed. The exercisers came off the ground too high; their heels came way up behind them and every muscle in their bodies moved, thus tiring them very quickly.

Browning thought of the days when he ran the hundred in college. He was always good for a third place with a ten; sometimes he was a bit under, but mostly a bit over. He liked to watch the other runners before the events started as they pranced up and down the infield, knees high, toes down, arms riding grooves in the air. He liked to prance as well. The difference was that once you came off the blocks, no one ran like that any more, not for the hundred. You wiggled every goddamn thing you could and went into your tape lean five yards from it. Today high school kids were blasting the ten for the hundred to bits. Browning wondered if he had had a son if he would have run track.

As he completed his second swing around the Reservoir, he started to look carefully at the other people who were walking. A heavyset woman in low, thick-soled shoes strode by, holding a book. A tall man went by, his eyes hidden by dark glasses, and Browning slowed, waiting, but nothing happened. Now he began to notice people lying in the grass listening to transistor radios. Once more Browning passed a gray-haired man who was wearing a checked cap. The man was peering with a pair of binoculars into the Reservoir. Browning slowed once again, anticipating that he would be stopped. The man continued to look at the ducks.

As Browning commenced his third turn, he noticed a rather chunky man striding toward him, his well-cut suit flowing about his legs and arms. Browning blinked his eyes and changed their focus to sweep the path further up. He was startled, therefore, when the man stopped, and smiling said, "Mr. Eugene Browning?"

"Why, yes," Browning said.

"Will you join me?" the man asked. His movements were almost feminine and his face approached being pretty.

"Certainly." They moved in the direction the man was going.

"Very warm today, isn't it?" the man asked. He had slowed his pace.

"Yes. But it's too hot."

"Really, I would have thought that hot weather wouldn't have bothered you?"

Browning looked at him briefly. The man was serious. "That's pretty silly, isn't it?"

"Well, now, I don't know. I will examine that theory, however, in the light of your reaction to my comment."

"Please do." Browning felt that he had been overwhelmed by the man's mannerisms to such an extent that he was suddenly aping them.

They remained silent as a Puerto Rican family walked by. Browning thought: For you too, fellow.

"I am told that you are interested in a business arrangement concerning a Mr. Carrigan, who's been in the papers lately."

"Yes. How —"

"Mr. Carrigan is very well connected with a corporation that has a great deal of influence in this city, Mr. Browning. And the present flurry of activity makes this venture highly risky."

"I can imagine," Browning said.

"However," the stranger went on briskly, "now and again our company, I am ordered to inform you, does undertake to perform charitable activities, that is, for cost only, with no profit involved."

Browning stopped and started to speak, but the stranger kept on walking and said pleasantly, "Don't stop, Mr. Browning. Let's keep walking, please."

Browning caught up with him. "But I don't understand."

"The business arrangement with Mr. Carrigan will cost you only fifteen hundred dollars, Mr. Browning — far,

far below our standard charge. When will you have the money, or do you have it now?"

Dazed, Browning replied, "I'll have it in a couple of weeks."

The stranger pulled out a small calendar. Browning watched the neat white finger slide along the card. "Do you have a pocket calendar, Mr. Browning?"

Browning fumbled for his datebook. "Yes."

The stranger peered at him with deep blue eyes. "You say two weeks from today, is that correct?"

"Better give me two days extra."

"Fine. We are very obliging. That will make it the twenty-eighth. Is that what you make it?"

"Yes." Browning had the feeling that this was not happening, but he marked the date and closed his book and returned it to his pocket. They walked on.

"On the 28th, Mr. Browning, you will return to the park. On the east side there is a road going north. About one hundred yards from the bicycle rental and the cafeteria, you will see a blue panther, a sculpture, crouching on an outcropping of rocks directly overlooking the road. Across the road from the panther, you will sit in the grass and you will have that week's *Time* magazine. In that magazine you will have an envelope containing fifteen hundred dollars. All cash. Thirty fifty-dollar bills. You will remain there until you are contacted. Is that clear?"

"Yes."

"I'm turning back here, Mr. Browning, but you will continue to walk around the Reservoir just once more. Goodbye." Browning did not look back. He walked slowly ahead.

four

A little before dusk on the previous afternoon, the Don had been sitting on the patio of his penthouse on Central Park West. Boxed baby spruce trees surrounded him. White garden furniture with its cumbersome scrolls gleamed dully in the fading sunlight. The awning was up now, its red and orange edge flapping softly in the breeze.

The Don was in his seventies, but his eyes were still sharp behind the non-prescription sunglasses. What remained of his white hair lifted and lapped in the wind. Most of his head was bald and browned with freckles. That head seemed to be made more of metal than of skin and bone, its shape was so precise. The Don looked down at the restful green expanse of Central Park, its trees and walks and roads and meadows, its Reservoir, its ponds. But from time to time he raised his eyes to the smaller but neater buildings across the park on Fifth Avenue. He grunted in contempt; he knew the people who lived on Fifth Avenue and how too many of them came to be there. He had not been involved in his kind of "business" for over fifty years for nothing. When he was young he sneered at them because he envied them; now that he was old it didn't matter. They too were victims of the human condition. Central Park West was quite good enough for him. Anyway, who could have known when he left Terrasina that he would have come this far?

No one.

And the journey down the long road was all in vain because there would be nothing to show for it, no wife, no children, just Peter. And they didn't like Peter; he would get nothing. Everything would go back to them as if they were a repossessing company. Not quite everything. There was some change for Peter, his only nephew. Peter was coming over for dinner, a fact that made the Don feel good.

The trouble was, the Don was too old. He still spoke with an accent; he hadn't tried so hard to get rid of it the way some of them had. Things had changed, but the Don had not. No more sharp clothes — the white-on-white shirts and hand-tailored suits and shoes — unless they were subdued; no more big cars, like Cadillacs and Lincolns and Chryslers. No more a lot of things.

The change had come when Tony left. Tony, who hated Sicily with such ugly venom. It didn't matter too much to the Don; he was too old to be involved in the silent power plays. He cast his vote with the safe majority, lit his cigar and leaned back from the table, staring out the window; he lived well because he did the right thing. Clarissa had been the only wrong thing, and only Tony, with his hatred of everything Old Country had been on his side. It hadn't been enough, two against the group. They extended their cautions and limitations to Peter. As his heir, Peter was out as soon as the Don was out. That was plain.

More and more the Village operations were being left to
trainees. But poor Peter had been in the Village for over ten
years. He wasn't a trainee any longer, he was an outcast. He
seemed to understand this because he never asked the Don
to intercede for him to get something else. The Don hoped
Peter understood it; he did not want to believe his nephew
was lazy. People with Terrasina in their blood could not be
lazy.

The village was on the coast road between Capaci and
Balestrate, 71 kilometers from Palermo. The misshapen
heap of stone and stucco houses crept gingerly down from
the broad mountain slope to the sea. The houses were burnt
yellow, dark brown and sometimes colorless; some were as
white as bleached skeleton bones. Dimly the Don recalled
the sirocco and how it had closed tightly about him, flailing
his eyelids and lips, smothering him until sweat began to
flush out of his skin. These last few years, he thought, New
York has been just like that.

From the park the cries of boys drifted up and they
made the Don think of the cheers that went up when the
brightly colored fishing boats sailed in from the sea across
the Golfo di Castellammare. The memory teased and the
Don found himself wishing vaguely for fish for dinner, red
mullet perhaps or rosefish or bass, and staring up at the sky
now and at the clouds filling with the light of the red sunset
at his back, behind the buildings that lined Central Park
West, he imagined he saw his mother returning home from
the market, the fish wrapped in old papers.

He hadn't really known his mother. He remembered
her as a very browned person who always wore black. She
put on newer black when his father was found shot dead on

the terrible road between Alcamo and Camporeale. The killer was never found and no one ever talked about why he was killed. Somehow it was taken for granted.

Then Anna Maria had become the center of attention. (The Don could no longer remember the events that separated his father's death from Anna's time.) She cried for two weeks and would not leave the house. Giuseppi, the Don's older brother, went about with a grim face. The mother wrung her hands and pulled her shawl far over her face when she went to market. The people in the street seemed to be waiting, waiting with little smiles on their browned, heavily lined faces. The Don did not know then that all this had to do with the young man from Montelepre over the mountain. The young man had kidnapped Anna for a few hours, leisurely having his way with her. It seemed that it took a very long time for him to ask to marry her, but he did, and Anna smiled once again, and Giuseppi relaxed and the mother stopped to chat on her way to and from the market. The pain of living according to custom.

The Don and Giuseppi worked the sloping land together, mostly in silence. Every thrust of the hoe was met with a snarl of yellow dust. Everything that had ever come out of this land came out sickly. One day Giuseppi threw down his hoe and shouted: "Who would want this land so filled with sulphur? And where there is not sulphur, there is marsh, and where there is neither sulphur nor marsh, there is rock!"

The Don liked Giuseppi. He had never seen his brother so angry. "The Phoenicians came and they didn't want this forbidden land. The Greeks came; the Arabs came out of the Sahara and *they* spat on it; the Germans came, the French, the Spanish, but none stayed. Is it any wonder?"

With the death of the father, Giuseppi had had to leave the church school altogether, and so he no longer brought books home and read to the Don, or showed him pictures. Giuseppi had tolerated the harsh patch of land as long as he knew he could leave it for the classroom.

The Don was just entering puberty when he followed Giuseppi down from the land. First they had to reassure the mother that everything would be all right, that somehow they would make a living. They tried to join the fishing fleets, but the crews would not have them, so they returned to the land. But more and more, the Don found that he worked it alone, while Giuseppi stayed in town, in the cafes. Sometimes he would not come home until very late in the morning. But there was money now.

The Don was not unprepared to move to Palermo; Giuseppi said there would be a larger house, more money and more food, and they moved. The Don and Giuseppi dressed better in Palermo, but the mother would not accept any of the new comforts and she did not spend any more time in the streets than she had to. Mostly, she divided her time between the kitchen and her bedroom, where she stared at the picture of her husband while telling her beads and looking at the one gift she had accepted from Giuseppi, a rosewood crucifix. But, the Don noticed, people did try to befriend her with a singular amount of deference.

The Don ran errands for Giuseppi's friends or delivered packages. He sat in the background while the men played cards, usually the game in which cardplayers insulted each other and offered drinks only to those they liked.

The books Giuseppi now brought for the Don were forgotten along with his desire to learn to read and write better. Those who lingered all day in the cafes or leaned against the walls of the piazza laughed at books. It was an accident that Vittorio Emanuele Orlando, being born at Palermo and now prime minister of Italy, ever got his hand on a book; books did not help many people born on Sicilian soil. Could they feed and clothe? Books were for the rich whom one saw only fleetingly being pulled about in their carriages, mostly to get the papers so they could read news of the war. And books were also for the priests, so they could learn how to steal from the poor. The Don understood that while the men in the cafe might have grudging respect for books, they feared them because those who knew books had always oppressed them.

At a very early age, perhaps hastened by the sun, the Don had begun to explore the mysteries of the female. He began, like other youths, with the daughters of outcast families or families without fathers or brothers. The girls were young, their loins browned by the sun, the first tendrils of black curling hair shrouding the secret places. Stealth gave way to bravado and these little girls gave way to the whores and furious bouts of wine-drinking. It was not long before the Don joined the clique of boys who circled the piazza, endlessly staring suggestively and whistling at females.

He was a stocky boy with a face that seemed to have been carved from one of the cliffs that stared out over the sea. His hair was a great shock of silky black, and people who looked at him thought of the Saracens who had come to Sicily centuries ago. The girls and the whores marveled that his body was so free of hair. He did not take this as a compliment at first. Later he did; it set him aside from his fellows.

He complained that he was getting too old to run errands and the men laughed and put him on watch while robberies were committed on hapless carriage passengers on the isolated roads inland. Giuseppi was now keeping the water count, the list of all the people who were allowed to get water for their crops. Once, while the Don was standing lookout for a robbery, a man had leaped at him and he was surprised to discover through his first paralysis of fear that he was stronger than the victim, and that when the victim understood this — his eyes gave him away — the Don was already the victor. After that the Don had no fear of using his body, and he gained a reputation for being good and quick with it.

When the police came around to ask their questions, with the timidity of inquisitors who already knew the answers, people shrugged. It was an important lesson to the Don; powerful men could make the police weak; silence could weaken them. Besides, the Don now understood that he was under the protection of Don Vito Cascio Ferro and therefore a member of the Friends.

With such status the Don could have the pick of the whores and Francesca was his choice. She was a slender, impossibly white girl from Carbonin and had dazzling blond hair. The Don had toyed with the idea of running away with her. The second night after they had discussed this with much kissing and cooing and tears, the Don whistled himself homeward through the darkened cobbled streets to find his house in disorder, his mother packing and Giuseppi furious because he was late.

"What are you doing?" the Don asked.

Giuseppi, gripping him by the shoulder, said, "Pack what you need for a couple of weeks. Leave all else behind. We are leaving Sicily, we are going to America."

"But —" The Don was thinking of Francesca and of the great world outside that he did not know.

Giuseppi smacked him hard across the face. If he had thought that Giuseppi had become soft working on the water count, the Don no longer believed it. "Do it!" his brother said. Quietly they slipped from the house and struggled to the end of the street with their bundles. A carriage was there, the two horses waiting silently and patiently. They climbed in and moved slowly through the streets. "Addio, addio," the mother kept whispering, holding her beads.

It was only when New York City loomed up in the west in the morning sky that Giuseppi told the Don why they had come. "They wanted you to kill. I am not saying that Don Vito wished it, but I am not saying either that he did not wish it. The Friends did not need us if that was what they wanted, and we did not need them. Now we start a new life."

The Don's thoughts had been broken off by the arrival of his nephew, Peter Vigianni. They had had a drink on the patio, while staring down at the park in that silence that often falls between people who know each other well. Peter, the Don knew, liked to sit on the patio and read. In that way he was very much like his father, Giuseppi.

Dinner, as always, was filled with light talk and laughter, with Carlo, the Don's man, joining in the conversation when he brought in a fresh course. Carlo was from Belluno and was short and chunky. His strength was belied by the angelic face and the blond hair. The Don guessed that on one of their many forays into Italy the Germans had paused long enough for one of their soldiers to father Carlo's eighth or ninth grandfather. He enjoyed listening to Carlo talk of

Belluno and its mountains and cold silver streams in which swam the delicious Belluno trout.

After dinner the Don and Peter took their coffee into the living room which overlooked the park. The Don lit up a Havana and offered one to his nephew. Peter refused. He preferred Parodi cigars. Someone had told him that they were made the same way they had been made fifty years ago, and when you smelled one, it was like catching a whiff of the Old Country. The Don wrinkled his nose at the smell of the Parodi. "Whew," he said, shaking his head. "You always forget how strong those things are until you smell one."

"It's not so bad," Peter said, removing the wicked-looking black stick from his mouth and studying it.

"How's things?" the Don asked.

"Can't complain."

"Rizzo giving you trouble?" Dominick Rizzo had changed his name to Donald Rich.

Peter shrugged. "No more than usual."

The Don knew that his nephew knew that it wouldn't have done any good for him to offer to speak to Rizzo. The Don carried no weight any more. Things should have gone better, the Don reflected. Peter should have been running one of those East Side French restaurants or managing a small brokerage house. Well, when the time came, there were the few big ones he had set aside. A man had to look after his relatives.

"I've been thinking of taking a trip," the Don said. "All I do is hang around here. Maybe me and Carlo can go trout fishing. Up in New England somewhere, maybe Canada. Can you get away?"

"No," Peter said.

The Don nodded. He had thought Peter would say no, but he said anyway, "It would be good for you. Bring a girl. Your best girl. No sluts. I don't like to be around sluts."

"I can't get away, Uncle."

"Maybe if I speak to Rizzo," the Don persisted half-heartedly.

Peter said, "I'll let you know as soon as I can see my way clear. How's that?"

"I suppose it's okay," the Don said petulantly.

Peter laughed. "You should have gotten married, Uncle. Then you'd have a son and a wife maybe to worry about and not a thirty-five-year-old nephew."

"You know they wouldn't let me marry her."

"I know it, Uncle."

"The bastards."

"That's the way the rules went, Uncle."

The Don was talking more to his cigar than to his nephew. "She was better-looking and cleaner and nicer than any ten or twenty sluts they were dragging around then and dragging around now."

"I remember Clarissa. She was nice to me," Peter said.

"Yeah, sure. We were up on 114th Street then. I could walk through Harlem and everyone on her block knew me. I gave the kids quarters and candy. A white man could pass the day in Harlem then without any trouble at all. There were nice people then. I don't know what happened."

The silence closed about them once again. The Don thought of Clarissa and her apartment on Edgecombe Avenue. Sugar Hill, 555. A real lady, and smart, too. She worried about a man, not for his money, like some of those blond bitches he used to be so hot for. What the hell, black people had always been nice to him. The whites laughed at his accent back in those days. Dago, Geechee, wop, pepperoni . . . And the Irish! Goddamn them. They wouldn't even let you inside their churches, that's how good Catholics they were!

"Uncle, I need a favor. For a friend. He used to live in the house where I was cooling it after that business with Jansen."

"Can't you do the favor, Peter?"

"No, Uncle. That's why I'm asking you."

Of course, the Don thought, of course. He was pleased that Peter had come to him with a problem he might be able to solve. "What is it?"

His nephew said, "My friend is a black man."

The Don rumbled deep in his throat. He raised the cup with the now cold coffee to his lips and looked at Vig, waiting.

"He's a good guy."

"I heard you," the Don said. "What's the favor?" The Don did not like to play guessing games. Peter would have to tell him straight out, bouncing it off his memories of Clarissa. That was all right; that was fair.

"The cop. Carrigan. He wants the cop."

The Don slurped his coffee. "Was that punk kid related to him?"

"No, only by color."

The Don raised his head and turned it stiffly in his nephew's direction. "An eye for an eye?"

Peter nodded.

Once again the Don turned to the park. That was the way it's always been done, one eye for another. That had been the life. People stood up and paid attention when the rules went like that; they didn't laugh at your accent any more when they thought that was the way you played the game. Maybe the colored were getting smart. At last. The Don relit his cigar. "Well, you know the way things are with me and the group now."

"I know, Uncle."

"I could give it to an independent, though. Lots of guys floating around without work. Your friend have any money?"

"I suppose so. Maybe he'll have to get it."

"How did he happen to come to you, Peter?"

"A wild guess. Maybe I haven't been too cool."

The Don glared at him. "Last month down on Elizabeth Street, two guys in the back of the head. One guy up in the Bronx near a dump, a bullet in the back of the head. One guy missing. If they decide one night, Peter Vigianni, what can I do, how much weight do I have these days? You know what, Nephew? Let me tell you how it is so you can start being cool. Once a week I get a check. It's a nice fat check more than covering my needs and wasteful habits. I don't go to the real important meetings any more, because no one calls to tell me about them. I haven't really been a Don since they deported Tony. I'm finished; they feel sorry for me, that's all. I rendered a service in the old days. I got the numbers and the whores lined up; I planned the restaurants; I took care of those greedy goddamn cops; but I'm through. Now you watch yourself. *You* get married and settled and I'll help you. Look what they have you doing. Any punk can do what you're doing. You've got to start planning to cut loose. I promised your father I'd give you my right arm if you needed it. Then he went in and hung himself. He never got used to this life. They'll let you out; you're not important. Other families are going up. You've got to cut loose."

Peter ran a hand through his hair. "One of those guys on Elizabeth Street was the night man at the club, Uncle. You could talk me into anything after what happened to him, but I'm sort of used to that kind of life. Settle down, get married and raise a family? That'd be such a square thing to do; still" — Peter broke off to laugh — "let me think about how to do this, Uncle."

"You gotta do it."

"But the favor?"

The Don waved his hand. "Tell me about it. I'm going to do it because you're going to do me a favor and get out. Besides, I don't like the Irish, especially if they're cops. Maybe Clarissa will feel a little better too. I wonder if she's dead or alive."

Peter always left his uncle a little before the old man's bedtime. Usually he kissed him on the cheeks and quickly broke the embrace. This night, however, he lingered in his uncle's arms. "Thank you, Uncle, for my friend. And thank you for worrying about me."

When Peter left, the Don had Carlo call Eugene Browning and arrange a meeting in the park. Settled in bed, the Don removed a little book from behind the bed and thumbed through it. Once he had seen a photograph of the man he wanted, but he could not recall the name. Page by page he moved through the book. He whispered aloud each name, hoping that the sound and rhythm of it would make him remember.

Itzhak Hod. That was it, that was the man they never used. He had been straight once, and that was held against him. Then he wasn't Italian or Sicilian. The days when outsiders were permitted to run certain parts of the business were over. No outsiders any more. Itzhak Hod. The Don replaced his book and turned out the light.

five

That same evening, on lower Second Avenue, Itzhak Hod was finishing a pastrami sandwich. The pickle that accompanied it slipped into his mouth after the last chunks of the meat and rye bread. Then he took a long, lusty swallow of his beer, set down his glass and looked pleasantly around. He belched loudly, picked up his glass and drained it. Much better, he thought. New York was never bad when you had a little layer of food around your belly.

Hod had been hungry for as long as he could remember. Perhaps this had to do with his size. He was just short of six feet, but he was massively broad and this made him appear shorter, stumpier. Brown, thin hair clung to the sides of his head, but the top was bald. Hod's was a friendly face, broad, with the planes of the cheeks very pronounced; you thought of Mongols or Tartars when you looked at him in spite of his blue, twinkling eyes. When people looked at his brutal body, they glanced quickly at his face and were relieved to see that it was friendly, even kindly.

He could be friendly, he liked to be friendly. When he was feeling good from drink, he liked to dance, moving in wild, knee-bending, body-thumping, arm-flailing abandon, like a Chasidic dancer. Such frenzy was perhaps the result of the way he had had to live for most of his fifty-odd years.

When he was six years old, the armies of *Dziadek* Pilsudski, lumbering their way into White Russia, destroyed the village where he lived with his parents, forcing a move to Warsaw, to the Nalewki district, where only the bread and tea wagons of Beth Lechem kept them alive. Every day reports reached the district: here five thousand were killed by the armies; there seven thousand. Here the Jews were cordoned within their streets and machine-gunned; there hand grenades were thrown into all the synagogues. As report after report came reeking of blood into Warsaw, the Jews left the streets and huddled in their flats.

The father, who as a boy wanted to be a scholar but had developed instead into a brushmaker, slipped into the streets every day to conduct his business — if not with brushes, with anything at hand. Somehow the pogroms lessened. Hod divided his boyhood and early youth between his studies (for his father never really gave up having a scholar in the family) and brushmaking. It was necessary, for the parents had been blessed with a robust child only in their middle forties. In the village it had been the cause for a three-day celebration. Now the boy had grown into a strong youth.

The elder Hod, although he looked with suspicion on the times, prospered in a small way. The pogroms had taught him a lesson, and now he was very active with the Jewish Colonization Association. It was true that he was not one of the scholars or big businessmen or a Rothschild, but even they needed help and information from the small people.

The trouble did not begin again; it was always there. Sometimes it was more deadly than at other times, but in Poland, if one were a Jew, the patience of Job had to be multiplied a thousand times over. And then some. This time they called themselves the Endeks and the Naras; they were fascists like the Nazis, like the Blackshirts of Italy. If life was hard for the Jews before, it was impossible now. Smigly-Rydz succeeded Pilsudski. Jewish merchants, whatever their trade, no matter how long they had been at them, had to take tests that were administered by Polish officials, and they always failed those tests. Once again the elder Hod was reduced to peddling his brushes in the streets of the Nalewki.

Itzhak Hod, his son, became a member of the shomrim, a group of young Jews who patrolled the streets protecting other Jews from the roving bands of Jew-haters. Before long Hod became the leader of the group, having beaten Polish youths to bloody pulps on several savage occasions. While others of the shomrim were often caught and jailed for defending themselves against the Poles, Itzhak always managed to escape.

The younger Hod, being as impressed as his father with the role of the scholar in any society, had the hope that in the University at least, the fascists would have no influence. But it was 1936 and Hod was a student and the Polish scholars did not protest and the few Jewish scholars permitted there dared not. Before long, by a fascist decree, all Jewish students were forced to sit on the benches on the left side of the University classrooms. It was Itzhak Hod who led the protests of the Jewish students; they stood throughout their classes rather than sit in the seats assigned to them. They stood while the Poles shouted and hissed and threw books; they stood staring stonily at the professors who, after seeing that they would not sit down, tried to teach as if they were not there at all. The protests spread from the classroom through the working classes and the inevitable result was a step-up of the pogrom.

The summer of 1939, Hod, with his parents, disembarked from a ship that landed at Haifa. The parents were now in their sixties. They journeyed silently to Kibbutz Deganiya — Em Nakevutset — at the south end of Lake Kinneret, the Sea of Galilee. This, Hod kept asking himself, is the promised land? This place of sand, rock and swamp? This place filled with Bedouin? He found himself longing for the streets of Warsaw where a Jew might stand and face his enemy and prevail. This, this Palestine, promised land though it was, promised nothing. For himself he would have left Warsaw and gone to Paris. But there were his parents who counted on him now for advice, for comfort. Indeed, it was only because of his role in the student strike and in the shomrim that the officials of the Jewish Colonization Association even allowed them to go to Palestine. They needed, they said, strong young leaders like Itzhak, who would be the new generation of pioneers, the newest pioneers. And who could tell but that this war's end would create a Jewish Homeland?

Hod continued his studies on his own, when he had free hours after working all day. Sometimes he took his turn as one of the scouts to guard against marauding Bedouin with a Lebel rifle that had been found wanting — sometimes it fired, sometimes it did not. Only the sixteen-inch bayonet gave Hod confidence, but not too much; he knew that the French in World War I had counted on this longest bayonet, and had been slaughtered.

As if the start of the War had been too much for them, Hod's parents died within a month of each other in the fall of that year, and Hod, released from filial obligation, told himself one night while on watch at the eastern edge of the camp, "I think I am very tired of being a Jew."

Hod walked down Second Avenue to Fourth Street, turned and walked toward the west. He walked gracefully for a large man, and he liked the way he felt when he moved. No muscle refused to do his bidding; his stride was unfaltering. He whistled a tune from *Fiddler on the Roof*, a musical he had seen a few years ago and liked. He had seen it twice, in fact. He wished he had seen Zero Mostel in the American production. He had had a hard life, Mr. Mostel, and an American Jew at that; did nothing ever change? Deep in the bowels of the West Village, Hod slowed his pace. He always found himself hurrying to her little flat. It was undignified, but it had stopped being incongruous, his having a 21-year-old sweetheart. The truth was that she was his very first sweetheart. There had been many, many lovers in half the great cities of the world, but no sweethearts. He was breathing just a bit heavily after walking up the four flights of stairs. He took a deep breath to regain his composure and knocked softly on her door. He had the key to her apartment in his pocket, but he had never felt right using it.

"Itzhak?" Her voice was soft and low and close to the door.

"Yes, Mickey," he said. "It's me."

"Hello," she said. "I had a feeling you'd come, so I fixed dinner."

"What if I had not come?"

"Then I would have been sad."

"Then I am glad I came. I do not want you to be sad."

"Come in, come in."

Hod allowed her to pull him inside. He smiled tenderly. He could not bring himself to tell her that he had just eaten and he said, "I'm glad you fixed dinner. I'm very hungry." He bent and embraced her; he could not remember ever holding a body so filled with life. He kissed her because he was happy she was his.

"Sit down, Itzhak, sit down," she said, as if afraid she might frighten him if she spoke too loudly or quickly. She pushed him into the living room area with its brightly covered studio couch, Modigliani prints and rows of books and black and orange floor cushions. He must remember, he told himself, to bring her some Käthe Kollwitz prints, Mickey would like those; she might even cry over them, Hod thought, again, tenderly. Kollwitz was German, but she had had a feel for life that the Nazis couldn't take, couldn't like, for they were going in the other direction.

"How did it go today?" she asked.

He moved his shoulders and smiled disarmingly at her. "About the same. Some promises, but I am sure things will improve." He broadened his smile; he did not want her to worry. "I have been in America only eight months, and only two in New York. In two months I met you, how much more luck can a man have? As to the jewelry, it will go all right. But perhaps what I should try to start is a little store instead of selling out of a bag, no? Good Israeli stones and trinkets, like copper from King Solomon's mines and the polished stones from near Eilat. . . ."

Mickey smiled her shy smile.

Hod said, "It is time for me to settle down. Mickey, I think also that my accent is now not so pronounced?"

"Sometimes it is and sometimes it isn't."

Hod nodded, stood and took off his jacket. "Today," he said, "for the first time, I thought about settling in America."

"Oh," Mickey said. Somewhere in the back of her mind she had thought they would go to Israel together.

"I've got to think about it," Hod said. "I'm getting on, you know."

"Some of your phrases, like that one, sound very British," Mickey said.

Hod smiled. "The British have always been with us, Mickey, not on our side, but as a problem, a sickness."

They couldn't get the Arabs to fight with them because the Arabs were inclined toward the Germans, so the British, with reluctance, formed the Jewish Brigades, Hod joined a unit immediately; it was a change from the routine of the kibbutz and he could take revenge on the fascists. While others went to North Africa, he went to Ethiopia with a commando unit; Germans were hard to come by, but there were plenty of Italians. When it looked as though the Germans might take Alexandria, they were flown to Cairo and held in readiness for the trip north, but the Germans were rolled back; Hod had a leave in Cairo.

He had come to love the city, especially the wide, neat streets in the Zamelek section. That was where he had crippled three British soldiers in a bar when they insulted him. After that, he went around alone, spending hours in the museum walking in and out of the rows of sarcophagi, pharaohs' carriages, and peering at dynastic jewelry and weapons. Out at Giza he studied the pyramids with the eye of a man critical of the work of his forebears. We built them, he thought, we built them.

From Cairo he returned to Ethiopia where his group raided the Italian patrols and air fields between Asmara and Aksum; here was the browned, ageless spine of the world, curved high in the air, a mountain ridge frozen in the agony of cataclysm in a time without record. Always with them were the Africans, the Gallas, Somalis and Amharas.

The unit did not get its flag until 1944 and with British permission. Hod did not remember being moved when it was unfurled to catch the winds of the Ethiopian peaks. It was just another Star of David, a blue star on a white background. It should have been a yellow star, like the stars worn on the ragged coats of millions in Europe and Russia; like the stars that had been ripped from those condemned to the chambers and ovens so they could be given to still others. Alone, away from the British, away from his fellow Jews, but under the unblinking eyes of the blacks (for, what could they know of these things?) Hod sat and cried and thought of Warsaw and what had happened to the Jews there. He trembled in fury and his tears, angry tears, stung his cheeks.

At the war's end, when he returned to Israel and the furious maneuvering for a Jewish home for Europe's refugees began in earnest, he quietly joined the Irgun Zvai Leumi. Here were the vengeful, the survivors of the death camps, the sole broken members of hundreds of families; here were the victims of the world's indifference; here were the remains from a thousand ghettos during two thousand years. Here were the survivors of a holocaust the earth had never been witness to before.

And there were the British, that awful conglomeration of dour islanders, the descendants of King John. King John took Jewish money for his wars when the Italians would lend him no more, then he transferred his Jews to the sand bars in the Thames at low tide and let them drown when the tide came in. The British who let the Jews help rebuild Oxford, then beat, robbed and cursed them for it; the British who, unable to do it themselves, allowed Disraeli to go to Rothschild to borrow money so the British lion could rest its flea-bitten haunches on the banks of a canal called the Suez; the British, so bereft of symbols of power and masculinity that they had to borrow the lion from that worst of all places, Africa; the British with their Lawrence and their Arabs and the Arabs' oil. They were about to quit the land, but they were leaving all the high ground guard stations to the Arabs, a fact which surprised no one.

The Irgun had had that necessary historical view and to the Irgun the British were as much the enemy as the Germans had been, as much a debtor as any other people who had taken and given nothing or very little in return. There was a bill come due. The Irgun was collecting payment.

Now it was very late. Breathing heavily, Itzhak had just withdrawn. He turned on his back. Mickey's breathing was still rapid and once in a while when she swallowed, it sounded like a gulp for air. Itzhak lit a cigarette, drew on it, and handed it to her. They smoked in silence, Itzhak stroking her body, and soon her breathing became regular and he could feel the muscles in her body relax. He said, "I have the feeling tonight, and it is so close, so powerful, that my luck is going to change very soon."

And Mickey said, as if she hadn't heard, "Ahh, Itzhak, how wonderful you are."

six

Browning disembarked from the plane. At the rent-a-car booth he had to provide an inordinate amount of identification along with his credit card, but finally he was free to pick up the automobile from the watchful Negro car-jocks.

"Hey, brothers, how goes it?" he said to them.

They nodded and pointed out his car. Browning got into it and drove away slowly, carefully observing the traffic signs. He did this automatically and without strain; he had been in the South before. He passed through the heart of the city, glancing at the new luxury apartments that had replaced the Negro slums through urban renewal. Civil rights acts and new laws had not influenced this city much; no Negroes lived in the new buildings because they couldn't afford to, which made segregation just as effective as it had been since the *conquistadores* tracked through America almost four hundred years ago. "Urban renewal means Negro removal," the phrase used to go. No one was quoting phrases any more, for phrases did little good except to reinforce what you already knew about *Chuck;* you were already filled to bursting with what you knew.

Browning drove past the high-risers with their white marble facades and uniform green window awnings and air conditioners, and suddenly the city began to crowd him with tobacco shops, lunch counters and small stores; with gas stations and graying one- and two-family houses. This was the way he remembered the city, but he missed that chorus of black voices that used to vibrate on the corners before the luxury apartments came. Now the white faces were becoming mixed with black faces, and then a few blocks further on all the faces were black. He swung off Washington Avenue and paused for a stop sign. Each of the corners was occupied: there was a large liquor store, and Browning glimpsed a white man standing with his hands on his hips, while a young Negro washed the plate glass windows; there was a gas station, a supermarket and a medium-sized dry-goods store. Browning drove on down the street and the Negro neighborhood closed in behind him. There were no sidewalks now.

At the end of the street, he drove into the parking lot of Clarke's Motel. He braked near the office and glanced around. The swimming pool had been cleaned and painted; new units had been added to the motel. Indeed, the parking lot was now asphalt instead of dirt and gravel. Clarke, Browning thought, was prospering with integration. Negroes did not trust it, the new laws gave few heart; they remembered too well the old laws. No, they did not trust them any more than he did and that was why he was here at Clarke's (Negro) Motel and not downtown as Bill Barton would be. That was Barton's job and no drunk peckerwood would bother Barton; the downtown hotels would see to that. It happened that, on occasion, a nigger really did get big and to mess with him would be to bring in Washington with the Lincoln Memorial thrown in.

Once he was settled in his room, Browning called Lincoln W. Braithwaite II. No Negro in the state was as big as Braithwaite, who was both president and chairman of the board of the Crispus Attucks Mutual Insurance Company. Braithwaite's father had built the company from nickels and dimes, double-crossing and bottom-dealing his partners and his policyholders. The policyholders, when their policies came due, had not, he advised them with mock sadness, read the small print. What they collected was often one-third of what they believed they were entitled to, small print or not, but there was no other company that would accept them as policyholders. They stuck with Crispus Attucks. As to the partners, both now in their late sixties, one was an "actuarial consultant," and the other a "consultant in community relations," offices with as little meaning as their titles, but which carried a more than adequate stipend for both, and in the community, a great degree of respect.

The elder Braithwaite had been found dead under mysterious circumstances when the current president was still a young boy. The autopsy had revealed traces of sperm in his throat. It had been known for years that he was a football fanatic; that he often supplemented the meager scholarships of the football players with gifts of money, clothes and dinners, which were held in his spacious home not far from the campus.

Browning was put through two crisp-speaking secretaries before he reached Braithwaite II. Braithwaite II had received a call from Mr. Barton and was delighted to have Mr. Browning in town. Where was he staying, downtown?

Well, he would send a car at six to bring him to dinner, after a drink or so first, of course. Oh; he, Browning, had his own car. Okay. Would he mind if another couple was present? There would be ample time to discuss his contribution to IRJ.

Next, Browning called Herb Dixon who had also studied for his doctorate at Columbia. Dixon had sometimes gone to Albany with Browning to spend the days between classes. Dr. Dixon had returned South to teach sociology, feeling that he could do more here than in the North.

And he had. Dixon had coached the first lunch counter sit-ins; he had pioneered the classes in nonviolent techniques and had himself slapped, punched and provoked his students to the limits and then beyond. "If you can't take it, get out," he had said. Those who survived his classes could take it. Dixon had been a Freedom Rider and his bus had been burned out; he had marched at Washington and Selma and back to Washington after King's death, and had worked in the summer program in Mississippi that claimed the lives of Goodman, Schwerner and Chaney. Twice his own home had been bombed and one of his daughters had taken a bomb splinter in the hand. Herb Dixon had run out of nonviolence.

Of all the people he knew, Browning felt he could confide in Dixon, and he longed to do just that. But he knew he would not; his plan was irrevocable. If there were repercussions from the Carrigan matter, though the officials investigated high and low, as they usually did, imagining a conspiracy, there would only be himself, himself and some white men who were in it for money. One black man and not five hundred. So he would not talk to Dixon, although he thought Dixon would agree and be pleased. No, not a word to Dixon.

This was the way it had to be for those kids in the streets, who once they got on them became prey for every white fascist, in uniform or not, who spent his days and nights waiting for open season to begin on Negroes. This was the way it had to be to protect those who had managed by some black magic to own their homes or stores, which were often destroyed along with *Chuck's* stores in the frenzies. This was the way it had to be to keep the state legislatures and the Congress from doing what they did after every rebellion — draw the noose tighter and tighter with dangerous new laws as though they were seeking the final excuse to begin the exterminations. No, silence. No words, confidences or threats, which in the final analysis are put forth in a vain attempt to obtain legal redress. No, nothing but the deed.

Although they corresponded irregularly and even though Browning had last been in the city only two years ago, he was shocked to see how thin and drawn Dixon was. He chain smoked cigarettes, where once he had smoked a pipe. His hair was now thoroughly flecked with gray and his movements were jerky, as a man coming out of shock.

"Hey there, Gene," he said, cheerfully enough. "I see you folks there in New York are setting up another thing for the summer."

"What's the news on that, Herb?"

"Nothing big yet. The cops've been reinforced, twenty-four-hour call, the mayor and leaders appealing for calm . . ."

"The usual thing. Herb, what in the hell have they done to you, man?"

"It's whipping me. I'm trying to get this thing fixed in my mind with an answer, and the only one I get is that it's not going to work, Gene, because they don't want it to work."

When, Browning wondered, had he reached that conclusion, the same time he had? How many others were reaching it too?

"By the way," Dixon said, "you're not looking so hot yourself."

"Well, it isn't easy."

"So you think Braithwaite is going to give you some money, hey?"

"Isn't he?"

Dixon said, "Oh, he'll drop a little bread on you, all right."

"A little? I need dollars from him; I need lots of dollars from everyone I talk to. We just don't have any money, Herb. If this new street scene comes off because of that cop, we're going to have to bail those people out, then we'll be flat broke. I mean, the white cats are tired of having the basket passed forever and ever; they thought this thing was going to end in two weeks, so everything was nice. Now it looks like it's going to last another century, maybe, and they've given up. So, here I am trying to shake down Brother Braithwaite. How much will he give me?"

"If your luck is running high you might get five big bills. When I was into this thing, he gave us not one red penny for fear of upsetting the rapport he's got with the crackers here. He's the only one who benefits from it."

"I've got to make him understand that we need that money and even if I can't get it all, I've got to leave the door open so I can get back."

"Diplomacy, Gene."

"Let's get a drink and swim."

In the water Dixon said, "You'd have been welcome at my house, you know."

"I appreciate that," Browning said, floating in a circle, "but I always promise Val that I won't stay with you because she doesn't want me to get blown up. I don't want me to get blown up either."

A smile broke over Dixon's somber face. "Matter of fact, nobody stays with us any more; nobody drops in unexpectedly to eat up all the fried chicken and drink up all the bourbon. It's rather nice."

"Hey, Herb, you know something? I think Nora's shacking up. I mean she told me she wasn't and I believe her, but, man, it's only a question of the right combination of things."

Dixon breast-stroked down the pool. "She's what, eighteen?"

"Yeah."

"Well, Gene, what do you want me to tell you?"

"Nothing! I hope you drown down at the deep end!"

"How many girls did you screw who were eighteen?"

"I did all right."

"It's got to happen, man. The best thing you can do for Nora is hope she gets somebody who knows what he's doing, and if I were you, that's all I'd be concerned with."

They were floating in silence when a blue and gold car drove into the parking lot.

"Well, there they are," Dixon said. "Just a little behind schedule."

Browning looked at the police car and the two officers,

who were looking at them. "Now they know we're right here and not starting a rebellion."

Dixon said, "Hell, the minute your foot hit the ground at the airport they had you, and they'll have you until you leave town in the morning."

"Braithwaite will have a little explaining to do to the city fathers?"

"Yessir. And if he gives you, it's going to be cash so it can't be traced."

Browning watched the cops as Dixon continued speaking: "These people can turn down medical reports of the policyholders; the state can suddenly decide that even Negroes shouldn't be paying as much as they are for Crispus Attucks insurance; they can send in inspectors and make everyone nervous for months. So old Lincoln Braithwaite is going to hand you cash and then tell the white folks that he gave you nothing and everyone's going to be happy."

The police car cruised in a large, slow circle and then was driven out of the lot altogether. Browning felt an immediate sense of relief. "I just don't like cops," he said. "No where, no time."

Dixon swam for the side of the pool. "It's time for me to get out of here. They know I'm here and I don't want them to start thinking they can mess over my family while I'm away." Dixon dressed hurriedly in Browning's room and drove away. Browning lay down to rest.

Later, with a sense of weariness, Browning rose, showered and dressed. He wished Dixon back so that he could go with him to Braithwaite's. They could talk a bit more then. But it seemed as if they both had realized a couple of years ago that all talk led to the problem, all of it, and eventually even their ideas had become the same. The problem overrode all other considerations. Friends they were and friends they would remain, but to remain so meant that they could not force one another to look inside where so much hurt lay oozing like hot lava. Now they were at the impasse; which one would commence to act instead of think?

Braithwaite's lay at the southern edge of the city. Along the way there was a stretch of blacktop road that passed through an isolated section. Tall slender pines rose on either side of the road. It was on this stretch that Browning noticed a police car tailing him. On this road, Browning knew, if it was night, the cops stopped Negroes and worked them over. For the hell of it. They also raped, when they could, lone Negro matrons on their way to the suburban ghetto near Braithwaite. Browning watched the car carefully until he pulled in at Braithwaite's. The car made a U-turn and headed back for the city.

Browning pulled up in front of a three-car garage. The house itself was a gigantic split-level fronted by a large neat lawn. For shade there were oak and cypress trees. Browning felt a surge of jealousy. No man should live this well in the bosom of the enemy, no man.

A slender brown man with a pleasant face bounded onto the terrace as Browning approached the house, breathing deeply of the freshly cut grass. Braithwaite. Browning recognized him from photographs. Braithwaite smiled and Browning forced one in return. Was Braithwaite followed by the police? "I'm Link Braithwaite and you're Bill Barton's assistant, Gene Browning. Good to see you. Come on in." They shook hands and entered the house. Braithwaite shouted, "Barbara, Mr. Browning's here." To Browning he said, "Let's have a drink. Scotch? This is bourbon country, you know, but I can't stand it."

"Scotch," Browning said.

"Have a seat. Right there. The view is great." Braithwaite moved silently over the deep carpet and Browning sat down on the low couch. He could tell it was expensive; his backside had never felt so good. And the view was great. The house was on a slight hill; he hadn't noticed that before. Through the picture window he could see the green of the suburb fall gently away, down to the city itself.

Browning accepted the drink Braithwaite held out to him. His host sat down beside him. "Looks like Bill's got his hands full again up there. Do you think it'll come off, Mr. Browning?"

"We hope not, but it may. That's my reason for being here, Mr. Braithwaite. IRJ is flat broke. We'll have to bail those people out if this thing gets off the ground. Then in another month we can be out of business altogether. We can't count on white donors any more. The rebellions made them feel that their money and time were wasted. And then, too, they take to heart all the 'Get Whitey' shouts and go away pouting. We don't have any choice but to appeal to black Americans who have the means to help us."

"Yes, yes," Braithwaite said, lighting a cigarette. "I know. But I'm sure Bill told you that what well-to-do Negroes *say* they've got often is not *what* they've got."

"Yes, Mr. Braithwaite, but —"

Braithwaite leaped to his feet. "Here's my wife."

She was as Browning thought she would be. Very handsome and very fair. Her eyes were green and her features regular. "How do you do, Mrs. Braithwaite?" he said.

"So nice of you to come, Mr. Browning. Bill always speaks of you when he visits. How long will you be in town, long enough to give Link some exercise at golf or tennis?"

"I leave in the morning," Browning said. She sat down beside him while her husband mixed a drink for her. Browning didn't feel it necessary to say that he didn't play either game, hated them in fact.

"You folks are getting ready to have a riot," she said with a laugh. "That's almost old hat by now."

"Just the usual old-time slave revolt," Browning said, knowing that she would not make the distinction between riot and revolt.

"Aren't they terrible? The white people never learn. Congress will convene, committees will be formed, there'll be panel shows with all the usual spokesmen, studies will come out — and it'll be just like it was in the Sixties."

"I'm afraid so," Browning said.

"It's a pity you're not going to stay and see our town," she said. Braithwaite returned and handed her the drink.

"I already know your town. Herb Dixon is a friend of mine. We were at Columbia together. I've been down about three times before, and just in case I'd lost my way, a cop followed me out here tonight." He wanted to say it without sounding as though he was accusing them. He saw them glance at each other.

Braithwaite said, "They really check on people coming from out of town. But you have a rented car, don't you?"

"Yes, but Herb said they'd probably seen me at the airport. You know, I'm just as cynical as the next guy about this whole business, but it becomes a bit much when they put the tail on you like this."

They watched a car turn off the main road and drive

slowly up the driveway to the garage. "The Neals," Mrs. Braithwaite said. "They are very nice people," she said reassuringly, as her husband went to the terrace to greet them. "Young but nice." The Braithwaites, Browning guessed, were in their late forties.

Neal, as it turned out, was a mortician who had an arrangement with Crispus Attucks in the matter of death benefits. Mrs. Neal and Mrs. Braithwaite were sorority sisters. How incestuous were these southern Negro business relationships, Browning thought as he labored through more drinks, dinner and the Neals' leavetaking. The city now was a mass of white and green polka dots, streetlights. Browning was wondering if the cops were waiting for him on that lonely stretch of road back to the motel. Mrs. Braithwaite bade him good-night and suddenly he was alone with her husband. Now, the nitty-gritty. Now, for the money, the bullshit or both.

"What does Dixon have to say about us, Mr. Browning?"

I need this money, Browning told himself. I need it badly, which means that I have to put myself in the trick to get it. He said, "He said that you'd never made your contributions to his organization public, or to any other organization, either."

"Yes. Well, we find it necessary to deal in cash for reasons you must have found obvious this afternoon when the police followed you out here. It's not only the police, it's the entire system. I would rather contribute to an organization that maintains its offices out of the state, even out of the South . . ."

Browning listened to his reasons and was glad that Braithwaite had not pursued his relationship with Dixon.

". . . We provide quite a bit of employment for the Negroes in this community . . ."

Yeah, at minimum wages, Browning thought, and the debits of the agents are five times as many as a hard-working agent in a white company would dare to carry and keep in line.

". . . so you see, it's not the personal consideration, but the consideration for one hundred and fifty people in the office and three hundred agents throughout the state. These are the reasons I prefer to deal in cash and without publicity."

All right, all right, Browning thought.

"How much are you looking for, Mr. Browning?"

"Bill didn't tell you in his letter?"

"No."

Browning stared through the picture window at the city and said, "Mr. Braithwaite, we've got to get fifteen hundred dollars from each person on our select list, or we'll be in trouble. We are in real danger of going under. I know I said that before, but I can't stress it too much."

"Fifteen hundred," Braithwaite said.

"We're in trouble. You know the function we perform can't be duplicated by any other organization. It would take a new organization ten years with luck to get where we are right now. The whole Movement can be set back a decade if we don't pull out of this hole."

"Maybe the employees will . . ." Braithwaite smiled. "I don't suppose there's time to begin a drive like that?"

"No, sir, there isn't. We're going to the cream of black business because there's no place else to go. Mr. Braithwaite, I've got a lot of people to see. I don't want to let it be known that I struck out on the first pitch. You're my first stop."

Braithwaite stood. "Listen, Mr. Browning, I'm a businessman. I don't give away money for nothing; I want something for it."

"What?"

"I want Herb Dixon to stop agitating around here. He's not accomplishing anything. He's getting the people, black and white, so upset that we can't move forward. I want him to cut it out. He could bring the state people into my company for a massive economic reprisal. He tells the people that Crispus Attucks insurance is high and doesn't really bring them the benefits it should. He's a troublemaker. I want him stopped."

"You know he's not in IRJ, Mr. Braithwaite; we don't have any influence over him."

Braithwaite rubbed his face. "Mr. Browning, I've had a long, tough day, and I don't really care whether Dixon's with IRJ or not. You want fifteen hundred dollars, I want Herb Dixon quiet. Those are the terms."

"I'll see what I can— "

"No, Mr. Browning. You misunderstand me. Dixon quiet, you get fifteen hundred cash delivered to you at your motel before you leave in the morning. That's the big print; there's nothing more."

"Yes there is."

"What?"

"I'll need sixty days for Herb. In sixty days or less, I can quiet him. That's a promise."

"Sixty days. Two months," Braithwaite murmured to himself.

Browning was thinking: In fifteen days they'll have the money. Soon after that the deal would be consummated, and if Braithwaite wants, I'll cut it down to a month. He can tell his "people" then, promise them "peace" at least until next summer.

"Too much time," Braithwaite said. "A month. Five weeks at the outside."

"You've got yourself a deal," Browning said.

Braithwaite broke into a smile and came forward to take Browning's hand. "Now, I knew you New York guys were into some of everything. I knew we could talk business or Bill wouldn't have sent you. Have a spot of brandy. What room are you in at the motel?"

Browning had brandy. Tomorrow morning, in cash, he would have the money. Bill Barton had put him in the trick and he wasn't surprised. Deals, compromises, they made the world go round, he guessed.

"Will you see Dixon before you go?"

"Oh, no," Browning said, smiling. "He'll get the word right from New York. Directly."

Braithwaite grinned now. "Good. That's business. That's the way to work it."

Yep, Browning thought. On the day it happens, I'll send him the newspaper clippings. That'll do it.

They shook hands on the terrace and Browning walked slowly to his car. This was going to be an exhausting trip; he was going to have to get neck-deep in a lot of stinking stuff.

He stayed well within the speed limit passing down the lonely road. He saw a parked police car, but it did not follow him. Browning wondered if his host had called them off now that everything was going to be just fine. Browning laughed to himself. What the hell. It was going to be all right in the end, when that cop lay dead. Braithwaite didn't know just how fine it was going to be.

seven

A week later Browning left the South altogether. He had five checks amounting to four thousand five hundred dollars; and he had Braithwaite's fifteen hundred in cash. It was almost all he could do to keep from taking the next plane back to New York and handing the bills over to the strange man he had met walking around the Reservoir. But four thousand five hundred dollars . . . What had he expected anyway? You could go down the list of *Ebony*-style black millionaires, but when you were sitting down with them in a richly furnished office or home, you discovered that the millions were all potential, all tied up in paper and columns of red and black numbers; or they were tied up in real estate or some other business; or were in fact millions only because of rumor.

Yet Browning could not blame these men. Of course they lent themselves to *Ebony* publicity and to rumor; they lived as high on the hog as they could afford to or as their reputations demanded. Like white people.

Behind Browning were visits to the wealthiest mortician, B. B. Hudson (*Splendid Service for the Supreme
Sleep*, 18 Magnolia Street), a small, whispering man who
with his bent head seemed in perpetual prayer; Agnew
Washington Lincoln, publisher of the *Black Eagle*, who,
although but a jump or two from the company seeking to
repossess his printing press, gave Browning a check for five
hundred dollars; Billy Joe Turner, a hard-laughing, hard-
drinking real estate man who drove a lavender Cadillac ("I
want ev'abody to see me comin' ") and had a thing for lady
bartenders. Browning had worked hard to get Billy Joe
Turner's check for a thousand; he had had to drink as much
as he did and talk as pretty to the lady bartenders. Bas-
combe, the caterer (*You Call It In; We'll Cook It Out to
You*) was a small, dark man whose fried chicken, frogs legs
and sweet potato pie were much sought after by the white
community; he wore a snow-white chef's cap while he
supervised the orders in his spotless stainless steel kitchen.

Betty Blanton was a socialite. She belonged to the
Links, Jack and Jills, and the AKAs. In her fifties, Mrs.
Blanton, one of those divorcées who appear in the *Ebony*
pages, had a thing for young men, and young men knew it,
wanted to know it, because Betty Blanton's family was said
to be high up in Bolito circles. She made frequent trips to
Washington, Atlanta, New York, Chicago and Los Angeles
to keep in the social swirl of things and to meet new people
whom she could invite to her modern mansion complete
with swimming pool and glass sauna bath. Browning did not
get his check until the morning after he had made love to
her.

Now, three thousand miles away and some eight hours
later, Browning in a rented car found his way to the Bald-

win Hills section of Los Angeles and the home of Dr. Millard Jessup. It was Wednesday, doctors' day off, and Jessup was waiting for Browning at home. Back in New York there was talk about Dr. Jessup; he was almost too militant. Browning reflected on his thoughts: too millitant. Well, yes, that *was* the correct phrase; one could be too militant in Browning's eyes. One could create the shock waves, that was easy, but it would not be easy to survive in the desolation of the murderous reaction; that had to come. The militants were like people who could not stand stitches, and so ripped them out, to their own detriment and everyone else's.

"Browning," the man said when he opened the door of the out-of-place Tudor-style home in answer to Browning's ring. "You're Browning, right? C'mon in here, man." They shook hands and Browning was relieved at Jessup's informality. The South in many respects still moved on formality, everything was with title. Jessup was a large, good-looking Negro, fair in complexion. "How's old Bill?" Jessup asked. They were padding across a floor covered with a deep off-white rug, and then up a circular stairway, also covered. "We're heading for the bar, brother. I know you can stand a drink. I know I can."

Softly they passed down a wide hall of the second floor and Browning caught glimpses of the corners of beds, windows surrounded by plants which basked in the hot sun. "My wife and kids are out — shopping, lunch and a movie." Jessup was still walking with a peculiar crisp stride, as if he were stepping over patches of collard greens. "Here we go." The hallway opened on a large shaded room. Browning saw at once that it contained a bar, billiard table and Ping-Pong table. Jessup slipped behind the bar. "What'll it be?"

"Scotch, water and ice," Browning said.

"A very civilized drink."

Browning walked slowly down the room, his eyes fixed on the photo portraits on the walls. These were the people Jessup was supposed to be associated with. There: Morris Greene. Browning had met him a few times before their goals had become different; had met him and liked him because they thought alike. Greene was said to have spent five months training cadres in the Blue Ridge Mountains. To be sure, there was the great, bushy Afro and the beard, the *kente* robe. Greene was the guerrilla warfare expert. Did he really expect battles to be fought in the cities? Then what was he training in the mountains for? Crazy.

It was fitting that the next portrait was of Leonard Trotman. He wore an African skullcap atop his Afro and a part of his *kente* was visible. Why, Browning wondered, did so many of them have to go the African route? What in the hell did Africa have to do with the present situation? And wasn't this African business a kind of retreat or defeat, after all? Uniforms. Everyone had to have his uniform.

Browning had met Trotman also. Trotman overnight had changed from an innocent southern college boy to a complete black anarchist and then to an organizer. Under Greene's guidance he had grown, but then he had been ready material after his only sister had been dynamited through that classroom wall. Greene and Trotman were said to be inseparable, yet they were seen together only rarely. Either their ideas were alike or they complemented each other.

Browning took another step. Grant Malone stared

down at him with clear, twinkling eyes, and Browning almost smiled back. Everyone had thought Malone to be the burningest thing to come down the pike. Once. Then Greene and Trotman had come along and now Malone seemed to be almost as one with A. Philip Randolph. He was the same age as Greene and Trotman.

Serene described the expression on the face of Father Parker. The white collar curved around his throat, a strange slash between the black of his garb and the black of his face. Almost any day now Parker would be kicked out of his diocese. Catholic laymen around the country opposed the advances of their leaders; now the leaders were hearkening to the people who kept them in business; Father Parker would have to go.

Parker taught the history of slave revolts, the role of the Catholic church in slavery and the slave trade and reminded his followers that the Bible also said, in addition to turn the other cheek, an eye for an eye and a tooth for a tooth. Parker was only teaching what was there to be taught, but he was going, had to go. But then, men of the Book often had to go. The big problem was that not enough of them did.

"I see you like the gallery," Jessup said, coming up with the drink. "They're all there." He nodded toward Greene and Trotman. "Twin sticks of dynamite. Never know when they're going to go off."

"You contribute to them, too, I hear," Browning said.

"More than that, man. These fellows are where it's at. I mean all those people who went before — necessary — maybe even made it possible for these guys to be the way they are. They meet here when they're in town at the same time. And we've got some plans."

"We heard about them, Doctor."

"How much did you hear?" Jessup was smiling and Browning thought it was a smile of pride. The doctor took his elbow and led him out on the patio. Downtown Los Angeles was almost covered by a thin haze of smog.

Browning wondered if he should go into what he had heard. But then, he had to know, definitely, just how much time he could still call his. "We heard you were organizing. That you have some John Birch money behind you. You're working with them."

Jessup laughed, his eyes crinkling at the corners. He glanced downtown and shook his glass so that the ice tinkled. "Yep. We're organizing. What else can we do? Nothing has changed since the riots. If they open up chain stores out in Watts, none of them have windows, just boards. Now they want to take our money and give themselves maximum protection. We got Reagan because of the riots. Do you know that there are entire industries out here that have *never* hired a black person? Busdrivers wonder why they get robbed — but they never wonder what the reaction of passengers is when the drivers don't let them off at their stops. It's like the cabdrivers in New York. Maybe so damned many of them wouldn't get killed if Negro passengers were not treated so badly by them, not being picked up and all that. I mean, it's easier to kill someone if you're pissed off at him.

"We're organized and organizing. I'm going to take you up in the country. Not a long drive. I want you to see. I want you to tell Bill this is a whole new ball game. That's why this is my last check. The black middle class, if I'm a member, is returning to grass roots and the knuckle-to-knuckle. It's really the only thing these people understand, you know."

"And the Birch people?"

Jessup almost sneered into his glass. "As far as I know, it's just white money. It may be even more right than the Birchers, hell, I don't know. They know what we're up to, and of course they want us for their own reasons. Maybe they think they'll take over when everything's a shambles, but that's not the way *we* plan it. Like most white people, they don't give Negroes credit for having an ounce of brains. But believe me when I tell you: we've got those cats cased, and like Uncle Tom got a lot of mileage out of his role, certainly more than Nat Turner ever did; we're cooling too. We will have ours at the very moment Whitey thinks he has his, but he won't have the ghetto; he doesn't want it, he's afraid of it, and the ghettos of every city in this nation will be our fortresses.

"Look at it this way, Browning. Ever since Negroes have been Negroes in this country, they've taken white money, Rosenwald, Ford, Rockefeller, so why not us? I mean, is Whitey going to be comfortable if he *isn't* giving away money to niggers?" Jessup laughed. "Man, we have got butlers, maids, drivers, laundresses, handymen, planted in the home of every white man we have contact with. You have a nation of people with a penchant for living well as cheaply as possible, cheap labor, and that means Negroes and Mexicans and Puerto Ricans — we've got them too — so our network is natural. We are into something this time."

Browning was digesting it all. Could Jessup be believed? No — he, Browning, was thinking like a white man now. Why not these things?

Jessup leaped up. "How about that drive? We can eat

up there. I'm pretty good with a steak and there'll be some cold beer. It's a relaxing drive. Besides, you can fill Bill in."

They went downstairs and Jessup, now wearing a Dodger ball cap, backed his Jaguar out of the garage. As Browning got in, the doctor eased on a pair of sunglasses. They headed toward Pacific Coast Highway 101.

"How much is Bill looking for this time?"

"As much as a man can spare and then some," Browning shouted back.

Jessup smiled. It was a strange smile; it twisted up the very corners of his mouth and his eyes crinkled. But the rest of his mouth remained the same and Browning remembered that no smile-light had entered Jessup's eyes when he smiled on the patio. "You're in a real hole, is that it?"

"Like the kids say, Doctor, it's pretty up tight."

"Those kids are catching the imagination of Negroes all over," Jessup said. He handled the car indolently.

"And a lot of white people, too," Browning said.

"That's fear."

"That's exactly what I meant," Browning said.

Jessup said, "Tough about their fear. For eight generations Negroes have lived, bred and died in fear. Now they think they have a monopoly on it, or are they just using it for something else?"

Cautiously Browning answered, "Yes, there's that to be considered, too."

They raced up the highway, the ocean on the west, the mountains on the east, until Jessup spoke. "Did you like our house?"

"Yes, lovely."

"Lived there seven years and none of our neighbors

have spoken to us, not the Caucasians or the Orientals. Seven years." He laughed suddenly. "To hell with them. If I turned Greene and Trotman and a few others loose on them, they'd wish they'd kissed my ass every morning and ate my shit at night. If they had any more money and if the ocean wasn't just a few miles away, they'd try to move again. But Los Angeles is the last stop for the bigot. They've been backing up, backing up, all over the country, but they can't back up any more; that goddamn frontier they're always talking about has been gone for a long time. It's like Joe Louis said —"

"They can run, but they can't hide," Browning cut in.

"Exactly, and I think they know that now and that's why things are getting sticky."

"Pretty country," Browning observed some moments later.

An hour from Los Angeles, Jessup picked his way eastward, spinning the steering wheel easily between his hands, ever climbing. "Look behind you," Jessup said.

Browning turned around. The mountains fell away behind them, long, brown, falling slopes frizzled with the green of trees and grass. The blue sea, foaming white, fell wave after wave upon the smooth tanned beaches. They reached the crest of the mountains and the blacktop road narrowed and then ended altogether. Jessup barreled down the dirt road, dust exploding behind them. They drove, it seemed to Browning, for a long time before the road opened on a clearing.

"Are those barracks?" Browning saw the buildings. They were austere and faced with split logs.

"That's right, they are barracks," Jessup said.

There were four buildings. "How many men do they hold?" Browning asked.

"Each one, fifty to sixty men. Maybe more. It depends."

They were past the buildings now, the car rocking gently down a dirt road.

From time to time Jessup turned and glanced at Browning's suddenly strained-looking face. "It had to come, you know."

They pulled up before a large log cabin-type house and the mountain silences swept over them. The sound of the car doors slamming seemed unusually loud. Browning turned to stare at the tops of the barracks, which could just be seen from the porch of the house. He heard Jessup unlocking the door and he turned and followed him inside. The place smelled of seasoned pine and oak and fireplace smoke, all contained in a subtle, still odor which, as soon as the door was opened and the wind swept in, leaped wildly about the room.

Jessup closed the door and strode to the kitchen section. "Another Scotch and I'll thaw out these steaks." Jessup watched Browning hover near the windows. "Some place up here," he said. "All the privacy in the world."

"Must cost a lot of money," Browning said, taking his drink from the doctor.

Jessup had returned to the kitchen section. He said, "You can't imagine how much money all this is costing."

Of course, Browning thought, Greene would be in on this. He was to black would-be guerrillas what Che Guevara had been to Latins.

The steaks began to sizzle in the pan and Browning could smell the garlic salt and the mess of onions. He was, he reflected wearily, very hungry. He walked to the kitchen section. "You know, Dr. Jessup, I've got a lot of relatives. They're getting on. Worked hard all their lives coming up through the first big war, Prohibition, Depression, the lynchings, doors closed everywhere. But they worked hard for their nickels and dimes and when they were getting into their fifties, Joe Louis and Jackie Robinson behind them, the second big war, Roosevelt, many of them bought pieces of homes and spent the next ten years, if they lived, fixing them up. Yes, they worked hard, were humiliated, took it, fought back when they could and struggled on. Everybody comes from someplace, Doctor, and every black ass had to hump it. That's where we came from, out of that. There are others who came out of that who were not so lucky. The ones who're stretching out their hands, and finding nothing, turn to Greene and Trotman. We owe them something."

"That's the way we feel. But you don't get something for nothing. White people are getting richer and richer, and we're getting poorer."

"What I am saying, man, is what comes after?" Browning spoke angrily and found himself trembling.

Jessup took a curious satisfaction in noting this.

Browning said, "Watts lasted six days —"

"They were untrained!" Jessup roared back. "We'll be trained." The doctor put the steaks on plates and set them on the table. Viciously, he opened two cans of beer. "It was the same all over in the Sixties — no training."

After his first bite of the meat Browning said, "So that means you'll last for twelve days. C'mon, Jessup, you know that the same white guilt you're counting on to render them fearful is the same damned guilt that's made them determined to stop every really militant movement and in the stopping provide them with the paper-thin excuse to do exactly what the Germans did to the Jews. Besides, I'm not sure that you're back to the ghetto, back with the guys standing on the corners drinking wine. I think you want them to think you're back to get their support. But you haven't really got out of that middle-class groove you're in. Like most of us, black and white, you want to live good, comfortably, and in this country, as in most countries, it has to be at the expense of others."

"Browning," Jessup said, "I've listened to all the arguments. We're on our way. We are going to accomplish in two weeks what IRJ hasn't been able to accomplish in fifteen years. We are going to nullify industry and police power in this Southland. Then we'll get what we want, which is jobs, a clear, untampered political maneuverability, and a few other things that'll come later. Brother, that's not too much to ask for. You don't even know, but I remember when Pearl Harbor was attacked. Do you remember all those scenes from European movies about the refugees crowding the highways getting out of town? That's the way they were here, too, man, getting their hats, making it on the road back east, scared the Yellow Peril was going to catch up with their white asses. I remember and we can do what we have to do."

After the steak, Jessup declined to show Browning the interiors of the barracks, and they drove back to Los Angeles in silence. Jessup parked in front of Browning's car and took out a checkbook. As he wrote he said, "Mr. Browning, it's been — well — *interesting* and I hope you'll pass on what you saw to Bill Barton." Jessup ripped off the check and handed it to Browning.

"I've been wondering all afternoon," Browning said, "just what would be accomplished by my telling him."

They both got out of the Jaguar. Jessup stretched as he looked at the lighted windows of his home. "It'll save time," he said. "He'll know when they come running to him, to help stop us, that he can't. He can play a good hand for himself by letting nervous whites know that the situation is no longer in his hands. Well, I see my family's home. I'm sorry about the check, being the last one, but Bill will understand, I'm sure. Goodbye, Mr. Browning. Keep an eye on the West."

As he drove to the Los Angeles International Airport the next morning, Browning could hear the planes taking off and landing. Outbound flights he saw go lunging into space to be swallowed at five hundred feet in the smog that already covered the city. Browning was well rested. He had spent the night in a downtown hotel, eating and watching television. The afternoon with Doctor Jessup had left him nervous and fretful. He had called Val and the girls; Nora was going to join in another demonstration at the precinct house where Sergeant Carrigan worked. But Jessup kept returning to Browning's mind. Time was of the essence. Not that Jessup's crew would be ready in quick time. But some word of it could get out; that in itself could trigger the excuse. His, Browning's, own little act of violence became more imperative.

A short time later his plane landed at Las Vegas. Browning deplaned and walked quickly through the small, flashy airport building and hailed a cab. It was almost a straight shot from the airport into town. Within minutes he was in his room, high in the hotel with windows overlooking the tortured horizon. It took him an hour to reach Gary Drake by telephone — Gary Drake, singer, dancer, comic, actor. *Personalité extraordinaire.* Drake was all for the cause. He put his money where his mouth was and not many in his position did that. You could count them on one finger. Gary Drake. Drake was reserving a table for Browning and some friends; there would be a party after the last show.

Pleased that he'd managed to do so much in so little time, Browning went downstairs for lunch, passing through the lobby where glossy prints of Drake were pasted on every available flat surface. Long and lean, Drake was handsome and his complexion was even more fair than Jessup's. It was always funny to hear him joke about race, because Browning could never really conceive of Drake being black. It reminded Browning of Powell: "Us black men, us black people." The Negroes knew that black had to do with soul, otherwise so many other Negroes (like Jessup and Drake and Powell) would be left out. Marcus Garvey would not have looked at Powell twice; in fact, there were no fair Negroes anywhere *near* Garvey, that anyone knew about for sure. When Garvey spoke of color he didn't mean soul; he meant exactly what one could see with the naked eye.

Browning was addicted to cars once he got outside New York City, so he rented another and went probing about Las Vegas. The marquees of the hotels and clubs bore the names of Tex Benecke, Guy Lombardo, Frank Sinatra, Phil Harris, and a few baseball players who sang or played the guitar off-season. Along the sunny streets, showgirls and showboys, many of them still in makeup, sought the inexpensive bars. Browning drove aimlessly, turning into interesting-looking streets and back onto the main highway again. Then, tired of the city, he drove to Lake Mead and on to Hoover Dam. There was a plaque on the face of the dam dedicated to the men who had lost their lives during its construction.

He grew sad during his tour of the dam. Here, he thought, was tremendous proof that if men wished to do a thing they could do it, regardless of the cost in men and materiel. They could literally build a lake in the desert, throw up billions of tons of steel and concrete to keep it there and create electricity, but they couldn't build any kind of bond between men and make it stick.

He leaned over the lip of the dam and watched the rushing water crash into the concrete and become foam. Once more he wondered if he was right in what he was going to do. He told himself again that he was right, that Jessup, all the Jessups, were wrong. He should have told the doctor that he too believed in violence, but not madness. Browning longed to share his secret with someone, ached to set it down, itched to have it over and done with to see if his ounce of prevention could save anything. Climbing back in his car, he felt weary and heavy. He wished for Val, to hold her and hear her laugh or even to complain.

Almost sullenly he drove back to the hotel and turned in the car, and went to his room to take a nap. He did not understand the sudden weariness.

When he woke an eerie golden glow flowed in from the west. The hotel itself was filling with the muted sounds of the cocktail hour, and looking down onto the main street, Browning could see the traffic quickening. He dressed slowly and went down to the dining room for dinner, and when he was finished he walked along the boulevard and back, enjoying the cooling that had come with night. To-morrow night this time, he thought, Chicago, and the night after, New York. Home. He hurried back to his room to catch the television news and promptly fell asleep in the chair.

He woke after ten, threw water on his face and went downstairs to the show room. Cigarette smoke billowed through the halls as he approached it, and he could hear the sound of voices, the clash of cymbals, the taps of a chorus line. Inside the room he was shown to a front table; it was already occupied with a young white woman and a young brown woman, both, Browning observed, showbiz types. "I'm Gene Browning," he said. Both the faces swept toward him, teeth bared in precision smiles.

The white one spoke first: "Hi! We've been waiting for you. Gary asked us to keep you company. I'm Sam. She's Maya. Sit down. Gary hasn't come on yet."

Browning sat and immediately noticed that a waiter was standing beside him.

"We've got ours," Maya said. "Get yours, baby."

"Coming to the party?" Sam asked.

"Sure," Browning said. "Why not?"

Now Maya asked, "How's New York? Groovy town in the spring and fall."

"A little hot right now," Browning said, eyeing the line of long white legs clattering across the stage.

"I'm hip," Sam put in.

Browning glanced at her. She was snapping her fingers to the music; her bottom lip was clenched beneath her upper teeth, and her shoulders moved up and down in time.

"Gary comes on after this," Maya said, shouting above the applause that covered the exit of the chorus line. Silken curtains slid down and the lights came up a bit. An expectant hum of conversation and small laughter ran around the room. Sam leaned forward, flouncing her blond fall; Maya signaled the waiter.

Another flurry of excitement filled the room as the lights dimmed; a soft roll on a kettle drum nudged into the room. Even before the curtain was raised they could hear the sound of tap dancing, and then the silken folds glided silently upward, and Gary Drake, dancing at an incredible rate of speed, burst out of the wings, his lean body coiled as if to spring at the audience. Applause broke loose as Drake traded taps with the drummer's rolls. He danced to the mike stand and lifted the lavalier mike from it. Without a noticeable change of pace, although he had stopped dancing, Drake began to sing an upbeat number; now the full band swung in behind him. Snapping his fingers, Drake, under eyelids that carefully studied the house, moved to his own good rhythm.

Browning was aware of the two girls, one on either side of him; they exuded something like electricity. The number ended and Drake went into a ballad. Once Browning heard Maya mutter, "Sing it, baby! Rap!"

And, as if to remind him of her presence, Sam said, "Grip it, baby, grip it!"

Mr. Showbiz, Browning was thinking, somewhat enviously. Sharp as ratshit and knows it. Go on, brother.

Now Drake was engaging in what the critics called the "free form" section of his act; no one ever knew just what it would be.

"Tonight," Drake said, breathing hard from his exertions, "we gonna get kinda *nasty*." A drum roll filled in the pauses between his sentences, drum rolls that ended with a snap. "Friend of mine's here —" (ra-rad-rat-tat!) "— collecting *money*, honey —" (rat-tatty-da-rat!) "— tell

you something 'bout this money —" (raddy-dat-dat-tat-
tatty!) "— it's to keep this mother from going up in smoke,
dig?" (ratty-at-ratty-at-bap!) "So, I'm gonna help you
loose from some of that bread!" Drake laughed softly into
the mike, as though he was involved in a game and was the
only one who knew the rules. Browning tensed on the edge
of his seat and heard Maya whisper quickly to Sam: "Oh,
oh."

Drake went on. "We don't want this to be one-sided, so
I'm matching. Everything cool?" He flung up one arm and
with a brilliant smile shouted, "Game-time, baby!" He
turned to the band, making sure the mike was still close to
his mouth. "Gimme some of that alto, baby, make this thing
a little sweet." He turned back to his audience, patent
leather pumps flashing in the spots. "Now, we *ready!*" The
music rose up behind him, subdued; he moved his fingers.
"Remember that old game they used to have at the circus
and the county fair? They used to call it hit the nigger."
The drummer hit his snare: *wham!* "That's what we're
going to play right now. You good folks out there gonna
th'ow at Gary Drake. Ball up them tens, baby. Anything less
than a ten hit this stage, there won't be no next show. And
the first ten with an ice cube in it that comes up here, it's
gonna be me and whoever threw it." Now Drake swung
from side to side, furiously popping his fingers. "If you
haven't got a ten, a twenty will do." His smile broadened,
but his voice became a snarl. "Ready now, let's play hit the
nigger."

The alto man played an aimless series of notes; the
drummer went back to his rolls and snaps. Drake swayed
back and forth and occasionally his *"mop, beedy-op"* could
be heard over the mike.

Browning did not see the first tiny green ball flash out of the audience; he saw Drake slip his head to one side and the ball was on the floor behind him. Then came two, three, and soon, flying out of the hands of men and women who had risen to see and throw better, there came a flurry. On stage Drake was taunting, "Aw, you ain't hit the nigger yet. A fifty's bigger. Might have better luck. Th'ow one."

As the bills came flying up the drummer was trying to create the sound of their hitting the floor: *bam. bam. bam, wham, ram, tam, bam.* The flurry of bills began to thin out. Drake kicked the balled-up bills with his toe. "Hey, looka there! The nigger wins! He ain't been hit once! Ain't that somethin' else?" He signaled with one hand and suddenly went into another uptempo number and followed that with a ballad to soothe the restless crowd. Then he was off, the curtain falling and the applause was ragged and uncertain.

Browning took a deep breath.

Maya looked at him. "He's something else, isn't he?"

"Yeah," Browning said. "Yeah, he is."

"That," Sam said, bending toward them, "was like right out of Kafka."

There was already a small crowd at the door of Drake's dressing room. The big, mournful-looking Negro bodyguard saw them and opened the door, Browning following closely behind the two girls. Drake was just emerging from a shower wearing a thick yellow terry cloth robe. "Hey, baby," he said to Browning, taking his hand and shaking it warmly. "How's Billy Barton? Sit down, man. You chicks get him a drink."

Drake flopped face down on a huge couch and his valet, a small man who moved like a shadow, peeled the robe halfway down his back. He began to oil and knead the long muscled torso.

"Well, we got you some bread," Drake said. "I'll match whatever the count is." Maya handed Browning a drink. The room was silent then except for the sound of the valet's hands on Drake's back. Drake spoke. "How did you like them motherfuckers? These people are too much. They *had* to go for it; it was like running out in the South in the Twenties hollering 'Lynch me.' What they feel has got to come out; they want it to come out. I'm just glad they didn't have rocks or hand grenades. Billy keeping busy?"

"Busy as hell," Browning said.

"I can imagine," Drake said. "If you're dealing with Whitey, man, it's a full, fucking-time job." Now Drake looked back at them over his shoulder. "Which one of these chicks you dig the most, Browning?"

Browning was embarrassed. "They're both nice, Gary."

"I know *that,* man. I mean some cats dig gray chicks and others dig Soul. I just wondered what bag you were in. That's all."

Browning looked into his drink; all this was new for him.

Drake and the valet talked softly.

Browning lifted his eyes to the girls and found them smiling at him.

"You've made him blush," Maya said.

Drake looked over his shoulder. "Did I man? I'm sorry. Well, look. You just work it out yourself at the party . . ." He turned back again and Browning heard him say softly, "I mean, it ain't nothin' but pussy, man."

The party began as soon as Drake stepped offstage after his last show; it was two o'clock. The elevators whooshed softly upstairs to Drake's suite carrying movie stars, stage stars, entertainers from the other Vegas night spots; there were athletes, comics and girls in crotch-length mini-skirts. The drapes in the suite had been pulled back and the full moon shone on the rugged desert landscape. There was music, and the go-go girls from the chorus lines of some of the clubs, still heavily made up and with breasts urged upward by wire and pads, moved restlessly through the crowd.

Drake's valet and the huge bodyguard oversaw the fleet of white-jacketed waiters; Drake himself was surrounded by other celebrities, all heavily suntanned. Someone was talking about Aznevour and how he had stormed Vegas only a few weeks ago; there was talk of another Sinatra movie. This one would do for Frank what "From Here to Eternity" had done. Frank was really putting soul in this one instead of cooling through it the way he did in most of his films.

Browning found Maya at his elbow. She said, "You don't like this very much do you?"

"It's a little strange to me. I just came out to beg some money. I don't mind it."

She said, "Sam's in the other room, you know."

Browning placed his empty glass on a tray a waiter was holding and took a refill. "I don't care where Sam is."

Maya took a glass from the tray, smiled and said, "Friend, you've just got yourself a date for the night."

Browning gave her a cautious glance as they made their way to the edge of the crowd. She had an angular face, bright, clear eyes that now seemed to be laughing at him. "What do you do in Vegas?" he asked.

Maya laughed and Browning wondered, Why does she laugh so much?

"I just sort of hang around. I'm a part of what the columnists call 'the entourage.' It's all right isn't it?"

Browning said hastily, "Yes, I mean sure, if that's your thing. . . ."

The mournful-looking bodyguard approached them. "How goes it, baby?" he said to Maya.

"Going and going," she said, "but not gone yet."

"Rap on, Maya. I hear you." The man looked at Browning with dead eyes. "You're Browning, right? Gary says this is for you." Browning took the thick paper bag and the envelope that was being handed to him; he knew that it was the check. In the bag, the money of course, the hit-the-nigger money. "Gary says for you to have a good time, okay, Blood?"

"Okay," Browning said, realizing that "Blood" was short for Blood Brother.

Maya said, "What'll you use it for, guns or butter?"

Browning answered: "I wonder what it would be like to try guns. Just once."

"Let's go to your room and I'll help you count it," Maya said, swallowing her drink.

Browning felt his joint growing very heavy and very warm. They made their way through the crowd until they were just outside the circle that surrounded Drake. "Everything cool, Brother?" Drake asked, pushing through to them. "I mean, you got the things and I didn't get a chance to talk, but tell Billy to keep in touch. I'll help all I can." He chucked Maya under the chin. "See you later."

She stood close to Browning in the elevator. He asked, "Do you live in the hotel, too?"

"We all do. It makes things convenient."

"Yes. Listen, you don't have to help me count this, you know."

"I know. I thought you did, too."

Browning shifted the bag in his arm. They stepped out of the elevator, walked down the carpeted hall which smelled of strong disinfectants, and into Browning's room.

"Anything to drink?" Maya asked.

"No." He watched her walk to the phone and order a bottle of Scotch.

The money had been counted and they were sitting on the bed waiting for the waiter.

"You're married, aren't you?" Maya asked.

"Yes. Two daughters. One in college."

"Really. It's hard to imagine you with a college-age kid. You live in Manhattan?"

"Near Columbia."

"I've always liked New York. Grew up in Harlem, became a dancer, sang a little, then nothing. White people can be mediocre and get by; not soul folks, though."

There was a knock on the door and Maya rose, taking a twenty-dollar bill from the stack. Browning watched her walk to the door. She was well put together; very well put together. Nice of Drake. He thought then of guys who had been to Africa and told of having been offered women to use during the night. That was in the bush, not in the cities where Western influence had been the greatest.

Browning and Maya had two drinks, talking about New York all the while, and then Browning tried to embrace her. Maya pulled away and said sharply, "Not yet."

Oh, oh, Browning said to himself. Oh, *oh*.

She continued talking about New York. It was four o'clock and Browning was tired. Late hours never did him any good the next day. He got up and went to the bathroom, leaving the door open. He brushed his teeth, washed his face and put on his pajamas. He strode out, whipped back the covers of the bed Maya was not on and got into it. She talked and she drank. After a while she said, "I've got this thing, dig? After a while the booze cools it. I can feel it getting quiet already." She reached to the other bed where Browning was curled up away from her, and seized his joint. "Wake up, lover," she said. Browning stirred. "Not quite yet, baby," Maya said, "but I'm getting there." Browning glanced at the bottle; it was almost empty.

He said, "Maya, listen: why don't we just take a raincheck on this. I've got a plane to make in a very few hours and I'm kind of whipped. Not as young as I used to be."

"Don't be impatient, baby," she said, squeezing. "I'm getting there, really getting there." She stood and started to take off her dress. She paused to empty the bottle. "Man, is it coming." She unhooked her bra and her small brown breasts eased down. She laughed and clapped her hands. "Gene Browning, I *know* you haven't had nor will you *ever* have what Maya's going to lay on you this morning!" She stood naked and wide-legged, laughing down at Browning. "I just ought to see what you look like with a moustache on, baby," she said.

Browning thought, Christ. C'mon, bitch. Let's see what you got that's made you so hung up. Damn. These broads with all this great pussy. Like the man said in his dressing room, it's just that. Browning turned on his side, away from her. All right, she wanted to give it away, she was going to have to work to give it to *him;* he needed his rest. When that hot Chicago sun started to bear down, all the trim in the world wasn't going to help. He felt the bed give way beneath her and then her hands were at his pajama belt. Browning kept his eyes closed; he wasn't going to help. If she wanted it up, she was going to have to get it up all by herself and *keep* it up.

"Oh no you don't, you bastard," she said, snapping the bottoms from under his hips. "Get me all hot and bothered and then you lay up there and go to sleep. Man, me and you, we got some loving to do!"

On the morning of the 27th Browning returned to New York. His last stop had been Chicago. He'd felt comfortable there; it was a city he knew. In the South and West he had been practically a stranger feeling his way.

He had seen Big Bobby Odum, fullback for the Bears and the most outspoken black man in professional athletics. Another doctor, B. J. Wright, had been his second call. Wright was a pediatrician with offices on the Gold Coast.

Browning had met Odum in Mr. Stephan's for dinner; he was preparing to report to the training camp at Lake Bluff. He had almost finished his book on discrimination in professional athletics, the book that would tell how black athletes were paid less than white ones (except in his own case); how some college coaches, teamed with sharp attorneys, chiseled goodly portions of the monies offered by the pros to a promising college back; how white athletes and ex-athletes like Tarkenton, Cooz, Giff and Goldie Hornung got endorsements, but black stars (himself included) got nothing, not even Bill Russell, and Willie Mays had to make do with Alaga Syrup and Petrocelli clothes. Odum had backed the last Olympic boycott by black athletes.

Odum had not been as large as he appeared to be on

television, and Browning marveled that a man only a little taller and wider than himself, although much younger, could blast straight up the middle like a howitzer in flat trajectory. Browning liked the Bear screen, coupled with a sweep, that sent Odum goalward, trampling the opposition into the ground. But for all his fame Odum was a bitter man; if he had been white, or if the deals were fair, his life would have been different. "What the average fan doesn't know," he said, "is that the plantation mentality is still present in pro ball."

Dr. B. J. Wright was an ordinary-looking dark brown man who, it was said, liked fast cars and fast women. He was as cool as Odum was hot. His clientele was mostly white, but the black middle class from Lake Meadows and Prairie Shores was finding the way to his office. The rumor was that Wright did not feel too happy about this fact.

Wright came from a small town in the South to go to college in the North. He graduated with honors and became the first Negro to enroll in the medical school which was in the same city. After his honor-laden freshman year, the director gave him a tuition- and expense-paid scholarship to Howard.

"Why can't I study here?" Wright asked.

"We don't want you here," the director answered.

Wright interned at Provident in Chicago. A few years later, he was listed as one of Chicago's eight black millionaires. His check was for $3,500; Odum's, for $1,500.

Browning went directly to the office when he arrived in New York, slogging through the steaming, dirty midsummer heat. He traded stories with Sam Tate and Marvin Dunbar and Amanda, Barton's secretary, as he waited to see Barton.

Barton looked tired when Browning got in. "You look whipped, Bill," Browning said. "What's been going on?"

"Just keeping it cool. I think we're over the hump and it's just as well, Gene, because the last couple of days I've been talking to the accountant. Man, we're so low we'll have to use some of the money you collected for salaries. If we'd had to pay out a bunch of bail money, you wouldn't be able to buy groceries next week. How'd you do?"

"You mean money?" Browning asked with a smile.

Barton smiled, too. "Yeah, I mean money. The other stuff's always out there."

"I make it twelve and a half thousand."

Barton's smile widened. "Really? I was praying you'd manage eight or nine."

"Jessup's given his last check, Bill. He's into something out there."

"Is it what we heard?"

Browning nodded. "And he wants you to know. He's got white money. Greene, Trotman, Parker — you know the people. Barracks up in the mountain. I didn't see any weapons and he didn't — wouldn't, rather — take me close to anything. He says to tell you we're through; that it's where he's at that counts."

Barton rapped his fingertips on the desk. "Yeah. It makes you wonder. All the time and work we've put in here, doing nothing it seems, but really a helluva lot. And here we are forced to cadge around the country for our own weekly bread while Jessup gets the backing of God only knows how many big white cats, and corporations. Shit."

"I want to take a day or so off, Bill. I'm a little beat myself."

"Go ahead. You deserve it. Drop that bread in the business office. Hey, who did you have, Sam or Maya?"

Browning had risen; now he paused. He felt as though he'd just discovered that there is no such thing as a left-handed monkey wrench. "Maya," he said, searching Barton's smiling eyes.

"That chick's got some problems. Next time, try Sam. Not that she hasn't got them, but she's polite enough not to make you suffer with her." Barton winked and Browning left his office.

When he finally reached his own office, Browning called Val at work. "You sound good," he told her. "I missed you."

The kids were all right and she had missed him, too. Only one bad thing had happened: Mrs. Poole had quit without explanation. She had been the third cleaning woman to quit this year. "We have to face it," Val was saying. "Colored cleaning ladies do not like to clean for colored people; for white people, yes, somehow it's quite all right; for Negroes, no, because they don't believe that other Negroes should have it kind of good if they can't have it."

Of course, Browning thought when he left the office. Of course, that was where Jessup was going to fall down. How could he really count on a domestic secret service when it tended to be made up of people like Mrs. Poole who, for all their protestations, believed in the status quo. Jessup was a fool, Browning thought, suddenly relieved, suddenly almost jaunty. He, Browning, was still right; right after all. Well, tomorrow he'd take the next step in saving Jessup and all the others from themselves. Browning stopped at a newsstand long enough to buy *Time,* then went down into the subway, whistling.

eight

At the Don's irritable urging, although he had planned to do so anyway, Carlo served an early lunch. "After I meet him, Don, and get the money, I'll be in touch with Hod, perhaps tonight. The sooner out of our hands, the better."

The Don grunted. He knew that Carlo was puzzling over his attentions to the man named Browning. They had driven, at the Don's insistence, to the neighborhood and building where Browning lived. "These people, Carlo," the Don had explained, "people on the outside, you can tell what they're like by the places they live in."

They already knew that the Brownings were one of three Negro families living in their building, and that he had a wife and two daughters. The Don speculated that, like other tenants of the building, Browning would like to sit on the stone benches that overlooked Morningside Park.

Over the soup the Don said, "Well, today he puts up or shuts up. You come right back and let me know."

"Of course," Carlo said petulantly. "But I don't understand why you're suddenly so interested in him."

After a few moments the Don said, "He's different. He's got a cause. For the others it's money, revenge, something selfish. God only knows where he's digging up fifteen hundred bucks, though."

"In the end, Don, it turns out just like the others. He doesn't want to do his own dirty work."

"Maybe," the Don growled. "But there *is* a difference. You just don't see it." Now the Don chuckled. "Besides, a man should never do himself what he can get someone else to do for him."

The Don ate hurriedly. Why should he try to explain it to Carlo? Browning wanted nothing for himself. He was an educated man with a nice family. He was risking everything. Why was he doing this unless he felt there were no other answers? The life was hard for black people in this country. He knew. He knew through Clarissa and what he saw, heard and felt. If it hadn't been for the near serfdom of the black man, almost like Sicilians of the Middle Ages, a few million people like himself would have had to remain in the Old Country. And America was so bigoted that he had had to earn his keep through left-handed endeavors.

The Don was now on dessert, anxiously casting glances back over his shoulder to see if Carlo had changed his white jacket for one more suitable for walking in the park. Maybe Carlo was right; in the end it came down to the same thing. Here I am, the Don thought, without more than a few years of Sicilian schooling, and I've earned every dime through muscle. And there is Browning, an educated man, a man of some culture, I suppose, finally resorting to the same thing. Regardless of what Carlo says and feels, the Don mused, I've got to know more about this, how it came to be. I never knew any better; Browning does.

He was seized with a curious excitement.

"Are you finished?" Carlo asked.

Somehow the Don had known that Carlo was standing at his shoulder. Carlo for years had done that, perhaps hoping to make him jump. The young ones always looked for signs in the old, signs of fear and broken nerves.

"Finished," said the Don, pushing back from the table.

Carlo reached to pull out his chair. "I'll get you settled on the terrace," he said.

"No, no. I can settle myself. You get over to the park."

"There's plenty of time," Carlo said patiently.

"Well, walk slow. I want to do some thinking."

When they were on the terrace, the Don said, "You know something, Carlo? I'll bet Browning won't even show up. Cold feet. I'll bet you five."

"You're on," Carlo said with a smile. He knew the Don wished to lose; he wouldn't mind losing. Browning's activities were bringing some excitement into an otherwise dull life.

Browning had risen early after a sleepless night. Someone else would have thought of doing this if I hadn't, he had told himself over and over; there was always someone else. Back with his family, Browning remained far from them, deep in thought. He feared discovery. After all, what did he really know about Vig and his connections? They might take the money and not do anything; what then could he do? Even if all went well there was always the chance that at some point in the future there would come that awful knock on the door.

What would happen to his women? That was his major worry. He was resigned to the destiny that befell all black men behind the bars of white jails. But who would care for them? Browning recognized that this line of thinking could lead him into areas that would preclude his going to the park and handing over the money. No, he was, however deviously, seeking a crutch.

The fact was that Val was working, would always work; her career was as much a part of her life as being his wife, perhaps more. She liked what she did. Nora was of an age now, extremely self-sufficient, and even, Browning guessed, ready to marry at the first opportunity. Chris — what was he thinking of? They were his *women!* They were not babes or little girls who had to be led by the hand.

By dint of sacrifice and occasional good fortune there was some money in the savings account. It wasn't much when you considered all the years they had worked, but it *was* there. There was hospitalization (why does a man *have* to be concerned with such mundane matters?), and Chris, like Nora, would go to a city college, also meet a boy, and that was that.

The act itself was needed and not for Negroes alone; the whites needed it as well, perhaps even more. Browning wished he had thought of it when he was younger, but then there had been hope (he hadn't known then what he knew now); everyone had hoped and that now lay dead. The need was for now, anyway, not even for the future. The need was for now so there *could* be a future. History and time had created a wrong so complex, creeping into every American institution, that it had to be shorted with simplicity. That was the beginning. However, it galled him that he could not do the act himself, like a man. It was possible that that kind of manhood was as mythical as cowboy manhood. No, power, real power, resided in anonymity.

Browning had left the apartment and gone downtown to the banks in order to break Braithwaite's bills into fifty-dollar denominations, and now he was lying on the grass opposite the blue-green panther. More green than blue, he thought. The magazine he held was heavy with the money inside it. From where he lay he could see sections of the pond where kids sailed their boats, and all around him he saw Negro maids in their white uniforms and shoes walking white children or sitting beside ill white adults. At dusk, Browning knew, the maids would gather along Fifth and Madison Avenue, paper bags filled with tarnished silver, chipped glassware, ends of roasts and cakes, to begin their rides to Harlem or Bedford-Stuyvesant. But they don't like to work for me, Browning thought. Could a bullet start the change in their thinking?

From his vantage point from which he had been watching Browning for fifteen minutes, Carlo tried to see more than just a black man lying on the grass, other people a rather respectful distance away from him. Carlo had seen his first Negro in Belluno when he was a young boy. The Negro had walked down the street dressed in a cape and bowler, looking for all the world like a minister from Rome, except that he had a surprisingly innocent face. Someone later told Carlo the black man was a singer and had performed in La Scala in Milan. Carlo had not paid too much attention to black people in America. What for? Their place in the scheme of things was designed and settled long before he was ever born. Some Italians still feared to come to the United States because it was said that the Americans treated Italians like Negroes; it was enough to make one think twice. But in America all it took to get by was a white face.

Browning looked like an ordinary kind of man; Carlo remembered that from his last visit. What terrible ideas occurred in the brains of ordinary-looking men. Carlo hadn't yet figured out why the heat bothered him. Well . . . Carlo looked at his watch; one-thirty. He left his position and walked toward Browning, coming up behind him.

"Mr. Browning," he said, when he was close to him. Carlo noticed that Browning did not start; he looked slowly, threateningly over his shoulder. Carlo studied the face again. Yes, this was Browning. "How have you been, Mr. Browning?"

Browning turned over and drew up his knees. He, too, was studying. This was the man he'd met at the Reservoir. "I've been fine, thank you." He watched Carlo lower himself to the grass.

"Everything's in order?" Carlo asked, glancing at the magazine.

"It's here. Can I ask when?"

Carlo smiled as he held out his hand for the magazine. "You can ask, but I can't tell you. Of course, you'll read about it, or hear about it."

Browning gave him the magazine. "Yes, of course."

"I wouldn't worry if I were you. It's a business transaction, nothing more."

"And that's all there is?"

"Yes, don't fret; it's done this way every day." Carlo got to his feet, his fingertips sliding over the bulges in the magazine. "We're an honorable firm. Goodbye."

Browning lay where he was, watching Carlo until he

vanished along one of the paths, then, with a sigh, he stood, stretched and started to walk northward. A good day for walking, he thought. Hot, but it's all right. I'll go slow. Give me time to think.

When the Don heard Carlo at the door, he reached into his pocket and took out a five-dollar bill. He held it in his hand and scrutinized Carlo's impassive face. "Take it," the Don said, waving the bill. "You win, right?"

"No," Carlo said. "I lose, Don. Will you trust me until payday?"

The Don's face lit up with a great smile. "Forget it, Carlo. You don't owe me nothing. Take this and buy some cigarettes."

Grinning, Carlo reached and took the bill; he did not smoke and the Don knew it. Pocketing the money, Carlo said, "*Now* will you take your nap?"

The Don eased himself down on the couch. "Sure, sure, I'm going to get my rest now."

Across the park on the second floor of the Israeli Consulate, Itzhak Hod sat across from a young Israeli official. Yaacov Peretz was his name. The official was surprised to see him. "You say you wish to return to Israel? Hod of the Irgun? The man who was a more vicious killer than any Arab?" Peretz was all the more shocked because Hod did not look like what some of the records implied he was, a killer. Both men spoke in Hebrew.

"Yes, yes," Hod said. "I knew it would come to that, but I did not kill that Arab family at Deir Yassin. It is true that there was an awful slaughter, but you have to consider the times. You were too young . . ." Hod shrugged. "It was never proved that I killed that family, and it was never proved because I didn't do it."

"But Hod," Peretz went on, speaking in that British accent that severely compromised one's Jewishness, "There seemed to be, if I recall correctly, several coincidences involving your presence in areas where Arabs were found dead. There were never indications of provocation on their part."

If he recalled correctly, Hod thought. Of course, he knew the facts; he would not be in New York if he did not know the facts. "None of it proved," Hod said aloud. "The Government needed a scapegoat. I was it. I was one of them."

The official looked past him to the window. The small, slow-moving elevator opened and the sound of the door rang throughout the floor.

"We asked you to leave because the Arabs would have killed you a thousand times over if they had caught you. In their desire to catch you, they murdered several other Israelis. Then, of course, we had to destroy the Irgun and the Sterns —"

"While the Haganah remained whole and its members now have all the government posts," Hod said, bitterly.

"The Haganah operated with the consent of the whole people; the Irgun and the Sterns did not. They were giving us a black eye. All of Israel seemed to be like Chicago in the 1930's. Cigarette, Hod?"

Hod reached with thick, heavy fingers and extracted a cigarette from the pack of Dubeks. He leaned forward for a light.

Both men exhaled and examined their cigarettes. "Where have you been all these years?" the official asked.

All right, Hod thought. We will play games. "Rome, Corsica, Amsterdam, Paris, Copenhagen —"

"Doing what?"

"I've been a jewelry salesman."

A smile started across Peretz's face, then he choked it off. "In Rio, too, São Paulo. But you, a salesman of jewelry. Well. Is that what you're doing here?"

Hod hesitated and then nodded. The game still. If he knew about Rio and São Paulo, then he also knew that, like certain Israelis all over the face of the world, he had been looking for Nazi murderers; that he had been one of many who had delivered a tip on Eichmann. But, if he wanted the game?

"Why do you want to return to Israel?"

"To start a new life. I'm getting married and my wife would like to live in Israel, and to tell you the truth, I think I'd like to settle down in one place now."

"Congratulations. She Jewish?" It was a question to ask. Strange things happened to Israelis when they got loose here. And it would help if she were Jewish.

Hod said, "Yes. I've been many places and I've not been impressed with them. My — the woman I'm going to marry made me realize that. And I'm not getting any younger." Suddenly he felt a rush of anger. "Look, I did a service. I did it when you were still cowering in a shelter. It doesn't matter that the people now say they weren't with us; they benefited by what we did. I did a lot of the dirty work that made Israel what it is today. I tell you I deserve a second chance." I shouldn't have said that, Hod thought.

"What will you do there?" Peretz asked as though he hadn't heard the outburst.

"We'll open a small jewelry shop, I guess. My wife

likes jewelry. People have gone to Israel with nothing but the clothes on their backs and done all right. We'll not be a burden."

Peretz played with his cigarettes. "There is a new settlement opening between Ein Hatseva and Ein Yahav . . ."

Peretz's voice went on. Hod knew the region; it was three hundred meters below sea level, one of the favored routes of Jordanian terrorists. Why a "settlement" there? Or was there to be more? Anyway they'd want tough settlers, probably vets, the young ones and the old ones — plus, Hod guessed, scientists . . .? Hod tried to imagine Mickey living in such a settlement. There would be the chalk-white hills stubbled with dusty brush, the blasted rock formations of the Negev. In summer it would be hot during the day and freezing at night, and in winter it would be cold all the time. Hod did not think she would dislike it. And strangely, being out of the cities would please him, too. He said, "Peretz, that is a very odd place for a settlement."

Peretz looked up from his cigarettes. "Hod, I think now, with so much time elapsed, that we can do something for you. Please consider the new *settlement* —" He had emphasized the word, Hod noted.

"An old hand like yourself could help to whip it into shape in no time." He raised his eyes as if daring Hod to contradict him. "That's a region where there's some fertility and we want to expand the work of the Arid Zone Research Institute down there. When is your wedding?"

"In a month or so. I'd like to have permission to return as a wedding present."

"We'll see, Hod. Call me in about ten days, can you?"

Outside, Hod pulled off his jacket, loosened his tie and

rolled up his sleeves. Feeling better, he walked slowly to the park, swinging his sample case. He had not felt so good in years.

Once he gained a bench in Central Park and loosened his shoelaces, Hod considered his visit to the consulate. Amazing. Just a few weeks ago he was contemplating a rather bleak future, although he had not admitted it to Mickey-Siona. There wasn't much work he could get in New York; it was practically a closed shop. Not like other cities he had lived in where he could expect all kinds of assignments, assignments of the kind that would make the world think twice about what a Jew could do. No, there was not much in New York except Mickey. A strange girl-woman. The woman part had come recently, in the past two weeks; it had come on a night when black clouds boiled over the city and rain gushed from the skies, tapering off to a fine, steady light drizzle.

He had been lying in her arms thinking of nothing special, listening to the sounds of traffic rolling slowly, wetly along the roads, and she had said, "I want you to marry me. I'm not pregnant. I say this because I think you won't ask me because of the difference in our ages. I love you and want to have your child; I think we can, still. I also want you to know that we don't belong here. That this country has run out of promises. I want to go somewhere where there's still a promise. Israel."

Hod had not moved. Her voice blocked out the sounds in the streets below.

"I'm an American who never felt American, whether because I'm a Jew or because I've seen and understood too much, I don't know."

In the darkness her offer blazed brightly and he saw

instantly down the corridor of future time that he would never be alone again and inside himself, where it was quiet and she could not see; he wept with joy. Until that moment he had not realized to what extent he had deluded himself with his years of hedonism. A child!

"And what of your family, your friends here?" he asked.

"Ah, them," she said, and it seemed to Hod that there was a smile in her voice. "My parents left Europe, too, because of persecution. But they have forgotten. There is among them now an arrogance that persecution has bred. They call themselves Jews, but they are Americans pretending to be Jews, for to be American, Itzhak, it seems to me that one must not be Chinese or Japanese or Mexican or Puerto Rican or Negro. One simply must be white to be American.

"Yet I've never made much over being Jewish. All of it, all religions should aim for one thing: to breed the best possible people for getting along with other people. But —"

"Yes," he said, knowing what she was going to say. "I haven't answered you, but yes, we will get married. Yes, I will take you to Israel, if it is possible —"

She kissed him. It was a peculiarly tender kiss and she broke softly away from him, saying, "Last year I went to Spain. I went to Toledo. Not far from El Greco's house there is an old synagogue built during the days when the Arabs and Jews lived in peace in Spain. It is a magnificent synagogue, Itzhak; we must go there one day, maybe on the way to Israel."

Hod had buried his face in his pillow, listening intently to the risings and fallings of her voice, thinking of how to get permission to go back.

"The guide there told me that the Jews left in 1492. He said nothing about Ferdinand and Isabella or of Torquemada. He said it in that temple with its polished benches and ivory scrollwork, the sun entering from a queer angle, high up, shining directly on the Hebrew characters on the walls. German Jews were not the first to believe that they had integrated; the Spanish Jews believed it too. We get into these societies and start believing we're a part of them and then . . ."

Hod had reached over and cradled her head in his arms.

She said, "I won't miss my family or my friends."

"I am almost an old man," Hod said. "And my life has been strange."

"No matter, and you must have a son. No almost-old woman can do that for you. I can."

"It'll be hard, starting from nothing, without money, and I have very little of that."

"We will do all right. I have a little money; that will be my dowry and my parents will make us a gift of money, I'll see to that."

"I've been away from Israel a long time," Hod said. "There've been many changes."

"There are always changes, Itzhak."

"Yes, of course. It will be quite all right."

Then, the next day, he had had to call the consulate for an appointment. He broke it and broke the next one until, finally, he could lie to Mickey no longer and he had gone.

Now Hod sat in the park remembering. He glanced idly at a Negro walking slowly by, a copy of *Time* magazine clutched tightly against his body. Hod sighed; it was one o'clock, time to get some lunch, go to his room, make some calls and worry about where the money to get back to Israel was coming from. He bent to tie his shoes and noticed a man reading a paper as he walked. So eager for bad news, Hod thought. Americans read like Israelis; they bought edition after edition, just to saturate themselves with horrors they were better off not knowing. Hod did not read; did not care to read. It helped to keep bad news at arm's length.

He walked slowly, thinking of the official at the consulate. They had played a game, but it had contained a promise. There had been a promise, made as only an Israeli can make one. . . . *With so much time elapsed; please consider the new settlement; you could help whip it into shape in no time.*

Hod was both elated and furious. He was going home! But at the rate he was going, he wouldn't have two Israeli lira to rub together. No matter! He was pounding down Second Avenue now. Tonight it was going to be a bottle of Israeli wine, Carmel, and Jaffa oranges for dessert. Wait until Mickey-Siona tasted St. Peter's fish fresh out of Galilee! He bought the wine and the oranges and carried them to his room. He would take them over to her place later. Now he had to lie down and *think!*

Within moments however, his thoughts exhausted him and sleep came. His great body relaxed and his snoring reverberated around his room.

He woke suddenly, dusk just starting to fill his window, and heard the echoes of his snoring. At the moment of waking he sat up quickly, instantly alert. The knock came again, softly but firmly. Then a voice: "Hod," it said. And again, "Hod."

Hod slipped off the bed, one hand pressed against it to minimize squeak. He tiptoed to the door and listened. When the knock came again, he tripped the key quickly, stepped to one side and said, "Come in."

Carlo pushed open the door, paused, and walked in and closed it. He stood studying the room, knowing that Hod was behind him. They all live like this, Carlo was thinking; alone, in little rooms with one window that could scarcely admit air.

"Sit down," Hod said, indicating the single straight-backed chair. Hod sat on the bed, offering his cigarettes to Carlo. A queer or a sadist, Hod thought right away. His visitor was too neat, too prissy.

Carlo shook his head. He reached into his pocket and extracted a white envelope. Hod studied its bulk. Carlo took from the envelope a card and handed it to Hod. Next, he gave Hod a picture that had been torn from a newspaper, torn so that no text remained. It was a picture of Carrigan in civilian clothes.

"And here," Carlo said, "is the money. All of it at once. You have that reputation." He watched Hod count it and was gratified to see his face relax. Twenty-five hundred dollars, one thousand of it contributed by the Don himself. "Just to make it really worth Hod's work," the Don had said with a chuckle.

"All right?" Carlo asked.

Hod, thinking of Israel, of Mickey-Siona, replied, "Just fine." He rose and guided Carlo to the door. They parted without goodbyes.

nine

Carrigan was the son of a cop and, he believed, a keeper of tradition. He had been on the force since the late Forties, following service in the paratroops after the shooting war was ended. He'd done most of his work in the MP's and liked it.

He was boosted up the ladder quickly because there were many fond memories of his father throughout the department; and he looked like a cop. Over the years, Carrigan's memory telescoped until he could actually recall serving at Bastogne with the Screaming Eagles, when in reality he'd never left Benning. But no one cared or bothered to remember.

Carrigan's first citation came when he disarmed and arrested a car thief on Riverside Drive. The thief had crashed his car into another and then leaped out, fleeing through the park. Carrigan and his partner reported that the man had had a gun that was lost in the disarming; the gun was never found.

In the second incident to bring him a citation there definitely was a gun and it was fired at Carrigan as he advanced on the suspect, who was supposed to have committed a series of robberies in a block of Eastside buildings. Carrigan was advancing because he was unaware that the suspect was armed. When the man fired, only the discipline of his training kept him advancing; it was this that cowed the suspect enough for Carrigan to disarm him, which he did with a force that many bystanders, their sympathies instantly switching, considered unnecessary.

But his career had been assured not only by his work, but by his family life as well. He had married above his station, to a college graduate of a Catholic women's school, and four children had followed. Life became dull and sometimes agonizing and Carrigan took it all for granted.

Little vices came his way — Christmas gifts, ten-spots from doormen, free drinks at certain bars, the red carpet treatment at certain others, and girls. His was a voice and view to be listened to in the PBA meetings, which always seemed to be concerned with the influence of communism on crime. Hitches on the narcotics and vice squads enabled him to trace this influence. Behind what the City Hall liberals were calling the Negro Revolution lay the spectre of communism. Negroes had always been bad, he said, but they were worse now because of the Communists. PBA members always applauded his speeches; they knew that when Carrigan was on a Harlem beat he took no nonsense from the people up there.

Now Carrigan was approaching fifty. His children were stretched from grammar school to the army; his wife had grown large and he never made love to her without feeling that she wasn't really interested. Promotions were frozen and men who had started with him were moving further out on the Island; where the money came from to build those new homes, no one professed to know. It was always that the cop building or buying was a good saver. To Carrigan it only meant that they were more clever than he and it galled him to think of his own small home in Queens, but his contacts higher up had slipped or gone, forced out by the easy-with-criminals attitude of City Hall. Carrigan found himself on a robbery squad on the East Side, tasting bile with every belch.

There were altogether too many robberies in New York. You came with a complaint call, took down the name and address of the victim and listed the items stolen. You asked if they had insurance, and most did not, and you shook your head sadly. Then you left your card (the card business had come, Carrigan remembered, with Jack Webb and *Dragnet*) and asked the complainant to call if anything else came up. You would call when you had something, which was almost always never.

Carrigan really worked on the Lewis case. Betty Lewis was single and she maintained a large apartment that had a view of the East River. She had been clipped of a television set, an expensive portable typewriter ("You a writer, Miss Lewis?" Carrigan had asked, and she had smiled — grateful, obviously, for the question — but she wrote only in her spare time), and some jewelry that was moderately expensive. She was a pleasant-looking woman in her middle forties, a kind of sipper of drinks, Carrigan had observed, for she was drinking one on the rocks and offered himself and his partner one, which they refused, naturally. She wore her dark blond hair in a fall and had good legs; most women her age did not look good in miniskirts, but she looked more than all right.

Carrigan returned the next day with a lead, he said,

and went over with her once again the items that had been stolen; this time he was alone and this time he accepted a drink. It was, in fact, his day off.

Betty Lewis and Sergeant Carrigan had been seeing each other for several months. She was good for him. He had always looked with a curious and hungry eye at single Manhattan women. They're getting laid, he thought, but by whom? He saw them with their sleek young men, their rough-hewn types, their Negroes, their Europeans. Now he had one himself. She had been to France once, and she liked to use French phrases and to serve him dinner with candlelight. She would give him a drink and make him sit and listen to her read sections of the novel she was working on. All this prelude to getting into bed, where she was extremely good.

After the shooting of the Negro boy, Carrigan's superiors as a matter of routine suspended him pending an investigation. He knew what the outcome would be; every man on the force would turn in his badge if he were found guilty, and City Hall knew it. The suspension was just to make it look good. After a few days at home — his house was under guard, just in case — Carrigan became restless. He called Betty when his wife was out shopping. As soon as the furor quieted down, Carrigan, wearing dark glasses and carrying a small caliber automatic, began to drift in and out of Manhattan, anxious to spend time with Betty over candlelight. No, he told himself, not the candlelight, the snatch — that's what drew him.

Since he did not read the papers or listen to radio or watch television, Itzhak Hod could not understand why a man would want to spend all of his time at home. Didn't

Carrigan have a job? When Carrigan finally did appear, wearing dark glasses and moving warily, Hod was relieved. In his rented car he followed Carrigan into Manhattan, where Carrigan stopped first on lower Lexington Avenue to buy a loaf of French bread in a patisserie, and then to an elevator building in the East Seventies.

Carrigan's neighborhood was not one where people ate French bread, Hod reasoned; a French baker would starve in Queens. Carrigan was carrying French bread to someone with French tastes. It all added up to what the Americans called hanky-panky. Hod pressed his face against the self-locking building door and caught sight of the elevator indicator still moving. If Carrigan was the only person on the car . . . It stopped at six. Hod counted ten, then saw the needle swing upward, stopping at eight, then it came down, seven, six, five, four . . . Hod retreated slowly to his car and his back was to the door of the building when it opened up and an elderly man came out with an aged collie on a leash.

All right. There was a pretty good chance that Carrigan went to the sixth floor with his French bread. Back in his car, Hod carefully noted the address of the building, then he drove off, heading downtown. Tonight he would go to a neighborhood theater and think about Carrigan.

Upstairs in the building, Betty Lewis, freshly made up and wearing a miniskirt and dark stockings, set aside her Scotch on the rocks and embraced Carrigan when he walked in.

"I'm so glad you could come," she said.

"Me, too," Carrigan said. He already had an erection. Lately the erections started to come as soon as he entered her building. He kissed her, backed her up across the room to the couch. By now this was ritual. Love with clothes partly on in furious haste, then dinner, and after, love with clothes off.

Utterly sated, Carrigan left at eleven o'clock. Across the park the Don and Carlo sat watching the television news. Uptown, as casually as he could, Browning asked his wife to turn on the set for the news. Downtown, Hod was just emerging from the movie house. He stopped at a deli and had a beer and a pastrami sandwich. Tomorrow was the eleventh day; he would call Peretz at the consulate.

ten

It was Saturday and the auto traffic that had started to snake out of New York the afternoon before was still snaking, heading toward the cool mountains of the Catskills or to New England or to the beaches of East Hampton, Montauk, and Amagansett.

As they drove slowly uptown, the late morning sky already silvering with a throat-burning haze, the Don could see couples walking or sitting on benches in Central Park; clots of bike riders pedaled along in the roadways; kids, eagerly clutching balls, tugged their fathers along the grass. Once they reached Morningside Heights Carlo slowed. He stopped when they came to the stone benches that gave a view of Morningside Park and Harlem. The benches were only a few yards from the building where Eugene Browning lived.

"I don't like it, Don," Carlo said, opening the door for him. "Why can't you just leave it alone?"

The Don got out without a word, clutching the morning papers. He pressed an old but expensive Panama to his bald head. Carlo closed the door behind him, found a parking place two cars away, pulled in and turned off the ignition. He lay his head back on the seat and adjusted the mirror so he could keep the Don in sight.

The Don stared unseeing at one of the papers. Sometimes he worried about that Carlo; couldn't teach him to keep his thoughts to himself. Always with the two cents to put in. Maybe he's just worried about me, the Don thought; then he lighted a cigar and opened the *News*. One day soon it would be spread across the front page. Maybe even the *Times'* front page, too.

He was not worried about Hod's doing the job; that was nothing. Doing the job without leaving a trace was the difficult part and Hod knew how to do that, but it took a little time. From time to time, actually only from minute to minute, the Don glanced at the entrance to Browning's building. A man with a family, surely before the Saturday shopping, stepped to the park to look down at the city. Twisting the cigar into one corner of his mouth and staring over the top of his paper, the Don muttered, "C'mon, Browning."

"Look," Browning was saying to his wife. "These big bags are all ready. I'll take them down. You and the kids can bring the others when you're through packing them." He started, grateful to be out of the apartment and glad that for the time being they would be out of the city. He was too tired and dulled with nervousness to feel guilty. In another hour or so they'd be well on the way to Sag Harbor. He would drive them, and tomorrow night he'd take the train back to New York, back to the job, back to the waiting. It made him twice as nervous to have them around; they didn't know, so they expected life to go on as always. They had a right to expect that, he thought. But it was taking too much out of him to carry on as though nothing unusual was supposed to happen.

Downstairs, he placed the bags in the trunk of the car they had rented for the summer, then, lighting a cigarette, he strolled to the benches. He noticed an elderly man sitting down, Panama hat pressed squarely on his head. And he remembered from his youth that the hippest guys were the ones who wore their hats in the squarest fashion. Inside himself he smirked. No chance of that dumb-looking old guy being hip about *anything.*

"Morning," the old man said when Browning strolled past him to the edge of the parapet.

Browning nodded. He did not recall ever seeing this man here before, and standing with his back to him, viewing with distaste the haze over Harlem, Browning felt the man staring at his back. But when he turned to take a seat himself, he saw that the man was serenely reading his paper.

"No break in the weather," the man said. The weather was always a good, safe topic; it affected everyone and generally adversely.

"No, none at all," Browning answered.

The Don lowered his eyes to his paper, having noticed the frown between Browning's eyes. He'd had it when he came.

"Can I see your paper, the one you've finished?" Browning asked, stretching out his hand.

"Sure." The Don handed the *News* to him, filled with a sense of burgeoning confidence.

Beneath them, on the paths of the park, the voices

started to come. First there were the young boys who galloped shouting between the trees and over the rocks; then the squalls of infants and the tense voices of their mothers telling them to shut up. The winos and junkies pulled together into their respective groups, the junkies mumbling, the winos talking loudly; it was early in the day. Later the winos would be mumbling in their vomit, and the junkies, popped and high, would be loud because they would be feeling so good.

"Care to see the *Times?*" the Don asked, passing it over. Browning had finished the *News* in three minutes. He hated the paper and it galled him to see Negroes reading it, supporting with their pennies a newspaper that wished them little good. Receiving the *Times*, although he had scanned it at breakfast, Browning said, "Thanks."

"Saw you loading your car," the Don said. "Vacation?" That wouldn't be any good. Here he had just made contact with the man only to find out that he was going away for the summer.

Browning said, "Not for me. The family. I'm driving them to the country, but on Monday, back at the office. I'll be a summer widower." Browning had noticed the man's accent, but couldn't place it.

"Too bad," the Don said. "But it's nice that you think of your family." He was relieved. "Besides, the city isn't so bad with everyone gone. The restaurants aren't crowded, traffic isn't so bad."

"My family," Browning said, "would never let me forget them."

The Don laughed politely, waiting for his next opening.

Then Browning, his lip curled slightly, turned to the

Don and said, "I see where they're looking for trouble in the cities again this summer. Do you think there'll be a riot here?" Might as well clear the air, Browning thought. Then he'll leave me alone. Yeah. Riot talk ought to shut up this old man.

The Don hesitated. Of course, Browning was jabbing at him because he had intruded on his privacy; it was to be expected. "Your people think they have cause to riot, I say maybe they're right. The way it is now a riot wouldn't surprise me; we've had them before, you know. But they don't make much sense. There's got to be a better way . . ." The Don let his voice drift and he forced a helpless look up into his eyes.

Browning lowered the paper onto his lap. "What do you mean?"

The Don shrugged. "I don't know, but in a riot everything goes, good and bad, nobody cares; old and young; they get carried away by the fever. People who've worked hard and saved all their lives; their houses get burned down, too. And then, well, you know what the police are like today. Do they ask questions? No. Right away it's out with the gun and bang, bang, bang, like that cop with that kid." The Don now flung open his hands. "Sure, a riot, but who pays the most?"

Browning saw his family emerge from the building. He rose. "There's my family, I've got to go." He returned the papers. "You live around here?"

"I live in the neighborhood," the Don said with a smile. "I like to sit out here; there's a nice breeze and I like the sound of the kids playing in the park."

"Yeah," Browning said. "Well, I hope we run into each other again."

"Hope so," the Don said, waving.

He waited until Browning's car pulled to the corner and turned. Then he rose and stretched and walked to his own car. Through the window he saw Carlo readjusting the mirror. Carlo opened the door for him and said, "Well?"

Chuckling, the Don said, "He's just like us; he doesn't really trust anyone, but I think I scored, Carlo, I think I scored. Let's go home."

As they nudged through the thick traffic on 125th Street, Chris said, "Boy, am I glad to be getting out of this city." She glanced around the car at the others. Nora, she knew, would be unhappy away from the city until Woody called her from East Hampton and they had made plans to meet at the Sag Harbor or East Hampton Beach. Then Nora would be all right, her old self again. Mother was unhappy because Daddy had to return to the city the next day; they would see him only on weekends for most of the rest of the summer.

Browning looked forward to arriving at the summer house; just a few hours would do a lot for him. He was grateful for small favors. And he would manage two or three long weekends, get in some fishing. Bluefish and maybe some blowfish whose tender meat he enjoyed. An afternoon with a mess of littlenecks and Long Island sweet corn and cold beer would fix him up fine.

"Every brother and sister in Harlem's out today," he observed aloud.

Nora said, "Daddy, you're always talking about brothers and sisters and you know darn well that half these brothers and sisters you're talking about, you wouldn't even let in our home."

"Nora, stop it," Val said peevishly.

"You know what I mean," Browning said. Poor Nora; she almost always had reference to Woody Chance; he lurked behind her every thought and statement. "Besides," he continued, "you don't really know, do you, just how I feel about these sisters and brothers? No, you don't, and I might suggest that until you really know, you cut out the generalizations."

"Well —" Nora started, then stopped. It wasn't Daddy; it was Mother she should be jumping on. Always harping on Woody.

"Look," Browning said over his shoulder as they broke out for the approach to the bridge. "It's a hot day. We got started late and there's lots of traffic. I'm going to have only one night with you before I have to come back to the city. Peace, let's have a little family peace for old times' sake, before we all got so grown and wise. I sure would appreciate it."

Val touched him tenderly on the arm as they sped down toward the toll booths. She smiled back at the girls; they smiled at each other.

"You got a deal, Daddy," Chris said.

Val settled down for the ride when they left the toll booths. For days now she had felt that Gene was all wound up. He woke more weary than he had been when he went to bed. Sometimes when she was returning to bed after using the bathroom in the middle of the night, he spoke to her, a simple phrase or so, meaning nothing much, but it meant that he wasn't sleeping.

"Anything wrong?" she had asked at the breakfast table a few mornings before the kids came in.

"No. Just don't seem to be getting any rest. That's all. It'll come, baby, and I'll be just fine."

Now they were heading into the worst part of summer and his face was still drawn.

Browning drove skillfully as always, again reflecting that half the drivers on the road shouldn't have had licenses to begin with. That they had them was the way America was. The states needed money, so they licensed damned near anyone who applied for one. The car manufacturers kept pushing the cars off the assembly lines and they had to be sold. Car sales, related to the steel industry, formed the hard cash base upon which the American economy was structured. Then there were the gas and oil companies, the individual gas stations; the contractors and subcontractors who built the highways; the towns that wanted the roads to brush past their business sections. All those profits had to be measured in terms of the number of people licensed to drive and own cars, regardless of how many of them ill-deserved that privilege. Yet authorities kept moaning about the number of people killed and injured in auto accidents. Why was it that Americans, for the sake of a goddamn dollar, did everything ass-backwards?

Like the World's Fair site they were passing. They could put up a tremendous complex of buildings to be used for only two summers and then abandoned to deteriorate, but couldn't bring themselves to build public housing. Browning shook his head.

"What's the matter?" Val asked.

"Nothing," he answered.

Now he began once again to ponder the delay in those people's killing Carrigan. He thought about this every day; how many times he did not know. He had no doubt that

Carrigan's death in the light of the current unrest would make headlines the nation over. Browning counted on that. He could not pull Dixon off Braithwaite until it happened, and there was always the chance that Braithwaite, if he became too impatient — a month was gone already, one week remained — might contact Barton directly and ask what had happened to the deal he'd made with him, Browning. Then there'd be a shitstorm over that fifteen hundred cash. Browning almost shuddered; he could see himself being pilloried by Barton; he could hear the crackers laughing already: "Niggers supposed to be raising hell with us, but too busy stealing each other blind." And of course he could never tell why he had taken the money or what he'd done with it. He felt a fresh burst of sweat on his forehead; he wiped it away with the back of his hand. Even so, he told himself, he felt more sure now that he'd done the right thing than he had any time before.

Val was speaking. "When I think of some of the truly nice cities we've lived in, Gene, I just wonder why we continue to live in New York."

"New York is groovy," Nora said. "I don't mind the heat."

"You don't mind anything as long as —" Chris started to say before Nora cut her off with a vicious, "Shut up!"

Browning glanced in the rearview mirror and saw Nora fling herself back against her seat, sulking. Chris had been about to throw Woody's name into the hopper and Nora did not want to give Val the opportunity to jump on her — which she did almost every time Woody's name came up. She ought to calm down, Browning thought. He thought of all the times he and Val had made love in the summers in small, hot rooms, body slipping on body, sweat rolling, puddling between the breasts, faces slick, arms and hands as damp as any other part of the body. You remembered making love in summer. It wasn't like winter or in cool rooms. In summer your perfumes and colognes went; you were just there sweating and smelling, grinding in the nitty-gritty. Maybe that was what Nora was thinking about, one of those potato fields out there; maybe some student's room, borrowed for an hour, back there in hot, steaming Manhattan. He tore himself away from the images. He thought to her: It's always rough going through the first time, baby.

He was passing through Riverhead before he knew it. Two or three nightclubs, shuttered against the day, stood along the road, sandwiched between barber and beauty shops and two churches. Then there were the Negroes themselves, walking with long, country strides, great smiles slashed across their faces. They walked along paths; there were no sidewalks.

They lived out their lives back from the road, mostly in shacks and some even in chicken coops that had been haphazardly reinforced to keep out the winter winds. The Long Island farmers had brought migrant workers up from the South to labor in their fields, but every year when the trucks loaded up for the trip back South, cool autumn winds racing hard over the flat landscapes, some remained. They spilled from the fields to the gas stations; they became domestics in the great gray-shingled houses that clung to the inlets; they became messenger boys, manure packers, or loaded groceries in Bohack's or the A & P. Once they had been like a summer squall, coming fast and going even faster. No more; poverty had been added to the wealth of the Island; black poverty, mean and ugly poverty. All for a lousy stinking dollar the problem had been created. Cheap labor, more profit. Now that cheap labor was eating up the profit in fear, increased welfare budgets.

Then there was Sag Harbor, the old whaling port with its black middle-class summer community spread on both sides of 114. Teachers, doctors, lawyers, social workers, and more recently, upper-level business executives — what were their concerns *now* with the brothers and sisters living in chicken coops? A few years ago, nothing. Today, a lot; they were coming together; had to come together.

The white blur came up slowly and moved softly across his forehead. Val was wiping the sweat with her handkerchief. "You're sweating something awful, darling."

"Yeah," Browning grunted. "Pretty hot today, even out here. The first thing we get in, I'm going for a swim. Who's for swimming?"

"Me," Chris said.

"Me too, I guess," Nora said.

"How about you, baby?" Browning asked his wife.

"Somebody's got to get lunch ready."

"Let's just pick up some potato salad, stop in at Bohack's and get some franks and cold beer. What's the problem?"

Val didn't want to tell him that it wasn't quite that simple. The bags had to be lugged in; clothes had to be hung up right away. And while they were swimming, she could drive into town and get groceries, and they sure needed more than potato salad, cold beer and franks. They had to eat tonight and tomorrow.

"Tell you what," she said. "We'll drive right to the house, unload, and I'll drive you to the beach as soon as you get ready. Then I'll go into Sag and get some groceries and pick you up on the way back."

A silence filled the car; Val had succeeded in making them feel guilty and she realized it immediately and said quickly, "It's the best way to do it and maybe we'll be finished soon enough so I can join you later in the afternoon."

"I'll go to the store with you," Nora said.

"Oh, you don't have to —"

"I'll go."

Browning said nothing. He pulled off 27 to 114, slanting through a small part of East Hampton, and poured it on going down the smooth, little-traveled road.

A Citroën, its front end low against the road, its rear slightly higher like a hunched scorpion about to sting, rushed past them in the opposite direction. A dark blond woman was driving. She was wearing dark glasses and her red lips were parted in a smile. Browning saw a flash of well-tanned shoulder. The man beside her also wore sunglasses and his shirt was a loud plaid. Browning saw this in a blur, then it was gone.

He pulled off the highway and drove in low gear down a bumpy, sandy road. He stamped down hard on the parking brake and turned to his family. "Val wants to get groceries, I want to go swimming. Darling, if you don't mind getting the groceries, go ahead. Nora, did I hear you say you would help?"

"Yes, Daddy."

"All right. Chris, you and me will go swimming." He tried to force an intense earnestness into his voice. "I'm having a very rough summer, ladies, so cool it. No squabbles; save them until I've gone. In other words, I'm asking you to help me a little. The old man needs rest and quiet. Okay?" He banged out of the car to the trunk. He carried the bags into the house, which smelled of pine, dried sand and sun.

What a splendid idea it had been! Two days on Shelter Island with Sean. (She preferred to call him that instead of John.) Two lovely nights with the smell of the sea around them, hours in the boat listening to the waves lap against its sides. She'd loved watching Sean's eyes go wide and his mouth grim whenever he had a bite. How he'd laughed at her squeals when he brought something up, especially those dreadful blowfish. Two days of drifting out of the world, forgetting everything in it. There had been only one bad moment.

They had been lying on a small, almost deserted beach, the boat pulled up, the motor jacked over at rest. Sean was lying on his stomach, gazing out to sea, sipping slowly from a can of beer. He said, "You know what I've been doing, Betty?"

She shook her head, shook it so the long hair whisked in a dark golden trail after the curl of her neck. She watched his face through her dark glasses; she liked them dark enough so her eyes could not be seen.

"I've been thinking about that boy."

She reached down and touched him automatically. She was kneeling in front of him. Now, still on her knees, she raised herself and arched her back, felt the stays firm up her breasts.

"I wish I hadn't been where I was that day. I wish I'd been a thousand miles away. Maybe it's being with you that makes me think like that."

Carrigan made himself think of his wife, with whom he could not think like this. Penelope. Penny. She thought it would be good for him to go on a fishing trip with the boys, to be out of the city for a few days just in case the colored still had ideas about getting even. Penny now gone fat in the thighs and almost formless in the breasts. For years now it seemed that she had said the same things in bed. "Hurry, dear, I'm not going to make it." Or, "Are you close, dear? I'm starting to hurt."

Carrigan glanced quickly up at Betty. He couldn't see her eyes, just the little smile on the edges of her mouth. She was still on her knees, but they were spread now and the little puff of crotch, neatly collected into her bathing suit, was thrust directly at him. He glanced at it. Was it his imagination or did it really happen — that her crotch was always somewhere close to his face.

"Don't fret about the boy, Sean," she said. She didn't want him to waste his time on thoughts of others, but she was always making the mistake of bringing others up, like last night, when she had said teasingly, "Honestly, darling, doesn't your wife ever give you *any?*" And he had smiled that tough cop's brutal smile before plunging into her.

Now, rushing back to New York, nestled in the soft interior of the Citroën, Betty reflected that they would have one more night together. He had never spent a complete night with her in the city. She would not have to release him until tomorrow, about noon.

eleven

Carrigan rode down the elevator in Betty Lewis's building.
Nervously he ran his fingers through his close-cropped
brown hair and wiped the sweat from his face. He felt
humiliated. Betty was now running things between them,
but he reflected with even deeper shame that, while he was
doing it, he had enjoyed it. He wondered — God! He didn't
have to wonder about that! He knew what Penny's reaction
would be if he ever — Jesus! Better stop thinking like that.

That bitch Betty liked it that way. That was why every
time he turned around there was her crotch practically in
his face. It was what she wanted all along. He imagined her
voice again and her face gone cruel. *"Go ahead. Go ahead!"*

Her way to humble a man. For the rest of her life,
Carrigan thought bitterly, she could laugh about the cop,
the big bad cop who'd gone down on her. All that Sean
business . . . crap! I must've been crazy, he thought.
Crazy.

Now he flexed his right hand; it hurt, but that had

been quite a backhand shot he'd given her afterward. Should've done it first. He'd left her bleeding at the mouth. Well, it was over. Or was it?

The door slid quietly open on the ground floor and a heavy man, moving lightly and fast, stepped in as Carrigan was just coming out of his reveries. Carrigan flushed with anger. "Okay, Mac, do you mind if I get out?"

He almost choked on his own words. The man had pressed the "door close" button together with an upper-floor button.

"Hey," Carrigan grunted, surprised that the man had not recognized the authority in his voice, but the door was already closing. Carrigan's jumbled thoughts immediately conceded the presence of an investigator hired by his wife, then a member of the investigating squad, then back to the private investigator. Automatically he reached to his back pocket for his wallet upon which was fastened his badge. His fingertips had just touched the worn leather when he felt the awkward piece of metal thud against his breastbone. He glanced down and saw the silencer, the gun.

Now Carrigan stared at the man in sudden fright, a fright which lashed and curled about him like the leather of a whip. The man did not look like a Negro, he thought in a panic which melted easily into a quivering fear. No, not Penny then, but the niggers, and here was a nigger who didn't look like a nigger.

"Turn. Turn around," the man said. "Do not move."

Carrigan forgot about his small automatic. It was only in the movies or on television that a man goes for his gun while staring down the barrel of another. Carrigan caught at the man's accent as he turned and noticed that they were only just now going up past the second floor, the muzzle of the silencer now resting gently against the base of his skull.

Carrigan just had time to silently curse the niggers, every stinking nigger he'd ever seen, read or heard about. He stiffened his fingers which were against the metal wall of the car and tensed his body. He was damned if he was going like this. But it was too late. You do not hear the gun go off before you are struck by its bullet.

Upstairs in the building, from her bedroom window, Betty Lewis peered around the curtain down at Carrigan's car. She wondered what was taking him so long to get to it. She was nude and in bed, still tasting the blood in her mouth. She laughed quietly. He was some guy, that Sean, really, still a babe in the woods when it came to sex. But she'd taken that robot spring out of him. Where was he?

Idly, she watched a blocky, bald-headed man, walking rapidly, cross her line of vision. She'd never made love with a bald-headed man. Well, the older she became, the greater chances for that! She released the curtain, thinking she would hear the car when it started up. She closed her eyes, waiting.

Betty did not know which woke her first, the low growls of the police sirens or the murmur of shocked voices in the hall. She woke slowly at first, as confident as any other New Yorker that the noises had nothing to do with her. On an impulse she sat up and thrust back the curtains, saw that it had grown dark and that Carrigan's car, directly under a streetlight, was crouched where it had crouched before.

With shaking hands she lighted a cigarette. What had all this to do with her? She turned on the bedside radio.

Nothing. She began to breathe easier. She dressed hurriedly, listening with growing dread to the sounds in the hall. At any moment she expected some of it to move down the hall and stop at her door. A drink, she thought, and went to get it, straight. Between the cigarette and the liquor she got her makeup on. Once more she peered out at Carrigan's car, wishing it far, far from where it sat mute and accusing. Now it was being stroked with flickering red lights. She saw the ambulance with its door open, and uniformed policemen holding back a small crowd. Attendants shuffled into view carrying a stretcher on which, covered with a blanket already suspiciously stained, lay a body. Betty felt cold, clamped with circumstance. *Was* it him? Quickly she poured another drink and drank it in a gulp. She went to her door, opened it and said in a light voice to the people still talking at the elevator, "What in the world is going on? Why are the police and the ambulance here?"

"Somebody found a man dead in the elevator, lady," a man said. "He was shot in the head."

"Ugh," Betty said, averting her head and allowing her lashes to fall momentarily. "A tenant?"

"If he is nobody knows him."

"Oh, this city," Betty said. "You go along thinking that these things will never touch you and one day there it is, right in front of you. It's awful." She backed inside and closed the door. She looked out; the car was still there.

She flung herself into a chair and cried.

Within two hours she was at the door again, answering a knock. The two men pushed forth their badges and asked if they might come in. Betty smiled and stood aside; they reminded her in some vague way of Sean. She saw both their eyes loop downward to her legs and she spun toward the kitchen. "Let me get you a drink. I suppose you're here about the noise in the hall and that man, whoever he was."

"No thanks, Miss," one said, his eyes springing up to her face. He brought forth a small note pad. The other detective leaned against the door, chewing gum. "You're a tenant here, right?"

"Yes," Betty said. She sat down and crossed her legs.

"Name?"

"Betty Lewis."

"Miss or Mrs.?"

"Miss."

"Home all day?"

"Since early afternoon. Just back from out of town."

"Did you hear a shot about five-thirty?"

"No."

The detective leaning against the door came forward, removing a picture from an inner pocket. "Ever see this man in the building?"

Betty took the picture and studied it. Her mind screamed, *It's Sean, it's Sean!* She handed it back. "No. Was he the —?"

The detective nodded and leaned back against the door.

She put her hand to her mouth. "Was that an officer's uniform he's wearing? He's an officer?" Then, almost too late, she remembered that Sean had come to her through a robbery investigation. "Wait," she said. "He did look a little familiar. Can I see the photo again, please?"

The detectives exchanged glances and the photo was returned to her.

She pored over it. "Ah, yes," she said finally. "He was

here several months ago. I reported a robbery. Oh! I just can't believe it! He was so nice and kind."

"He hasn't been back since then?"

"Here?"

"Yeah."

"Oh, no."

"All right, Miss Lewis. Did you notice any colored people in your building today?"

"Colored people? Negroes?"

"Yes."

Betty frowned. "I haven't seen any . . ." Her voice drifted with uncertainty, although she was quite sure no Negroes lived in the building; the tenants had got up a petition against the leasing of an apartment to a Negro couple two or three years ago. But . . .

The detective closed his pad. "Miss Lewis, we'll have to ask you not to make any trips until we get this all cleared up. It'll only take a couple of days. We'll be talking to you again."

Smiling, Betty closed the door behind them. The detective who was chewing gum said, when they were in the hall, "Shit, that's a good-looking piece."

"Yeah, Larry, and there might even be better in a building like this."

They were poised in front of the door of the next apartment, "This is a waste of time," Larry said. "No one heard a shot. A silencer. Back of the head, no chance of just a wound. Professional job, looks like, but I don't know — let's face it — there's a good chance the spades did it. I didn't know they were this good."

"Well, one thing sure. There's been a lot of rumors

that they *would* do it, and they had reason to do it. Poor bastard never had a chance to get his gun."

They knocked softly on the door.

The Sunday traffic rushed south on East River Drive, sounding like water flowing steadily over a falls. The mayor found the sound strangely relaxing and he was irritated that the police commissioner had had to call him. This goddamn city, the mayor thought; not a minute's peace, not a second.

But he smiled when the commissioner came in, and shook his hand warmly. "Leonard, why have you come to crap up the day?"

The commissioner took the seat the mayor pointed to. "Sorry, Mr. Mayor, but I thought we'd better talk about this one right away."

"*Which* one, Leonard?"

The commissioner joggled around in the chair until he found a comfortable position; he never had liked period pieces. "Late this afternoon one of our men was found with the back of his head blown off. In a building not far from here. It was Carrigan."

"Oh, my God!" the mayor said, stabbing at his head with the heel of his hand. "Well, what do you make of it, the obvious?"

"Looks like a very professional job," the commissioner said. "And everyone *does* think it's a revenge killing."

"Goddamn it, Leonard. What kind of klutzes do you have on the force in the first place? That sonofabitch didn't have to kill that kid. Jesus, bigots appear suddenly right out of the woodwork. And he'd have gotten off after the investigation —"

"No, sir," the commissioner said quietly.

"Well, damn it, it would have been nip and tuck, with the whole of Queens, the cops, the firemen and the sanitation workers behind him, spurred on by the Police Benevolent Association. There's never been anything benevolent about those bastards."

"Mr. Mayor, I know how you feel, but the fact is, sir, this is a whole new ball game. We're going to press this investigation as we would press any other —"

"— but with perhaps just a little more diligence, eh, Leonard, now that a cop's been killed? And don't give me that business about if a cop's not safe how can an ordinary citizen be. I know that one."

The commissioner almost sighed. "I wanted to say, sir, that we'll conduct it like any other investigation. But we have got to consider the involvement of a Negro or Negroes. If this proves to be the case, then you won't have to worry any more about whether the summers are going to be long and hot. There's something new, maybe, like the Bible says, an eye for an eye, but it could prove to be even more dangerous."

"Somehow, Leonard, it's always made more sense to me, that eye for an eye business."

"Yes, sir, but the men on the force may want to get an eye, too."

The mayor jabbed a finger at him. "No, Leonard. Your cops are public servants. We tax people in this city, tax them to death, to help pay your boys. I don't give a damn what they were like under somebody else's administration; under mine they are to serve the public, not beat the hell out of it. And there'd better not be a single case of police retaliation. For Christ's sake, man, all we need is a private war between the cops and the blacks. It would rip this city apart from river to river." The mayor stopped and listened to the sound of the rushing cars for a moment. "By the way, what's happened to those two cops who didn't answer that mugging call?"

"Suspended pending investigation," the commissioner said, clearing his throat.

The mayor asked mildly, "Did they or didn't they respond to the call?"

The commissioner took a deep breath. "It looks like they didn't."

"Then what's the problem? Why are they only suspended?"

"The PBA. Naturally."

"Naturally," the mayor said. "Leonard, I don't know. We don't seem to be getting through to the police. Their function has *changed*. They're creating more tension than they can ever hope to ease. Now. What about this Carrigan, married?"

"Yes, sir. Four kids."

The mayor slapped his thigh and said in a cold voice, "Four kids of his own, yet he could shoot down someone else's. Leonard, it's all shit, I tell you, and stinking more and more. Send over some flowers for me, will you? I'll do a letter. Call me later and let me know what's up."

The mayor stood and walked with his commissioner to the door. He watched him go down the walk and climb into a black limousine. "Goddamn it all," he said to himself when he reentered the house.

Within hours every on-duty cop and most off-duty cops in the city had heard of Carrigan's death. Almost immediately the officials of the Police Benevolent Association posted a five-thousand-dollar reward leading to the capture and conviction of Carrigan's killer. Some of the fixed, hard-eyed grimaces of the cops on duty in the black sections slipped slightly, and some of the cops in those same sections, saddled with a sudden weariness, plodded through the streets, worry budding in their minds.

The million black people they guarded slept righteously that night, grateful that the boy's death had been avenged, grateful that at last one of *them* (they all assumed) had gained the answer without destroying the neighborhoods. But they too hazarded a worry. They did not doubt that a Negro had killed the cop; therefore, they girded their loins in preparation for the retaliation that must come. For the moment, however, the score was one and one, and they wished the black killer godspeed. Tomorrow would just have to take care of itself; that was the way they'd always lived.

Newsmen left their desks in television studios or news offices to huddle over the last drink of the evening before heading home. They were more reflective than usual.

"Let's face it," one of them said. "If the blacks have progressed this far, it'll work. No one's caught up with the Mafia yet, and this is their kind of operation."

"Sure beats burning up the ghettos," another said.

"Shit, the ghettos were never theirs in the first place —hey, that's a piece for the Sunday Magazine: 'Who Really Owns the Ghettos?' "

"It'd take you five years to plow through all the holding corporations down to the real owners. Rockefeller, maybe."

"Yeah, then where would I get it published?"

"Muhammad Speaks."

"Hey, Flip. One more round. The last one."

"Tell you. I'd rather have this than the National Guard. One of those stupid kids almost put a bullet in my ass over in Newark back in sixty-seven. This is cleaner. Fairer."

The train ride in from the Island had almost sapped Browning's energy, but he had timed the trip to catch the late news. At the sound of the Teletype machines, the signature of the show, he set the paper he'd been reading aside.

The lead was the news of Carrigan's death. The words of the newscaster sank in slowly. A bubble of fear grew within Browning; it burst quietly and created other, smaller bubbles of fear. He willed himself fearless. It's done, he thought. Then realizing that he was alone, he spoke to the room: "It's done."

Although he felt drained, he went to the kitchen and fixed some coffee. He wished he were not so tired. He would go out and listen to what the people were saying in the bars; the people, the brothers. Now, he thought, *now*, let's see what's going to happen.

Carlo snapped off the television set with a flourish and started for the Don's room and stopped. He would tell him in the morning, what was the rush? After all, it was merely a report on a job they knew would be done one day soon. They had paid for it, so there never was any doubt. Now, perhaps, was a good time to get Peter and the Don away together for some fishing. But Peter would have some excuse, of course. Carlo stood on his toes and stretched, peering down into the park which was laced through and ringed by green-blue lights.

twelve

Itzhak Hod woke in his small, almost airless room and reached immediately for a cigarette. He had slept soundly. Only now, as was the pattern with him, did his mind recall the face of the man he'd killed yesterday. In a couple of hours the brain would refuse to conjure up the image any more.

He felt some relief; this had been his last job. From now on the work would be for free and the victims maybe Arabs. After so many years. New roads, new buildings, whole new cities, but the killing continued. Maybe, just maybe it might be different; killing close up with a silencer, so close you could smell your victim, have his last expression stamped on your mind was one thing. Picking him off at a thousand yards was something else. It was cleaner that way, or seemed to be. You saw no expression on the face, and as for the body, it could be *imitating* the last violent snap of death. Kids did it all the time, loved to do it. You killed for money, as he had been doing, which was better than doing it because you liked it, but not nearly as honest as killing in a rage as he had long ago. Or you killed for country. And that could involve killing for all the other reasons.

Hod snuffed out his cigarette, rolled out of bed, washed and lit another. Dressed in a few minutes, he left the room for breakfast in one of those bleak Second Avenue eat shops. Then he walked to Astor Place and took the uptown subway and dozed behind his sunglasses. Today for the first time in several days he would see Mickey-Siona; she believed he had been out of town on business. On business he was, Hod thought, and in a way, also out of town. Now he was back.

He burst into the office of Zim Lines, walking on the balls of his feet, almost dancing to the desk of a good-looking, solid young woman.

"Well, why don't we begin a beautiful day with a beautiful woman," he said in Hebrew. The woman looked up smiling and greeted him in Hebrew.

"It's too nice a day to do business," Hod said. "Let's take a walk in the park. What do you say?"

"Ah, one of those from Tel Aviv," she said. "Quick with the tongue, quick all the way around."

"And you?"

She said, "Tel Aviv, too."

Hod pretended to be taken aback. "A nice girl like you? No, no, you must be fooling. You are right out of Jerusalem, maybe even a kibbutz in the north?"

"Never mind. Buy something and maybe I'll walk in the park."

"Let me buy it in the park," Hod said with a hearty laugh that caused everyone to turn.

"But I am only selling tickets, nothing more," she said, her smile lessening. "Come on, be a good boy and sit down. What can I do for you in the way of legitimate business?"

Hod, feigning disappointment, sat down. "Young lady, when money is exchanged all business is legitimate. Now, you can sell me two tickets to Haifa. I want to stop in Barcelona. How long?"

"A minute." She riffled through a folder. "A day and a half."

"Good, good. Time to go to Toledo."

"To the synagogue," she said, knowingly. "There's one now open in Barcelona. Not nearly as old, not nearly as nice."

"Toledo," Hod said.

"First class," the woman said.

"Oh no," Hod said hastily. "Tourist is more fun."

"That's true, that's true. September fifteenth, all right?"

"Couldn't be better. Say, will you be sailing then?"

"Name?"

"Hod. Itzhak Hod."

"Mr. Hod, remember you are buying two tickets."

"I know, I know, but sometimes I get greedy."

The woman was smiling as she wrote. "Round trip, Mr. Hod?"

"No, no. I think I'll stay home this time."

She said, "Good. You will be there waiting when I come."

"Listen you, you better hurry up. You see this bald head and big belly? How long do you think I can afford to wait?"

Reaching for the money he held out to her, the woman answered coyly, "Isn't old wine the best wine?"

Hod popped his eyes. "Give me the tickets. Another minute of this and I can't be held responsible for what happens, I promise you. Just give me my tickets and let me run for the cold showers."

Late in the afternoon Hod, breathing a little heavily, knocked softly on Mickey's door. He clutched a dozen tightly budded yellow roses, the kind vendors sell on the streets, and a bottle of domestic champagne.

She opened the door at his first knock and rushed into his arms and found herself encompassed by the roses and the wine. She remained there, silent, as though she had just finished running a long race and was exhausted.

Hod asked, "What's the matter?"

"Until you called today, I thought you'd never come back and I — oh, come on in." She took his elbow and pulled him through the door. Inside, she kissed him.

"You'll make the champagne boil," he said.

But she went on, unhearing. "I thought all those silly, silly, middle-class things, like what would my parents say. And I thought that you didn't want to be forced into anything and you left, not to go on a trip, but to escape from me."

"After all we said?"

"Well — it's happened before," she said. "And you're the kind of man who'd try to be kind about it, and just go without any word."

Hod set down the wine and roses. "That's what you say, eh? Just feel my pocket here. *Feel!*"

Wonderingly she stroked his breast pocket. "Long, flat and thin. What is it?"

"You can't guess? Really, you cannot?"

"Could it be . . . ?"

He watched her eyes widen, soften. "Go ahead, guess."

"Tickets!" she cried. "My God, tickets to Israel!"

"Yes!" he shouted, whipping them out. "With a day and a half in Spain, time enough to go to the synagogue in Toledo."

"Itzhak," she said. "I am so, so very ashamed of myself. I missed you so and now it's all right. When do we go?"

"See? September fifteenth."

Still holding the tickets, she said, "Sit down, I'll fix you a drink and you can tell me all about Chicago."

Hod pulled off his jacket and sprawled on the floor cushions. He pruned his mind in preparation for her questions about the trip he'd never made. He'd begin it; it'd be better that way. He sighed.

"Well, I did a little business on the trip, not much, but then again better than I expected."

"Was Chicago quiet?"

Hod hesitated. "Chicago was Chicago," he said offhandedly. "What do you mean quiet?"

Now she was back with his drink. "Around New York when the cop shot that Negro kid we all thought we were in for another long, hot summer."

Hod furrowed his brow. "I've heard talk, but I don't know what it means, this long, hot summer."

Mickey laughed. "I do forget. You haven't been here a year. And the news bores you. How shall I put it to you simply? The Negroes in this country are demanding full rights, which had always been promised to them, full opportunity in a lot of areas, which also had been promised to them. Let's say that the Israeli Arabs were cut off from other Arabs by a large ocean and couldn't wait for the Zionists to be pushed into the sea. Let's say that the Israeli Arabs wanted to be complete citizens of Israel in every respect that a Jew is. They'd be doing the same thing Negroes in this country are doing. Now, just yesterday, the cop who killed the Negro boy was himself found shot dead and everyone thinks the Negroes did it, that they are finally through with rebellions in the summers, burning stores and homes. I asked about Chicago because here people thought the boy's killing would cause more rioting and indiscriminate killing of whites —"

"For revenge," Hod said. "It's what we would have done." Something, some*thing*, was making his scalp itch.

"For many, many summers now there has been rebellion and killing, rebellion by the blacks and the killing by white cops. You must've read or heard something about it wherever you were."

"I'd heard something, but America is so filled with news, and when you're here, it storms you and makes you forget in one minute what you've heard only the minute before. It's not like that in Israel. What happens in Eilat makes headlines in Tel Aviv a few minutes later and stays headlines. But America is too large; you cannot really get too close to things."

"It is a bad time, Itzhak. A riot starts, say in New York, and by the afternoon there are other riots all over the country. With the blacks it's like that, and about time, too. Anyway, like the Sterns and the Irgun, I think yesterday they killed the cop who killed the boy. An eye for an eye."

"Hey. What do you know about the Irgun and the Sterns?"

"Darling, every Jew knows about them."

Hod scratched his scalp. He knew the name of the cop before he asked; he could hear the syllables of the man's name already ringing in his ears. "What was the cop's name?" he asked as casually as he could.

Mickey laughed at him. "Poor Itzhak. You must be the only person in New York who doesn't know it. Carrigan."

"An Irisher?" Hod asked absently, as fear came lunging up. A cop, a cop! Why hadn't the man who paid him told him he was going to kill a cop? No matter, on the one hand. A job was a job. However, didn't all cops, even the ones off-duty, carry guns? Hod cursed silently. If it had not been his habit to move quickly, the man, the cop, Carrigan, might have surprised him, whipped out his own gun and today it could have been Hod, *me* lying under the ground.

"Itzhak. Itzhak! Are you all right?" Mickey asked.

Hod wiped his forehead; cold sweat came off in his hand. He knew he must be pale. "Just a little tired," he said. "Perhaps another drink. Don't worry."

He pulled himself together the few moments she was busy with the drink. Now she was back, still talking about the blacks. Over twenty-two million people; that is a mighty nation! Hod thought. "But why haven't they done something about this before?"

"I think it's because up until recently they had more faith in what this country is supposed to stand for than any other people," Mickey said.

"And the Jews here?" Hod asked.

Mickey paused over her plate. They were at dinner

now, the champagne was open and the room was filled with the strong scent of rapidly budding roses. "America is a disease that many Jews've caught; they feel like other white people, the goyim, about the blacks. They ask: 'What in the hell do they want?' They are afraid, too, because they are guilty also, having done the same things, or not having done anything. Others have been traditional Jews; they believe it their duty to help the blacks, to work with and for them —"

"They'd damn well better," Hod said, "because it's clear that if it were not for the blacks, it'd be the Jews who'd be doing the suffering."

And that, Mickey thought, was the very thing that had set many Jews in the camp of the Gentiles.

"There are a number of Africans studying in Israel," Hod said. Someone had told him; there had been none there when he left. "And black Americans visit all the time."

"That's as it should be," she said. "I'd not feel so good if it were any other way."

It was, truly was, Mickey was thinking, a good thing, Carrigan getting killed. That it was terrible was outweighed by the good. Itzhak would have to agree; that was the very way Jews in part won their independence and Israel. For the blacks nothing else had worked. Patience? Well, not as much as the Jews', perhaps. Not two thousand years' worth. And something became etched in the minds of an oppressed people, something it never could forget when it witnessed the systematic world-approved destruction of still another oppressed people.

Dinner over, Mickey cleaned up and joined Hod in bed. Hod had been thinking that for the first time he wanted to share his secret; he wanted to tell Mickey he had killed Carrigan. Early on, in Palestine, there had been the group to share the secrets with. After, in Europe, you worked alone, sharing nothing, not even trusting yourself with too much to drink. No. Of course he could not tell her. Everyone approved in the abstract, if it was in their interests or coincided with their feelings of the moment.

I looked on my right hand and beheld, but there was no man that would know me: refuge failed, no man cared for my soul.

True. You lived alone and moved alone, mostly, and the very people who paid you to perform those acts that cemented you in loneliness often dealt with you as though you were dirt. They were afraid of you. You were Ishmael.

But now the dirty part of it was over! All those years with the last-minute expressions of fear and unbelief; all those packets of money with their little brown wrappers, all those stuffy little rooms and the hours of ceiling staring. He could sing now if he felt like it.

"I would be content," Mickey said, "if they next killed the man who murdered the three college girls."

Hod stirred. "What, what do you say?"

"A man made a bomb, put it in a college, and three Negro girls were killed when it went off."

"Was he caught?"

"Yes, Itzhak, but in the South a white man is never convicted for killing black people. He was acquitted or something. Anyway, he's free."

"Enough, enough!" Hod said. "All this talk of killing; it does not become you." He slid his arm around her. "Besides, it is time to talk of other things, Mickey-Siona; it is time to talk about us."

"Yes, Itzhak."

"We will not be in the jewelry business in Israel, at least, not right away."

"It doesn't matter. In fact, I thought it would be all right because it's your business."

Hod smiled in the darkness. Then he said. "We are going to the desert, deep in the desert. South of the Dead Sea."

"What will we do?"

"They're starting a new settlement. They need people to work there for the Arid Zone Research."

"Whatever is that, darling?"

Hod chuckled. "They make the rocks grow green with vegetables. One of your big American Jews got it started, Lehman. It'll be hard."

"I don't mind it. I just want to be there with you," she said.

"And dangerous."

"Dangerous?"

"It's near the terrorist infiltration routes."

"I'm not worried, Itzhak. Are you trying to worry me?"

"No," he said. "Of course not. I just want you to know how it will be." No point in telling her what he really thought. He'd have to be there and see for himself.

After a while Mickey said, "Will you meet my parents?"

Hod chuckled again.

"I owe them that."

"Yes, yes, of course," Hod said. "And the wedding?"

"I don't want the canopy, do you?"

"Whatever you wish. But it's true. I can do without the canopy, too. I do want to tell you, Siona. Israel in many ways is like any other country. I don't want you to be disappointed. And I suppose that if you're a state and want to remain a state, you've got to start behaving pretty much like other states that've survived."

"I don't understand."

"Well, it's not a fairyland. People work very hard. And there are politics and skulduggery, just like anywhere else."

"Oh, I supposed so. Don't you want me to come? You're telling me so many bad things."

"I just don't want you to run for the airport a week after we're there."

"Itzhak."

Hod sighed. "I'm sorry. Sometimes when I think about us, I think maybe it's unreal and I keep trying to find out if it is."

"It isn't. It really isn't, Itzhak." Mickey now smiled in the darkness. And she believed she was the only one who thought it wouldn't happen. She lay her head in his arm. Hod finished his cigarette, drew her close and they went to sleep.

thirteen

"I got the clipping and your letter, Gene, and I'm puzzled. Wanted to call you right away, but figured I'd better wait and call you at home. Now, what the hell's going on? What do you mean when you say maybe I ought to cool things a bit down here?"

Browning was glad the family was away. He would have found it hard to field Herb Dixon's call with the girls around. The office had fallen almost into chaos when word came of Carrigan's killing. But Browning had not forgotten to write Dixon as he'd promised Braithwaite. Dixon sounded angry and Browning knew it was going to take some talking to calm him down.

"You calling from a booth far away from home?" Browning asked Dixon.

"Pretty far, but I imagine that the telephone operators and postmen and everyone else is a part of the Gestapo system. But let's talk about this business."

"Herb, it's all moved into a new phase now. That's what I hoped you'd get from the clipping —"

"Did Soul do it?"

"Soul," Browning said. Yes, a Negro did it. Me. I got the thing going.

"You sure? Know who? Trotman's guys?"

"I'm sure," Browning said, wishing Dixon wouldn't mention names on the phone. "But I don't know who. Listen, Herb. Trust me. Call your kids off for the time being and let's see what happens with this. The whole idea of mass action is out now, I think. It's something else, like this; hit and run. Hitting the cat who's in the news; the latest Chuck to mess over Soul, all right?"

"Yeah, yeah. I think they got the message even down here."

"How about it, man?"

"Gene, first tell me how come you're so sure."

"C'mon, Herb." I want to tell you, man, but I can't. I just can't, Browning thought.

"But obviously, you know something."

"Herb, we're talking too long and the telephone situation in this country ain't so hot, you know. Promise you this: one day I'll fill you in. That's a promise. I just can't now. But I want you to promise me something, too. Call your kids off and sit tight. A deal?"

There was silence on the line.

"What do you say, Herb?"

Dixon's voice came back incredulous. "I can't believe it, Gene."

"Believe what?" Browning asked cautiously.

"I'll be goddamned," Dixon said. "I will be damned. Look, Gene. You got a deal. Oh, hell. I've got to ask. Man, was it you?"

Browning forced out loud and cheerful laughter. "Me?

Damn, Herb, why man, I don't even *talk* about things like
that; it's the other guy you mentioned who's in that bag."

"Okay," Dixon said, but Browning knew intuitively
that he did not believe him. What kind of clues had Browning left behind that prompted Dixon to suggest he was im-
plicated?

"We'll cool it. I don't like it, just because I know it'll
make Braithwaite happy. But we'll do it. Take care of yourself, Gene."

"You too, Herb. S'long."

Just as Browning replaced the phone it rang again,
startling him.

"Gene, it's me."

Bill Barton. Browning recognized the voice with a
bounce of fear. But he said, "Yeah, hi, Bill."

Barton had come rushing back into town with the news
of Carrigan's death, but still hadn't given Browning time
off.

"I want to talk about a few things, like really in
private. Can I come up?"

"Sure, Bill." Had he got to Dixon too late? Had
Barton been talking to Braithwaite about that cash? "I want
to talk to you too, man, about some goddamn vacation
around here."

"Okay, see you in about twenty."

Barton came in with a worried look. Browning handed
him a drink and sat down across from him. "Tell you what's
bothering me, Gene. Carrigan. I've been telling myself that
he was involved in some racket and got greedy and he got
his. I told myself that even on the way back. That's five days
now."

"That's right. It's Friday and my family expects me in

Sag tomorrow. Are you going to mess up and keep me here? Val's salty as hell already because I can't get this vacation thing together."

Barton waved a hand. "I know, man. I know. In two or three weeks we should have it together. I'm sorry. I'm staying in the office too, and my old lady's got her ass on her shoulders." Barton leaned forward and placed his drink on the table. "Look, Gene, we got a real problem. Everybody's saying the brothers got together and did Carrigan in. What brothers? Why can't I find out something about it? You hear anything new?"

"Well," Browning said cautiously. "I've heard some talk of Trotman and his group."

"Shit," Barton said, snatching his drink up. "Trotman was in North Dakota on some Indian reservation, having a conference with Indian militants. Now, that's where *that* is."

"Then who?"

"Man I don't *know*. If I knew, we could get *our* thing together and be ready when they catch the brother that did it —"

"You think they will?"

"Gene, goddamn it, you know niggers were never allowed to get away with anything. This case'll be open for a thousand years."

Suddenly Browning understood. "The cops have spoken to you."

"Man, you better believe it," Barton said bitterly. "And the FBI. They want to know what we might know—"

"Where was Morris Greene?" Browning broke in.

His boss rubbed his long, lean chin. "Nobody knows where Greene was or *is*. If he did it, I hope he's out of the

country. They ran Bob Williams out and he only went for
Soul taking care of Soul. They'll skin Greene alive and wrap
his dick around his neck. These whities ain't kidding, Gene.
Hell. We don't know if it was Greene or not. What's the use
of even talking about him. How about another drink?"

They went into the kitchen together. "Why all the
sweat, Bill?"

Barton spread his hands, played the tips of the long
fingers against each other. "We're at the bottom of the pile
anyway when it comes to getting donations and member-
ships. If this kind of tactic works and Negroes gain through
that what they haven't been able to gain through organizations like ours, then we're dead, and all the other groups
that work through existing legal means, existing institutions, are dead too, man."

Browning handed him a fresh drink. "The thing," he
said, "is to gain the objective and in this case maybe the
end justifies the means."

Barton glanced at him. "Yeah, yeah. Sure. But tonight
I drafted a statement for the press" — he smiled sardoni-
cally — "deploring violence of any sort from either side in
the drive for full rights for blacks."

Back in the living room, Barton sprawled out in his
chair again. He looked shrewdly at Browning. "You can
always go back to college and teach," he said. "But where
do I go?"

Browning stared past him, to a picture on the wall.
He'd always been cynical about the guys who'd given all
their lives to running Negro advancement organizations. At
what point did idealism give way and the hard realities close
in? At what point did one start thinking of raises and
suburban living and tailored suits and vacations in Europe?

And why not, after all? It was almost impossible to live in this society without being tainted by what it was made up of. Browning supposed he'd always known that for many a black man existence depended upon being rah-rah for the cause. Sometimes he forgot what he knew because there were other things that took precedence. Now Barton had brought him back to basic economics. For all the superficial worry about the continued existence of IRJ, Barton underneath was worried about what was going to happen to Billy Barton.

Browning said, "Take the example of NayCeePee. They ran into tough going a few years ago. Militants were taking over everywhere, and they were not only scaring Chuck, they were scaring Soul, too. So Soul returned to NayCeePee; membership there picked up something like forty percent. The human animal is the same all over, Bill; conservative."

"Man, I could wait the storm out, but we're up against it. I ought to talk to Jessup. He'd know something."

Browning stared at the picture again. "If you knew something, I assume you'd report it to the cops or the FBI? Is that what this is all about, Bill?"

Barton looked carefully at his drink. "For almost a week that's something that's been bugging me." He stared sharply at Browning. "For the right kind of information, Gene, we won't have to worry about funds for the next two years."

"Jesus," Browning said. "Jesus Christ. Does it mean so much to them?"

Barton pointed a long finger at him. "Chuck ain't no fool. He wants to get into this and break it up; doesn't want it to spread. Let two or three groups see that selective assassination has merit, failing all other tactics, and we're going to have some shit going."

Wryly Browning said, "Assassinations aren't exactly new. The Kennedys, Malcolm, King — not to mention the ones in other times and the ones we don't even know about. We've now got to consider, as others have before us, assassination as just another political weapon. The twentieth century, with its own history of political assassination, isn't set apart in time from other periods in history when it was an acceptable weapon."

"Listen to the political science instructor," Barton said.

"It's the truth," Browning said simply. "And they know it; otherwise do you think they'd be out trying so hard to buy information?"

"I can't excuse it on those grounds, Gene."

Browning shrugged. "I don't suggest you do, but I do suggest that you remember that we may be in a new time, one totally unfamiliar to us, but with the goals still the same. As for me, I'd be willing to let IRJ go down the drain if Negroes can get what they must have. You know that's the line of the Urban League and NayCeePee: they'll be glad to be put out of business by not having present the situation that brought them into being in the first place."

Barton finished his drink and stood. From his basketball player's height he looked down at Browning. "Man, we are going to be a long, long time in this shit. I don't see any changes, big changes, meaningful changes on the way."

Browning wanted to say, but didn't, that a big change had happened on Sunday last. Big change had brought Barton to his living room and it had caused Barton to worry about his own future to the extent where he would trade a piece of information to ensure that future. Big change was swirling around his neck, but Barton couldn't even feel it. Perhaps it was time to go back to college now.

"Have a good weekend," Barton said at the door. "And tell Val I'm sorry. Thanks for the taste, Gene. See you Monday."

Goddamn it! thought Browning, pacing restlessly in the street. It was the next morning and the streets were almost bare of traffic. I'll be late if I don't get a cab in the next few minutes, he thought. Damn them! Goddamn them! The cabs, spaced long minutes apart, hurtled southward, the white cabdrivers impervious to Browning's frantic waving. Disgusted, Browning walked quickly down Broadway to the subway, resigned to missing his train at Penn Station and to hanging around another hour; to calling Val and telling her that they'd got him again. Cabdrivers!

He turned at the sound of a hail and recognized the face and the voice with its accent right away. They belonged to the man he'd spoken to on the benches last week. He smiled and stood there with his neat suit, the papers folded under his arm, and Browning thought, The last thing I need now is a conversation with this old bastard.

"Cabs're giving you trouble, I see," the Don said, glancing at Browning's overnight bag. "Visiting the family?"

"Yes," Browning said, almost curtly. He strained to look over the Don's shoulder for approaching taxis.

"I'm on my way downtown myself. Why don't we share one?"

"Got to get one to stop first," Browning said. He saw one and moved out to hail it. The old man moved in front of him and raised his arm. The cab swerved across the street and stopped near them. Browning was chagrined. He knew that had the old man not been with him, the cab probably would not have stopped.

Smiling, the Don waved Browning into the cab before him. He knew that Carlo, sitting in his own car, was watching and would follow them wherever he went.

"I guess I owe you some thanks," Browning said. "I'd have lost an hour if I'd missed the next couple of cabs. Penn Station for me."

"Fine," the Don said. "That's not far from where I'm going. Your family is at — I forgot?"

"Out at Sag Harbor."

"That's a nice spot," the Don said. He twisted around and casually looked behind them. Carlo was right on their tail. "How's the fishing been so far?"

Browning said, "I hear it's great, but I haven't been. Just too tired once I get out there."

The Don laughed. "But it'll relax you; loosen up the brain."

The car hurtled downtown. Browning glanced at his watch; he was going to make it all right. He heaved a sigh of relief. He saw himself down in the subway waiting for a train. The trouble with them was that you never knew when they would come on weekends. Feeling momentarily expansive, Browning extended his hand. "I'm Gene Browning. I'm grateful to you."

"I've done nothing," the Don said. "I was looking forward to seeing you again, anyway. Just call me Mantini."

Browning turned to watch the city rush by and heard the old man speak. "I see that cop, Carrigan, got himself killed. Maybe that'll make things a little cooler this summer. Do you think so?"

Browning glanced at the sturdy face, the bald head that was revealed with the man's hat in his lap. He was surprised to see that up close the man's eyes were not black, but blue. Browning said, "I think it'll help a lot. What do other people think?"

"I haven't spoken to other people about it," the Don said.

Browning shook his head. "I see." He wondered if the man was one of those people who just had to befriend a Negro with whom he could discuss the situation. Why didn't they talk with other whites about it? Or did they know they would never get any real answers talking to each other? But that's where it was, with Chuck.

The Don felt Browning's hostility. "I hope you don't mind my talking about it. I don't know any colored people and I am interested in what goes on. I'd like to understand and even help if I can. I don't mean to butt in."

Browning found himself softening. "It's a very complicated situation Mr. Mantini — is that Italian? I noticed your accent, but I couldn't place it."

"Italy," the Don said. "But I don't understand why it's complicated," he said with a shrug. "You get hurt, you hurt back. That's not complicated."

Browning tried to explain. "You don't hurt back the way you were hurt first because the next time around you get hurt even more. I mean, two times out of three Goliath would have smashed David. He was lucky."

"It does make sense," the Don said, "to hurt in such a way that you don't have to take the blame for it." He allowed his eyes to slide past Browning's and to the rear window again. "That's smart. That doesn't make a man a coward."

"We like to work through channels, the courts, making people aware of their rights so certain situations can be changed —"

"That's not working so hot now," the Don said. "Even I can see that."

"It's true," Browning admitted. "Those things are not working so hot. I guess they never did."

"I'm a lot older than you, Browning, and to tell you the truth, I don't think they ever worked."

Browning glanced at him. The old man was the first and only white person he'd ever met who admitted that. "That's a very strong statement," Browning said with a half-smile. "I'll bet you're a philosopher."

"I'll bet I'm not," the Don said. "I'm retired. I was in business. What about you?"

"I work for an organization that prefers to go through channels. Like I said, courts, and voter registration and so on. It's the Institute for Racial Justice."

The cab was slowing up as they approached the station. The Don touched Browning on the arm. "I'd like to have dinner with you one night when you're free. Are you in the phone book?"

Browning nodded. God, he'd never get the man off his back. Never. "Right now," he said, "I'm kind of busy. A couple of weeks and the crush should be over."

The cab swept in beside the walk and Browning got out. "I'll look for your call, Mr. Mantini," he said, and rushed into the station. Well, he thought, that's one dinner I'll never be able to make. He gained his seat on the train and sat back. But it would be just my luck to find him sitting on that bench every time I came out.

Well, he'd see. There might be a sizable donation from the old man, and a good hunk of bread would do the IRJ a helluva lot of good.

Browning leaned back and took a few deep breaths as the train moved through the trainyards with their rusting rails and battered old cars. Should keep going, Browning thought. Pick up the family, drive back to the ferry, Connecticut, Massachusetts, Vermont, Canada. And never come back. Now he had to tell himself that Barton had frightened him. First, it was because of Braithwaite's cash. Then that passed. Now the fright was even deeper. Barton would pass along anything he discovered to the FBI just to keep himself in a job for another couple of years or so. But obviously Barton knew nothing and was puzzled and angry because he didn't. He'd taken the hook at the mention of Morris Greene.

The trouble with Barton was that he was thinking white; he'd started thinking right away of the most obvious blacks. Browning almost smiled. No one, so far, and even Dixon wasn't *sure*, seemed to be *able* to peer past the militants, forgetting Guevara's important statement about picking up the ammunition instead of the medicine. Only Che *had* picked it up; he hadn't let someone else pick it up for him, and he had a family, training and a practice. Latin temperament, Browning thought. Now, *I'm* thinking white. The situations were different; on Che's "home ground," Cuba, there had been a chance to win and they won. There's no chance to win a shooting war here. Browning glanced out the window watching the houses flash by as the train leaned into a curve. Face it. Guevara was less afraid of the consequences, more committed not to some action, but to being the focal point of the action.

Browning continued with his rationalizations. And this was an urban society. Cities. Streets. Large concentrations of armed men, the police. Everyone who lived in Manhattan could be screened at the bridges and tunnels. So? Don't live in Manhattan.

Ours has been, he continued, a tradition of resistance so secret that even we have been unaware of it. The black man appearing so dumb that he couldn't understand the simple job the white boss explained to him; the black man always breaking his hoe, broom, shovel and claiming surprise that he'd done it; the black man shuffling, murdering the time away; the black man speaking English upside down to keep from understanding, to block communication that would further enslave him; the black man discovering boll weevils and transplanting them from cotton patch to cotton patch; the black man blowing snot in the white folks' tapioca and pissing in the tea and coffee and stirring spit into the roast beef and chicken gravy; black hands hard on tiny white hands, quick on little white bottoms.

And Gene Browning slept a while, a little smile curling his lips.

Nora Browning sat in the parked car and watched the train ease up to the station. Her mother had let her drive alone. Finally. Hard making her realize that she was a woman now. Eighteen, but a woman. Daddy would be surprised to see her, and she bet Mother was sitting next to the phone waiting for the East Hampton police to call and tell her of an accident. And of course she suspected that she was driving to meet Woody. Natch. Well, Woody hadn't come out yet; she expected him to call tomorrow. Daddy would be there. Good.

She leaned her head on the back of the seat and smoked a forbidden cigarette. He was looking very tired these days. Maybe Mother was right; he was working too hard. God, for what? The place was beyond saving and it had to be almost that way when Daddy got it. We don't want any part of it, she thought, not the way it is now. No, thank you. But they wanted you to be a part of it, the parents and older people. Do you take The Pill?

Nora smiled. Of course I take The Pill. I had to lie. Don't mind hurting Mother, but Daddy's something else again. A special kind of guy. He hurts inside, you can tell. Even she can tell now. After so many years of being married, too.

She glanced around her. The cars were pulled up, noses toward the station. Behind them was a lumber company and the smell of freshly cut wood seasoning in the sun hung cleanly in the air.

Peaceful. Out of it. Forget the business with China and how Woody and millions of others were threatened by it. Forget the forests of H-bombs aimed down our tonsils our honored parents left us, along with an economic system that builds in obsolescence; you never know when they're going to call your car back in to put the wheels on. Forget that once people dreamed of a working democracy where a vote really counted for something. Now what do you have? A succession of genuinely mediocre men as Presidents, a Congress made up of millionaires or people trying like hell to become millionaires.

I'll be damned. And all your parents can think to ask

you, one, are you taking The Pill, and, two, who are you going to marry?

She leaned forward and gripped the steering wheel with both hands. I am taking The Pill, she thought, and I'm going to marry Woody. Their thing didn't work. Now it's our turn. Later.

She opened the door and ran to meet her father.

Browning glanced once at the car and saw that Nora was alone. He concealed his surprise. "Hey, baby, I see you got wheels," he said. He kissed her. "And been smoking, too."

"You look really whipped, Daddy," Nora said. "Let me drive back. You rest."

"Sure. I want to see just how well you handle this thing anyway. How did you get your mother to let you come alone?"

Nora smiled. "Persuasion. Logic. Anything you want to call it, but it worked."

"Woody out yet?"

"Tomorrow."

Browning winced. "I was sort of hoping he wouldn't be here," he said. "I'm still looking for peace and quiet."

They dipped under the railway trestle, sped past Schwenk's Dairy. Nora said, "I planned it this way. I hope you don't mind, Daddy. I just didn't want to get into a thing with Mother."

Browning turned in his seat so that he was looking directly at her. "This thing for Woody, it's supposed to be real, huh? At eighteen, huh?"

Nora smiled her smile again. "Can I put it this way? You and Mother have known each other since you were eighteen, right? Okay, what's *wrong* with eighteen and liking somebody? The other thing is, suppose Woody isn't it, just suppose he isn't? Is my seeing him going to kill anybody?"

Browning sighed. "Seeing Woody now and maybe marrying him later are two different things and I think you ought to know that everyone isn't as tolerant of mixed marriages as me and maybe, I don't know, Woody's folks. Not by a long shot."

"I know," she said, chin high, peering steadily at the road. "But that's the way you've left things."

Now Browning lighted a cigarette. "I've noticed," he said, "that the ocean air does something to you. Nothing seems to happen to you in the city, no growth, no special wisdom or anything. But as soon as we get out into the country, things start happening to you; you start growing and in a very subtle way you start snapping at me. Now, I know the system's bad. I can't begin to describe to you just how bad it is. I haven't yet quit trying to change it, you know, and I don't suppose I will. I'm still here. I haven't gone anyplace, so, I haven't left you any of these things yet. These things were left to me, too."

He felt as if he had reached her. They continued on, riding in silence until he said, "Tell me something, Nora."

"If I can, sure."

"These are strange, strange times. I mean we may actually be at the point where all of it is going to blow, yet you have to consider that, being at that point, suddenly something could happen to make things better."

"Yes?"

"Rotten way to begin, honey." He smiled at her and patted her shoulder. "I look at you and I wonder. Everyone these days is into some militant thing. Discovering black, reveling in it. Even your mother's got this haircut." Browning took a deep breath. "And there you are with Woody." Browning watched her chin come up even higher. "That was a statement. Not a condemnation, you know. I'm wondering how you can have this thing for the boy with all the other insane things going on."

Nora shrugged. "I just do. For me that's the way it is. And I know all about the black bag, Daddy. Really. And thanks for being the way you are. I know what people think about Woody and me; about me especially. But you and Mother gave me a life and I mean to live it the way it feels best. You taught us that being black was not being inferior and also that because a person is white he is not superior. Now, I believe that. I think I am all the blacker because there is Woody."

"Aw, rap, Nora. Is that what they're saying these days?"

She laughed. "Daddy, you know, it's sometimes just too much to bear, all this horrible past. Maybe you don't know it — do fathers ever know it? — but I'm pretty tough, even for a girl."

Browning was staring at the fields, unseeing. What he did see was himself telling Nora. He saw her shock. Love was life, and life, although attached to death, wished very much to be incompatible with it. She would not be able to understand that in order to have life, to treasure it, one must rub elbows with death, to summon it, to cause it.

He turned and smiled at his daughter. "I know you're tough, honey. Hang on to it. You'll need it. You can't do without it."

Nora had turned into the driveway; the wheels were now crunching on the sand. She looked at her father, a long, searching look, and saw in his face only weariness and worry, and suddenly, deeply touched, she took his hand. "Daddy, please don't worry. It really is almost our turn now."

Browning smiled his thanks, and opening the door, prepared to embrace Val who had run out to the car.

She felt good, very good, and he gave her a heavy kiss and then, an arm around Nora and an arm around Val, walked to the house.

"Darling," Val said nervously. "Billy Barton called up in a sweat. He wants you to call him right away."

Val brought him a beer while he telephoned. He sipped it and listened.

Morris Greene had sent letters to the New York police and the New York papers saying that it was obvious now that from here on out it was going to be an eye for an eye. No white man was going to kill a black man without getting killed himself.

"Where is Greene?" Browning asked.

"The letters were posted in New York. Nobody knows where he is now. And the police are looking for him. They think he got Carrigan."

fourteen

Morris Greene shifted the Italian racing bike into high gear and, pumping hard, rushed past two parked blue-helmeted scooter cops. He hardly noticed the sign that said *Short Cut To The West Drive*. It told the cyclists in Central Park that they did not have to go farther north along the road that brushed Harlem. A few of the early-morning cyclists were peeling off on that road.

Greene pedaled on alone except for the few pros who whirred past him at a steady, driving pace, padded helmets on, feet strapped to the pedals. The park was just past the peak of green; the grass had taken on the hint of a brownish tint. Now the walks were either of dirt or broken concrete; the grass was not cut as it was at the south end of the park. Greene, heaving over the handlebars with his huge, awkward bulk, came swiftly up to the curve, sliced it and headed back due south, rushing downhill now past the pale-green swimming pool which in a couple of hours would be flecked with brown bodies. He missed his beard and Afro and he felt the wind slashing against his newly shaven face and barbered head. He felt younger without the hair on his face and head, somehow leaner, but more vulnerable.

He pumped furiously downhill and leaned dangerously into the curve around the swimming pool and swept northward again. Seventh Avenue opened before him, great gray buildings lined up on either side of the street, the center strip bearing large trees. Sunday morning. The church folk would be out before long, Greene mused, and for a moment he was lost in the nostalgia of his childhood days in church, the black-robed choir, the steady motion of fans which advertised the local Negro undertaker, the smell of perfumes, the perfunctory *Amens!* A different time; an altogether different world.

Now Greene shifted into a lower gear and attacked the hills. He wanted very much to walk his bike up, but it was a question of some obscure honor that he pump all the way to the crest, and he did with a steady pace that sent blood pounding in his ears. At the crest, breathing heavily, he circled two or three times, then dismounted and walked the bike along a path that gave a direct view north of Harlem. Gratefully he sat on a rock and luxuriously lighted a cigarette. He smiled, thinking about the cops he had passed. Not only those two; many others. They sought a Greene with a bushy head and a thick beard, not a Greene in sneakers and plaid shorts, expensive cotton shirt. The Greene they wanted also wore African robes and haunted the corners of Harlem.

He glanced up at the sound of someone coming along the path, then smiled at the newcomer. "You look like a plucked chicken, Len," he said.

The newcomer was breathing heavily. "Let me tell

you," he said. "I feel like one. And you've got a lot more face to wash, too."

Leonard Trotman drew out the kickstand on his bike and shook hands. He too lighted a cigarette, and sat down beside Greene. "Ahh, it's a great day. Just right. Not too hot yet."

"How are the redskins?" Greene asked.

"Well, you know. I'm black, they're red, and there's all of history. But the young ones are something else. It'll work out. Say, how long did it take you to go around the park?"

"Forty minutes. You?"

"About the same. These hills at this end killed me. I thought I was in shape."

"Me too."

They finished their cigarettes in silence. Trotman stared glumly down at Harlem, a slight frown on his face. It really was a gas, meeting in the park like this. All the way in from Chicago Trotman had been thinking about what Greene said he was going to do, and by now, of course, he'd done it; every cop, sheriff and state trooper in the country was looking for him, not to mention the government people. He glanced at Greene to find Greene laughing at him. "What's funny?"

"Len, do I look as funny as you without all the hair?"

"I feel strange, Morry, damned strange, let me tell you. I feel like a billy club could bend my skull right down to my chin; I felt a little better with that bush."

Greene leaned over and punched him lightly on the arm. "The Man is looking for beards, Afros and dashikis. Wait until this afternoon when I put me a suit on and some polished shoes. I'll blow his mind I'll be so clean."

"I got me one of those double-breasted jobs with high-flying lapels, brass buttons and twelve-inch vents and boots, baby. Plus a tie like my granddaddy used to wear; must be half a foot wide at least."

"You can wear that shit; always looks good on skinny cats," Greene said. "I thought I'd lose like hell in the mountains, but all I did was get hard."

There was a brief silence after this exchange and then Trotman asked, "Morry, what's the program?"

Greene offered him another cigarette, took one himself and lighted both. "The program," he said.

"That Carrigan thing," Trotman said. "Sounded Italian to me. The cat was in the rackets, got greedy. None of those cops are worth a dime."

"I don't think so," Greene said. "Between the cops and the Mafia there's a special thing going. Gentlemen's agreement. In the first place, a cop has to really get shitty; in the second, they'd never leave him around to be found. So we take advantage of the situation. Part of the program. I claim I did it. That gives the cops an out; they got a suspect but the brothers have got a hero, I mean a violent hero. A Shango. We have got to make these Chucks believe that they can no longer kick black asses with impunity; that blacks will get back. That's like A-number-one in the program."

"Yeah, baby, I understand all that. Makes good sense, but you know if they catch up with you, you won't get a chance to say you were only fooling. They'll put so much lead in your ass you'll look like a lead mine. Then they can wipe Carrigan off the books."

"Yeah, I know," Greene said. This was for real. Climbing up and down mountains, meeting in out-of-the-way places, little conspiracies here and there, speeches, threats, demands — all that seemed now like a game. "But game-time is over," Greene said aloud to Trotman.

Trotman nodded. All over the nation he had felt the sense of disaster hastening up. There were people ready and willing to act, but in indirect and often wasteful ways. Few sought a genuine closing with the tread of events. Greene was one of them.

"Over," Trotman agreed. How many nights had they reviewed the actions of the Congress, state legislatures, white spokesmen; how often had they dissected newspaper, radio and television reports, all to find it mandatory to strike, to attack the system physically somewhere near the center of power. That is what would make the revolution a genuine revolution. And unless that were done soon things would begin to slip back into old molds — as whites wanted them to; and blacks grew tired of talk, no action and the one-at-a-time murders of their leaders. Game-time's over.

"Number two," Greene said. "It's a two-part program with a demand. Labor Day, think of Labor Day weekend."

Trotman stared out over Harlem seeing Labor Day weekend. Cars rushing up and down the traffic arteries bumper to bumper. Bright sun. Last holiday of the summer. Parks filled. People everywhere. New York City steaming.

Greene went on. "You travel around this city very early in the morning, very late at night, and on the buses, at the toll bridges and tunnels, brothers, mostly brothers, working those same bad hours Chuck always gave them, while Chuck's home in bed getting his sleep. Len, we got people on those bridges and tunnels. A year and a half ago before I went to the mountains we got some brothers and sisters in civil service in both New York and New Jersey.

We need to demonstrate that we can cripple this largest city in the world. We can make what they did to Paris a few years back look like a picnic. Only we don't hit the streets. We stay cool."

Trotman did not have to ask what the demands were; he knew them. They had spent at least two years separately and one year together drawing them up.

The first was the immediate resignation of every senator and congressman from any state where Negroes did not have full enfranchisement. This applied to state legislatures, too. Interim elections would be held to fill the vacancies. The mood of the country, while rifle-hard now, would change. If a legislator was stupid enough to get caught out in the old games in this new time, he was expendable. People were going to be very willing to trade now — a number of legislative bigots for peace for the whole society.

The second demand was the immediate allocation by executive order of ten acres of land, one intermediate-sized car and five thousand dollars to the head of every black family who could establish his need for such a grant. Forty acres, Trotman thought, was what we *should* have had. Nobody needs a mule any more, and the cars could be purchased at the special government price, the one they paid for military cars. And wouldn't this help big steel and big auto manufacturers? Five thousand dollars was little enough to pay for what we also should have had and even then all those five thousands would total up to less than what the military budget would be per month if the U.S. invaded China. Didn't need more than five thousand, like some Americans. A people freed without food and only the clothes on their backs, who have bred from tough greens and hog leavings superathletes, don't need big money; a people who not only survived but multiplied could make do with a teeny bit. The five thousand dollars was like a handful of damp seed. But it would do.

Land. There was plenty of it in the "disaster areas," areas from which the youth had fled, going to the bright lights of the cities. Old men tended the cattle and farmhouses leaned with every strong wind, gray clapboard shingles flapping. There were abandoned dairy farms by the hundred thousand, and there were government reserves. Land, capital, and transportation. Basic items. A modern Homestead Act. Chuck wants peace in this land, he's going to have to pay for it, just like he's paid to keep the peace everywhere else on this globe. And it was little enough they were asking; they called them demands, but they were really a challenge, a last chance.

The third demand, Trotman knew, was a strike at the core. No longer would teachers, social workers and other professionals who were qualified be paid the same wages as policemen, firemen and sanitation workers; they would get more and the others would get less. Thus there would be an immediate review of wage scales and a redefining of values. This demand recognized that many of the black problems were also the problems of whites, and allies were necessary. Included in this demand was the establishment of a civilian review board in every city in the country with a police force of over fifty men. The people had that right; their taxes paid police salaries. Plus, commencing in 1975, these same cities would gradually begin to hire only college graduates who had completed the requisite number of courses set down or approved by the civilian review boards. At that point salaries would start to become commensurate with those of other public servants who were also college graduates. The level of

education in the nation had risen, but the educational re-
quirements of the police hadn't been upgraded in half a
century. Some cops didn't understand or even know the laws
they had sworn to uphold.

Trotman and Greene had long ago recognized the
inequities that gave sanitation workers, for example, the
same take-home pay as many teachers. Qualified, experienced teachers, to whom the children of the nation were
entrusted for almost two decades, had no business being
jealous of the money drawn down by a dropout in the
sanitation department. Of course, the trade labor unions
tended to be tougher and stronger than white-collar unions
and this had a great deal to do with the inequities. The trade
labor unions, many of them guilty of discrimination, would
have to come under review by the communities in which the
locals functioned.

In foreign policy, U.S. forces would have to leave Asia
at once, even if the invasion of China had already commenced by Labor Day. And U.S. investments in South
Africa, Mozambique, Angola and Rhodesia, in addition to
all the U.S. government defense money that made its cir-
cuitous way to those countries, would have to be withdrawn
or blocked or cut off at once.

Finally, back home, there would be a ten-year tax relief period for the heads of all Negro families who could
prove their need for it. Black people didn't want things for
nothing; they weren't Freedom Fighters sulking far from
home while making good money and living in decent neighborhoods, neighborhoods in which Negroes were not
wanted. The tax relief period would help to overcome to
some small extent the deficit of generations.

Trotman sighed. The demands were legitimate. Would

Chuck think so? Five bridges or tunnels would remain after the first phase of destruction. That had been the plan and still was. Or was it? He said, "There'll be five things left, right?"

Greene nodded. "That's the plan. Five left, that's right." We'll leave them. We want to strike the right balance, if that's possible with the Devil. One thing's sure: we've got to live here, too. Our people can wire up any bridge, any tunnel, no sweat. You know where they got their training, and everything'll be cool. Nobody in the street. We want black America to behave just like white America behaves when there's catastrophe — like nothing's happened. They have to understand how cold and deliberate we are. The guys at the top will."

Now Greene felt exhausted, but he could imagine green river water pouring through the gaping holes of tunnels; see bridges shuddering in their moorings and then toppling into the waters or streets below.

Trotman remained silent. Greene was remembering back to the time of the first sit-ins in 1960, remembering meetings in middle-class black apartments, with people shuffling back and forth to the telephones to talk to the students down South; he was remembering the Freedom Rides and the burned-out buses, the beatings; remembering the Martin King marches, the SNCC voter registration drives in the Deep South, and the plunging fear and disintegration that had come after the murders of Goodman, Chaney and Schwerner. Remembering all the years, the false starts, the false hopes, all the waiting, all the killing, and now it was 1973 and game-time was over. It had to be over.

Greene glanced at Trotman who was chewing a blade

of grass. He was the only person in the world he had ever confided in, and then, not completely. But more than in the younger people. They were harder, willing to take orders and often spoke about the "ultimate act" until they had come to believe it. It had taken a long time to find and train them, steer them clear of Chuck's traps that lay in wait for every black man. The bastards could buy you off so smoothly sometimes that you believed you were still fighting them.

"And Jessup?" Trotman wanted to know.

"No. Not Jessup. From jump I didn't trust him because he was trying to begin a black revolution with white money. And those cats Jessup's hanging out with have no plans for us except graves. Fascists. He still believes he can outsmart them before they outsmart him. It's bad enough when you can't trust a brother these days, but I never meant to go the whole way with Jessup and those Birchers. He talks to too many people and too many people tend to guess and even know too much. The man's a fool; he still believes pure revolutionaries can come out of a system like this one, and he thinks that because a man's black he's an automatic revolutionary. Not true. He took Gene Browning up to the camp. That was a mistake. Anybody working for Billy Barton, you've got to watch him. Besides, Browning was a professor in a white school. What in the hell does he know about what's going on out here in the street?"

"Oh, he's all right," Trotman said.

In the silence that came between them again, Greene heard more voices out on the road and saw cyclists walking their bikes to the crest of the hill. He saw that Trotman was perturbed. "What's the matter, Len?"

Trotman shook his head. "One month, then, most

likely, all hell's going to break loose, and I got me a job to do before then."

"Yeah," Greene said.

"I got to get him," Trotman said quietly.

"I'm going to need you, man."

"I got to get him," Trotman said stubbornly. "Sometime this month."

Greene said, "What can I say?"

"Nothing," Trotman said. "She was my sister and he's still free. He's got to go, Morry. If I die the next minute, he's got to go."

"Okay, Len. I understand. It's the way it ought to be."

Trotman gave a low laugh. "Now it feels lonely, like being back in the mountains again at night. I guess it always is when you've made the decision you should've made a long time ago."

Greene said nothing. It was always lonely, always. For example, here he was in New York on Sunday. How great it would be to take a shower, dress and go to the Red Rooster for the early dinner of roast duck! A couple of martinis, stuffing, tantalizing gravy. But no, he'd eat in a cafeteria someplace, or in a Village restaurant that served mediocre food or maybe even canned goods in his room. He said aloud, "Yeah, cold and lonely and one month to go."

"One month?" Trotman asked with a sad smile.

"One, an ace."

Greene didn't look at his friend as he spoke. "Len, maybe this isn't the smartest thing to do. But do you think we could bop to the Rooster this afternoon, sit in the back when most of the crowd's gone and latch on to some of that roast duck? Could I get away with it?"

"Let's not take the chance," Trotman said. "You just can't tell who is who these days. The cat talking all the shit next to you may be the Man. I'll go by and pick up duck for two. Where will you be?"

Almost shamefacedly, Greene told him. He never should have gotten that weak, Greene told himself. Not over martini glasses beading with sweat or plain old superbly cooked duck; not over the hum and swing of Negro voices, male and female, or sleek, action-seeking foxes; not over blues from the box. Never. Greene sighed. He stood. "I'll leave first," he said.

A revolutionary. A goddamn duck dinner and cold martinis and I'm a washout. A forty-five-year-old washout. Side dish of stewed tomatoes, hot rolls with butter, another side dish of collards or turnips, homemade apple pie . . .

Greene passed over the crest of the hill and began to pedal. The bike picked up speed with every stroke and soon the wind was rushing against his body, slashing at his face.

fifteen

Browning lunged for the ringing telephone with mixed feelings. He wanted to talk to someone, but not someone from
the office. The days had piled on days and the office talk was
all about Greene. He was both puzzled and nervous about
Greene's act, but he thought he understood it. He had never
underestimated the man.

And there was the increasingly irritating Billy Barton
casting about for one of the top-level jobs that the city, state
and federal governments were always holding out to the
right black. In addition, increasingly his thoughts returned
to teaching, to going back and telling the department head
that he was going to teach political science the way it should
be taught.

He was also vaguely jumpy about the confused reports
of U.S. troop increases along China's border, as if there had
not already been enough "accidental" ground fighting at
patrol strength. This was the year the Chinese were believed
to be capable of sending nuclear rockets to the U.S.

This information, however, slipped and slid around in Browning's mind, for there were other things. Like the five thousand black militants across the country who were being politely interviewed by government agents seeking information about Greene. IRJ had been asked by many to seek a halt to the harassment. IRJ would do its best, but it was in the American tradition to hunt down the "bad nigger" and kill him before his wild ways polluted every other nigger. Damned fools, didn't they understand that it was already too late, that the "pollution" had already spread like clap on a destroyer? Trotman too had vanished, so chances were that something was up, something big coming.

Things were already happening. As if taking a cue from Greene, the assassinations of policemen went from zero to fifteen in just a few days; it was something Browning had not anticipated and he read the reports with both revulsion and elation. It must have been these reports that prompted Herb Dixon to apologize for thinking Browning had killed Carrigan.

In less hectic moments Browning found that he envied Greene. He had done nothing, but he took the blame; he, Browning, had had it done, but in such a way that he would not have to take the blame. He approached each day's news with quickening breath; *he* could have been in Greene's place with the history of the United States howling down *his* track.

Although he missed his family more with each passing day, Browning was grateful that they were not underfoot now. God, how would he have been able to conceal all the emotions he was sure kept crossing and recrossing his face? He was sleeping badly and he was sure that he would have had at least a dozen pitched battles with Val if she were in the apartment.

"What's the matter?" she would have asked several times a day.

"Nothing," he would have answered. "Tired."

"Something more than that."

"No, nothing more, baby."

"You've been like this now for days."

"Sorry. It'll pass."

"What're we supposed to do in the meantime beside walk on eggshells?"

And perhaps he would have said, "I don't much give a damn what you do as long as you leave me alone."

And they would have been into it. No. Good they were away. Maybe things would straighten out by the time their vacation was over.

Now Browning spoke into the telephone.

"Mr. Browning? This is Mantini — hello, are you there?"

Browning had been momentarily surprised, now he stuttered, "Yes, yes, how are you?" He continued without waiting for a reply. "Have you called before? I've been pretty busy —"

"It's all right," the Don said. "I understand perfectly."

Browning got the feeling that his caller did understand perfectly.

The Don went on: "An old man like me, I've got nothing to do, lots of time on my hands. You, I can see you must be busy. Anyway, I thought we might have dinner tomorrow night. Are you free?"

"Why, I —"

"If you're not," the Don said affably, "just say so. We can do it another time."

Browning leaped to make amends for his bungling effort to get out of it. "Oh, I can make it all right," he said. All he needed right now was to sit around talking to some old man whose accent made his English hard to understand. Why was he so goddamn persistent anyway? Some white people were like that; they insisted on your being friends even if you didn't want to be.

"That's very good," the Don said heartily. "Where would you like to eat?"

"Oh, I have no preferences, Mr. Mantini."

Browning picked up a pencil and wrote down the details of where they would meet and at what time. He said goodbye with a sense of uneasiness. Perhaps he should have told the old man right out that he didn't want to eat with him.

"Just couldn't," he said to the telephone as he hung it up. "I guess I'm soft as babyshit."

"Okay?" Peter Vigianni seemed relieved when his uncle nodded that everything was all right.

"What a nut that guy Greene must be," Peter said. "It must be great for the other guy who really did it, but Jesus, who in the hell walks up and hangs a murder rap around his own neck, especially a cop's murder?" Peter shook his head.

"If you ask me, they're all crazy," Carlo volunteered, ignoring the Don's impatient frown. "And I think maybe your uncle's catching it."

Peter's head came up with a snap. "Yeah, Uncle, why bother with dinner and all that? What's going on?"

"Nothing. Nothing's going on," the Don said impatiently.

Peter said, "Pretty soon you're going to make him interested in you, too, and then maybe me and —"

"Don't think I haven't already said it," Carlo said.

"Relax, relax," the Don said. "After all these years you think I don't know what I'm doing? Come on, now. Just take it easy."

"How is *he* taking it?" Peter asked.

The Don shrugged his shoulders. "That's what I'm trying to find out. Carlo bothers me; now you come around asking questions. I'm curious to know how a man acts who's not — you know . . . but gets himself all twisted up. What's so bad about wanting to know, huh, Carlo? Huh, Peter?" The Don muttered under his breath as he unwrapped a cigar. He stopped suddenly and pointed a finger at Carlo. "And another thing. If I was really a part of things in the group, I'd have a few black soldiers around. It's good business, and it's the style, now. Maybe Rizzo — pardon me," he said with a sneer, "*Rich* — is already thinking about it. The trouble with the people in this country is that they think killing can only be done by white guys. Well, I can tell them a thing or two about jigs with knives *and* guns during the days after the first war when I came here. Make a Sicilian knifeman look like he was playing with a toy.

"And let me tell you about those colored boys in the ring, talk about your killer instinct. Jack Johnson, like a big black clumsy tank; none of the white guys wanted to fight him. And that Joe Louie, what a beauty, and that damned Jew, Mike Jacobs, had him all sewed up; must have made a fortune off him. Lots of colored guys," the Don said, his eyes shading with memory. "That kid Clay, with the Arab name. A real happy kid in the ring, a real champion, what moves!"

Carlo sneered. "And Benvenuto, Graziano, LaMotta, Marciano, what about them?"

The Don was puffing his cigar now, and he said, "I notice you didn't say anything about Carnera. Graziano and LaMotta fought like colored guys, and I'm in this country long enough to tell you that's the way white people talked behind their closed doors. Now the Italians aren't hungry any more; they go to college. Boxing is still for the colored guys and the Portos."

Peter said, "I don't think you ought to bug Gene, Uncle. He's not a dumb man. He wanted a favor; you did it for him. Let's leave it alone. You know, the guys downtown are all talking about it, asking who set the job. They're going nuts trying to figure out what's going on."

"Good, good," the Don said. "That'll teach 'em. As for your friend, he doesn't know, and a little dinner together won't hurt."

Browning was weary and irritated with himself, mostly, when he arrived at the restaurant. There had been several heated discussions with Barton on how best to duck handling the cases of the militants who'd been questioned or would be questioned by the government agents. No money, Barton had said, so they *had* to duck out, leaving behind as good an image as possible. The money could have come from someplace; it always had in the past. Now Browning, for perhaps the hundredth time, wished he had told Mantini that he was too busy to have dinner with him ever, but he hadn't and here he was. Approaching the table where the old man was sitting patiently, Browning was suddenly aware of something familiar about him, but in the next instant the distance shortened between them, the shadows changed, the old man became himself.

The Don rose to greet him and they shook hands. "I'm glad you could come, Browning. Please, please have a chair." The Don could tell that something was bothering his guest. Better get a drink in him quick, he thought. "How is your family?" he asked.

"Better than I am," Browning answered, hoping to communicate to the old man that he was not really pleased to be here.

"But that's the way it's supposed to be, isn't it?" the Don asked. "Let's have a drink or two before we eat." The Don beckoned the waiter.

"Good," Browning said with some grimness. "I've had a very hard day."

The Don understood what Browning really meant, but no matter. He had gotten him here. "I gather that you're a well-educated man, Browning. I mean, college and all that, am I right?"

Browning had got this from cabdrivers, the ones who had picked him up and wanted to involve him in conversations maybe to keep his mind from wandering to the possibility of robbing them. He said simply, "I went to school at Columbia and taught college before taking the job I have now."

The Don had known about Columbia from his nephew; he didn't remember anything about Browning's teaching. The drinks were on the table now and he watched his guest pick his up; it seemed to be with a gesture of relief. It and another would help them through the dinner.

The Don raised his glass in a toast without name, tasted it, swallowed and said, "It's August and so far, so good. No riots. What do you think about that fellow Greene, wasn't that something? And they can't seem to catch him."

"Oh, they'll catch him," Browning said. "They'll turn over every brick and pebble in this country until they do."

"Would you happen to know him? I don't mean to make you responsible for every other Negro. But if I knew him, I'd have to take pride in his having lots of guts if for no other reason." He sipped slowly from his glass and his eyes crept over the rim of it to seek out Browning's suddenly troubled eyes.

"I don't know him well," Browning said, "and yes, I think he's got lots of courage. He's an intelligent, well-educated man, and it's hard for me to think of him killing that cop. Maybe we're a people who have a long patience and who come to the use of violence only after we've suffered a great deal from it."

"Yes," the Don said, twisting his glass in a circle in his hand, "but you make it sound as if because a man's intelligent, he has no use for the tough stuff."

The Don saw Browning glance up at the last remark. Browning said, "You're right. Intelligence doesn't have anything to do with how much a man can take. It can help him to rationalize away the use of violence, thinking about his own skin, but that same intelligence will tell him, finally, that he's got no choice but to be as tough as the next guy or tougher." Browning knew he was speaking of himself.

The Don knew it, too, and was embarrassed by it. He covered by ordering a second round. "It's the way life hands it to us, Browning."

They ordered dinner and the Don was pleased to

observe that his guest had started to relax. "What did you teach in college?" he asked.

Browning said, "I tried to teach political science."

"Politics," the Don sputtered. "As dirty as the day is long."

Browning said, "Not just politics. Political history, how our institutions work and if they don't why they don't. Also what we can do to improve them. We call it a science, but some people call it an art."

"It's a lot of crap, that's what it is," the Don said. "I'm in this country a long, long time. Longer than you're alive, and the things I could tell you about politics; it's like an octopus, in everything."

It'd taken Browning a long time to reach that same conclusion. "What kind of business were you in, Mr. Mantini?"

"I had a small chain of stores here and in New Jersey. Every time I turned around, I had to buy off the cops, the firemen, the water inspectors. They put the bite on you for every jerk who's running for office, and let me tell you, they've got you so hooked up that you've got to go along with them or get ruined. If the people of this country really, *really* knew, as *I* know, how rotten their governments are, they'd bounce them and start all over again. That's why I'm not at all sorry Carrigan got his; he had his hand in a pie somewhere. How do you feel about it?"

"An eye for an eye," Browning said, "and a cop for a kid."

"Right," the Don said emphatically. "And the cops who're getting killed probably deserve it."

Those assassinations, Browning reflected, would bring the tensions to the snapping point. *This* was the time of

crisis, not the Sixties as everyone thought. Forms of amelio-
ration had set in then; enough to push back the boiling
point. But there was no pushing back now.

Browning was unaware of how the thought came. It
was as if someone had reached up and turned on a switch,
and he found himself glancing more closely at his host. He
forced up Vig's image to fit it to the old man's face. Not
quite; no, not at all. Vig twenty years from now? No,
but . . . He found this frightening and he sipped his
coffee. But of course, Vig had been responsible for setting
up the Carrigan deal; he never doubted that. But who was
this man before him, this Mantini? Although the coffee was
hot, Browning felt it was iced going down. What in the hell
was going on?

"Coffee all right, Browning? You've got a kind of an
upset look on your face."

Startled, Browning said, "It's all right. I guess I was
thinking about all the work I have to do tomorrow. And I'm
still tired from today. Mr. Mantini, what do you think is
going to happen now?" It was time he started to size up the
happening here.

"What do you mean?" the Don asked.

"With Carrigan dead and other cops getting killed."

Quietly the Don said, "I think we're all in for a bad
time, but maybe after that we'll have good times."

"Maybe," Browning said. "Italy is a very violent land.
The Romans, during the Renaissance, violence with refine-
ments, Mussolini —"

"Mussolini was a clown and you forgot Sicily," the
Don said.

"So I did," Browning said, and he thought he detected just a hint of a smile on the old man's face. Dur-

ing one of those marches a few years ago — I forget what this one was all about or where, somewhere in the South — an Italian woman, Italian-American, was killed by a bunch of crackers riding in a car. She had been participating with the blacks. I think she was a mother. I remember talking to some other blacks then and we all thought other Italian-Americans would retaliate. We gave those crackers three days more to live —"

"Call out the Mafia or something?" the Don said.

"Yes. We really thought they'd be found dead somewhere. But no."

The Don was quiet for so long that Browning thought he was not going to make a comment, but the old man said, as he finished his coffee, "I am told on pretty good authority that the Mafia is strictly a business organization."

"No causes at all?" Browning asked.

"Only the cause of money, which is power."

"Not even bargains?" Browning persisted.

The Don said, "Of course I'm not in the organization, even if I'm Italian. All I can tell you is what I've heard. No bargains." He called for the check.

Outside, the rapid transition from the air-conditioned restaurant to the humid evening air made Browning perspire, it seemed, at a faster rate. They stood together and Browning heard himself ask, "When do we see each other again, Mr. Mantini?"

"Whenever you like," he said.

"I've found it very interesting to talk to you," Browning said doggedly, "but I suppose I'll wait for you to call me." He wanted to say that he assumed his host never gave out his number, but that would have been a violation of whatever game was going on.

The old man said, "Then I'll call you very soon. I've enjoyed it, too."

Browning sat back in the cab the restaurant doorman had hailed for him. He had escaped nothing, he thought, nothing at all. That old man, Mantini, he knew; Browning was certain he knew. Well, then, now what? What did he have that Mantini would want?

He shifted restlessly in his seat. Wasn't he imagining things? From all he'd heard, they didn't work like this. And hadn't Mantini himself said that there was no charity and no bargains? But if he was imagining things, why did he feel so keenly this grating sense of uneasiness, as if he had taken a wrong turn somewhere and stumbled on something he shouldn't have? And the man's conversation: Greene, riots, intelligence versus violence, intelligence *plus* violence?

Glumly now, Browning gave himself up to the motion of the cab. Besides Mantini, who else? Goddamn it, *who else* could he expect to have to play games with? If only, if *only* he'd had the courage to have done Carrigan in himself there would be no games. Now he had to play out the string with Mantini, find out where the old man was at, and in the process, find out where *he* was at and for how long. Browning grimaced; only a few hours ago he had been worried about Greene and how the whole of American history made it mandatory that he be found and, at least legally, lynched. But there had been an aspect of the conversation, Browning thought, suddenly sitting upright, his heart pounding with the possibility of reprieve. Greene for Browning. Maybe he would be safe once they caught Greene.

He got out of the cab at his apartment building, paid the driver and walked slowly to the elevator. Just what in the hell was he thinking about? Hadn't he already made his plans in the event that he was discovered? Then why in the hell was he in a cold sweat, leading the cheers for Greene to get picked up?

Chickenshit nigger. Like a whole history full of niggers at the moment of crisis. All the high-blown thoughts the thing had begun with, Browning thought once he was in bed, listening to each sound that came through the night. They were noble. Thought I could cut the mustard. No? Maybe that was the difference between hipsters and hippies, between men and boys, between sprinters and runners.

The sharp, piercing ring of the telephone made him realize that he had fallen asleep after all. At first the ringing seemed to be part of a confused dream, then he rushed from bed, glancing at his watch. He had slept only an hour. Val was on the other end of the line.

"Did I wake you, darling?" she asked.

"I hadn't really got off. Is everything all right?"

"Oh, sure."

Browning thought he detected a certain quality in her voice, but he couldn't name it. He said, "You don't sound so hot. What's wrong?"

She sighed loudly. "Just lonely, I guess. Tried to reach you earlier. Can't Billy give you some time off?"

"Baby, the whole thing's shifted. Billy's trying to get out and into something else. And I've got to get out. We're really riding the skids this time around. The government offered to help us keep going if we found Greene, but Barton's as lost about him as the cops. Maybe it's about time I got back to a college, Val, and really started to teach my thing the only way it can be taught — just throwing out all the old books and getting hold of something else. I can't teach it the old way any more, with the old stuff."

There was new life in her voice. "I'm glad, baby. When you get out we can talk about it. We'll figure something out."

"Yeah," Browning said, feeling a great deal of relief himself, now that he had shared his thoughts with his wife. "How're the girls?"

"They're out on the beach. Weenie roast or something. Chris has got herself a little friend now. Seems to be a nice boy."

That means, Browning thought, he's black.

"Gene, I wish you were here."

She hadn't said anything like that in that tone of voice in years, and Browning found himself instantly moved and frightened as well. "It's lonely as hell here, too, Val. Terrible. I think this week I'll come out on Thursday. To hell with Barton."

"Promise, Gene."

"That's a promise, baby."

Troubled and afraid he would not get to sleep, Browning hung up and took a couple of aspirin and returned to bed. Val, he wondered, Val, what in the hell's going on?

sixteen

"I'm sorry," Mickey was saying. "But they put it to me in such an awful way. The only child and all that." She laughed and kissed Hod, who was lying on her floor with one of the cushions under his head. "And they think that because you're an Israeli, you should want to do it a little according to the rules, too."

Hod held her by her hair. "Will it make you happy to make them happy?"

"Oh, Itzhak, yes. We're going to be far from them and who knows what could happen —"

"Hah!" Hod said, sitting up. "They'll be in Israel every summer, I'll bet —"

"So? They can contribute to the economy. Will you do it?"

He pulled her to him and wrestled her beneath him. "Only for you. I wouldn't dream of doing it for anyone else. But I don't have any family or friends here."

Mickey said, "How about your friend from the consulate?"

Hod smiled to himself. Friend? Yaacov Peretz, the man who'd arranged for him to return, was a friend? Peretz was a recruiter. *Aliya* was going to the dogs and the *yordim* had to be enticed back home, no matter what they'd done. Peretz a friend! But he said, "I'll ask him."

"And he'll do it," Mickey said confidently. "It'll be simple and small, so don't worry. No fancy clothes, just dark suits, okay? Itzhak, Itzhak! Can you imagine? Here I am cool, real cool. What's exciting about a marriage, but I'm excited!"

"Enjoy it," Hod said, and he wanted her to. He was getting to his feet now.

"Aw, so soon?" Mickey said.

"Well, I told you I had this appointment today, but I'll come by tomorrow and we'll go see your parents."

"All right. I'll go down with you." At the bottom of the stairs she kissed him goodbye.

Hod, alone now, made his way to a bus stop, picking up a paper on the way. At the stop he thumbed hastily through the paper. Nothing about Greene. Nothing except the reports of cops being killed and others being armed more heavily.

"Did you hear?" Mickey had said to him one night. "Morris Greene killed that cop. The whole nation is looking for him." Hod had listened patiently while she explained who Greene was. A guerrilla, Hod had thought when she was finished, taking credit for what I did. Whatever the reasons, he thought in anger, they could never be good enough. He didn't give a damn why Greene had said he'd done it; he just shouldn't have. He, Hod, had no fear that he would be found out.

He was a professional and professionals didn't think

like that. It was a rule among his kind of professional that one never took credit for a job he didn't do. Greene, obviously, was not a member. He was a political opportunist. It was Greene's "confession" that had sent Hod running to the newsstands and the radio.

Over the days, however, his anger lessened and he became intrigued by what was going on, all made possible by his murder of Carrigan. The American cops were as nervous and frightened as the British soldiers had been before Partition. Yes, there was a familiar scent here, the look of recognizable things.

What Mickey had told him about the three black coeds and their killer entered his mind almost unbidden when he became aware of Greene. He now knew the names of the girls: Rena Trotman, Mary Owens and Christine Jones. Days of poring over back issues of New York papers in the library had given him this information. The killer's name was Herman Mahler and he had been acquitted for insufficient evidence, but later had publicly admitted, in a copyrighted article, that he had placed the dynamite in the building and set the timing device.

Hod had checked the Montgomery, Alabama, telephone directory for Mahler's address and one night he called, asked for Mahler, discovered he was speaking to him and hung up. There was one thing left before he went to Montgomery: study a map of the city. This would be another business trip and he would have to take it just before they were married. Hod planned to send a note to the Montgomery chief of police. It would read: "Dear Sir: In regard to Mahler's death, color me Greene." He would type it on a typewriter in the library. The note would make Mr. Greene a pretty popular fellow, and at the same time Hod's mission south would rid the world of someone who obviously shouldn't be allowed to live. It was Hod's turn to have some fun.

He boarded the bus with a spring in his step and found a seat, opened his paper and searched through it once more. Nothing. It was almost the end of August, he reflected as he folded the paper, and soon he would be married and taking the ship to Israel. He would be bringing one American Jew back with him, his wife, and they should plan to give him a medal. Americans weren't easy to come by these days.

Hod did not doubt for a moment that the Israelis, out in the desert somewhere, had a nuclear setup. And why not? All the wars they'd had with the Arabs had shown that the Gentile West was perfectly willing to make another Ethiopia out of Israel. But Israel had to survive, and more than that, flourish. Therefore it had to be expected that it would take every necessary step to make that survival and flourishing fact. Was this what Peretz's "settlement" was all about? Arid Zone Research indeed! At least not that kind. He had heard of the first reactor from a visitor to Israel nine years before.

"The reactor sat way back from the road, perhaps a good mile in the desert, looking for all the world like a brown tit, you know, the building it was in."

Nine years ago. What else was new, perhaps a lot. Extend lines out and around whatever was of most value to the "settlement" so that the terrorists — maybe they weren't even *there* any more — wouldn't get too close to become suspicious. All dreams, maybe, but over the years pieces of news or rumors had found their way to him. Yes, the Israelis had been active all over Europe, and at one point he'd even heard of a certain deal made with West Germany. God, what you had to go through to survive. He'd see, he'd see, that's all.

He looked forward to returning, whatever the circumstances. In Israel there were still real causes, a few of them tainted around the edges. Since leaving it, he had discovered that the world did not move along reasonable lines. There it was simple: fight or be driven into the sea. Develop or be swamped in the Arabic miasma of European-style, middle-age feudalism. Whatever had happened to the golden years in Spain, Jew and Arab almost inseparable? In Israel you were forever seeking a Martin Borman, an Adolph Eichmann, because the world forgets too easily, and there are things no one should ever forget. The world is reminded because there are always people to remind them. Like a Mr. Greene. What was that figure Mickey had given him about the number of black people killed in the slave trade? One hundred million over the centuries. Mr. Greene should not forget or permit anyone *else* to forget.

Now Hod thought of clouds chasing the sun over Masada, that terrible mass of fortress rock on the western edge of the Dead Sea; the Dead Sea almost always placid, and strange when it was not, with its ugly green waves, thick with salt, roiling up along the shore. He thought of the mountains in the Negev, still cluttered with bolides from sometime not quite beyond memory when fires lashed at the land and the earth heaved and opened and closed again with a groaning snap. Going north in his mind, he saw the Judean desert, even the peaks of its hills chalk white as if they once had shrugged off the Dead Sea waters, but not their salts. And Jerusalem at sundown, the stone of the buildings uniformly absorbing the golden sunsets. What did the rest of it look like now? He almost smiled when he recalled that he'd heard of people buying skis for the Golan Heights now. The new Jordan area territories? What new cities had been carved out of rock, sand and ocean edges?

To consider Israel fairly, you had to consider the Arabs and if you considered *them* fairly, would you then have an Israel? They stood in such great, great numbers, overwhelming numbers, at the very gates of the nation. And what of those already inside, the ones who, although prospering as Arab-Israelis, would always remain loyal to Cairo or Amman? When he was younger Hod thought he could kill them all. He undoubtedly would have to kill them again, but one thing was clear: you couldn't kill them *all.* There had to be a way, and the first step was that both sides had to be honest. The word brought a smile to his face. He had not thought Mickey could influence him so deeply so quickly.

When he left the bus and walked the block to the library, he entered the cool halls gratefully. He paused long enough to call Peretz, who came on the line sounding like a benefactor who was acutely aware that he was one. "Hod, what's up? Everything all right, or is there trouble?"

Always looking for things, Hod thought. "No trouble, Peretz, unless you call an invitation to a wedding trouble."

"Ummm," Peretz said. "Yes, that could be big trouble. You're inviting me? Your wedding? I'll come."

"One minute," Hod said. "I have no family here. Will you walk with me and stand under the *chupa?* It'll be small. My girl is an only child and we agreed to do it for her parents."

"What does the father do, Hod? He's rich, I hope."

"He's in fabrics and he's only four years older than me."

There was a pause on Peretz's end of the line, then he said, "Aha! Hod. You've got yourself some very tender fruit. And you want me to be your family, is that it, me representing Israel?"

"Yes, yes, that's what I'm asking."

"I'll do it, Hod. It should make the Americans stand up and take notice. Maybe we can get a few to go to Eretz, eh? Five thousand from America this year; that's the estimate, and we'll be lucky to get a thousand who'll stay. Can you imagine? Once we estimated as high as fifty thousand a year."

"Look," Hod said. "Leave them alone. They're probably better for Israel right here than they would be there."

"Okey dokey," Peretz said. "You let me know exactly when. Right after Labor Day, you say? By the way, have you discovered what Labor Day means, nobody works or everybody works?"

"A holiday, that's all I know," Hod said. "I'll let you know."

Hod hung up and walked up the stairs in search of the map of Montgomery. Soon he would be done with this great, mad country; he had seen it, felt it, and with the Carrigan job and the one he was contributing for free, not even at bargain rates, for Mickey, for the blacks (but weren't they the American Arabs?) and to show Mr. Greene that he wasn't the most clever man in the country, he would have massaged the very soul of America. That was something even Americans avoided doing. So it was time to leave, time to return and concentrate on leaving an heir. Perhaps in a way he was drunk, like Lot, and Mickey was one of his daughters. So be it.

The next evening, retracing in his mind certain routes

that seemed best to take in Montgomery, he called on Mickey, taking the steps two at a time.

"How awfully wonderful you look," she said as they went back down to take the subway to the Bronx.

"Never mind wonderful," Hod said, striding powerfully, proudly, with this young woman on his arm. "Do I look prosperous?"

"Prosperous enough," she said. "They'll be so impressed with your being an Israeli that they won't look for anything else."

"And," Hod said, "we will go with the story of the jewelry in Israel?"

Mickey held his arm tighter. "You have been raising capital to expand your business, okay? You already have shops in Tel Aviv, Eilat and Jerusalem —"

"I'm really prosperous," Hod said. "But when they come to visit, what do they find?"

"Once we're there and settled, we'll simply write back and tell them we decided to go back to the land, that's all."

Hod found himself nodding approvingly. Who would ever think such an innocent face capable of such slyness? A face touched on the cheeks with the faint blush that always seemed to be embarrassment, yet nothing embarrassed her and all things excited her. She was a woman very aware of life. He teased: "Good, good, what a sly wife I'll have."

"Not sly," Mickey said seriously, "resourceful."

"What is resourceful?"

Mickey pondered as they walked. "It means," she said, "being able to do the right thing at exactly the right time."

She felt his pressure upon her arm. He spoke. "When

we walk around your Village and I see all these young men, young and good-looking, with full lives to offer you, I have to ask myself time after time, what is it you want with me."

They walked on in silence and when he finally looked at her she was smiling. "What makes you smile in such a way?"

"Because I'm thinking in answer to what you said, that I don't know *what* it is you have, but whatever it is, I want it."

Sometimes, Hod thought, she was terribly capable of embarrassing *him*. "Do you know something?" he said. "I'm nervous. Your mother's going to turn out to be my age or maybe a few years younger, and your father's mouth is going to fall open, maybe, yes?"

Mickey tossed her head. "That's their problem. Besides, they already know you're bald."

"Little woman, you have a very large mouth," Hod said with a laugh.

"This large mouth has prepared them."

The subway was hot and filled with sharp flecks of dirt which flew and stung with each passing train. When their train came they got on holding hands and joked just beneath the roar of the train. Hod had never seen such filthy subways. Barcelona, London, Paris, wherever; any underground was cleaner than New York's.

When they reached the Bronx, Hod said, "Now we must find a flower shop."

"That's not being resourceful," Mickey said. "That's being very, very sly. My father never gives my mother flowers."

"I counted on that," Hod said pulling her into a shop

which they left minutes later with a dozen roses. "He sounded like a man who didn't give flowers."

At the door of the Friedman apartment, Mickey's father first inspected Hod's full, smiling face, and then the roses, both with a deep suspicion the kiss from his daughter could not erase. "Beware," he muttered, "the Greeks bearing gifts." But he had said it with a probing smile and Hod said, also with a smile, "Beware the Trojan who looks a gift horse in the mouth." Shaking hands all the time.

In the vestibule Mickey's mother stood waiting, now joined by her daughter, her hands clasped before her, her eyes on the roses. Hod walked to her smiling broadly. "For you, Mother," he said, kissing her cheek. "Would you call me Itzhak? I knew you would, anyway. You Americans are so informal, it's nice."

"I'm told you Israelis are pretty informal, too," Mr. Friedman said, rocking from heel to toe.

Mrs. Friedman had accepted the flowers with a soft murmur and bright eyes and Hod now turned to her husband. "Mr. Friedman, it's true. We don't have time for it; too many other things to do," Hod said.

"Let me offer you a drink," Mr. Friedman said. "What would you like?"

Hod rubbed his face dubiously. "I'm not much of a drinking man, but in honor of this occasion, maybe."

"Scotch, rye, bourbon, vodka?"

As they settled in chairs, Mickey said, "Maybe you'd like a little slivowitz, Itzhak? Daddy buys some wonderful slivowitz." She smiled and Hod smiled back, remembering an entire night and part of a day when they had made love after drinking slivowitz.

"Good idea," Hod said. "I'd love to try some."

"Me too," Mrs. Friedman said as she patted the roses into a vase she'd already filled with water. Hod thought her an attractive woman and it pleased him to think that when Mickey became her age she would look like her.

"All around then," Mr. Friedman said, leaving them.

"What's for dinner, Momma?" Mickey asked. To Hod she said, "Momma's absolutely the best cook in the world."

"Everything I know I taught her," Mrs. Friedman said. "She's a good cook and you'll have the best meals in Israel. I'm glad she's marrying an Israeli."

"There're bums in Israel, too," Mr. Friedman called out.

Hod said, "He's right, you know. I know a few myself."

"Pay no attention to Meyer. Like a father, he doesn't want to lose his daughter."

Mr. Friedman returned carrying a silver tray on which sat glasses and the bottle of slivowitz. "A father doesn't mind if it's the right man."

The room fell silent until Mr. Friedman had filled and passed out the glasses, then Mickey danced forward holding her glass aloft. "To the right man, Itzhak!"

Timidly, but with much beauty, Mrs. Friedman lifted a glass also and touched it to her daughter's. "To my new son, Itzhak."

Hod, seeing and understanding the liaison between mother and daughter, leaped at once to the father's side. "But wait. Let's drink to something for all first."

"Yes," Mr. Friedman said. "How about *l'chaim?*" Dryly he said to Hod, "You look healthy enough."

"— for my age, you mean," Hod said.

"*L'chaim!*" Mickey said, and they echoed her: "*L'chaim!*"

"You're right about my looking good for my age. But in a year you'll have a grandson. Wouldn't you like that?" Hod roared with laughter and nudged Mr. Friedman with his elbow. Mr. Friedman hastily filled the glasses again and Mrs. Friedman looked at Hod with new interest.

Mr. Friedman said, "The big thing, Mr. Israeli, is where you going to be at his bar mitzvah?"

"To Itzhak," Mrs. Friedman called out.

"To my Itzhak," Mickey said.

Mr. Friedman sipped his drink with a nod.

Hod now said, "You know what I was going to say, Mr. Friedman? I was going to say I'd be putting flowers on your grave at my boy's bar mitzvah time, but that's not a nice thing to say. I come in friendship because I want to marry your daughter. I'm a little old; since when is it bad for an old Jew to marry a young Jew? Tradition, no? Or maybe you wanted Mickey to marry a nice tall blond boy who looks like a goy and has a goyishe name. Could be? But let me stop. I want to be friends."

"Friends we can always be, but we're talking about family —"

"It's not for you to talk any more, Meyer." Mrs. Friedman's voice had cut through small, but clear, filled with sadness tinged with determination.

Mr. Friedman blinked his eyes and said, "One more drink, hey, and then you can run the house, the business, everything all by yourself, hey?"

Mickey spoke then and her voice was empty of all the pretense of being a dutiful daughter. It made her think of the talks and then the arguments she'd had with her father before finally leaving home. "Daddy, you know Momma's right. We *are* going to get married. We'd like for you to say, 'Okay, great, have my blessings,' but —"

"Okay, great, have *my* blessings," Mrs. Friedman said.

Friedman, going red in the face, almost shouted. "What is this? A man walks into my house and says he's going to marry my daughter. A man with not as much hair as me. A man I've never seen or spoken to before tonight, and what am I supposed to say, 'Okay, boy, okay Mr. Israeli, you want her, you got her,' is that what I'm supposed to say?" Friedman's glance burned around the room. The women lowered their heads; Hod studied him. Friedman flung his hands in the air. "Anyway, enough. You and you," he said pointing to Mickey and her mother. "Get dinner ready." To Hod he said, "You, Mr. Israeli, we'll sit here and talk." He glared at his wife and daughter. "That is, if nobody minds?"

Silently, with little smiles playing around their mouths, the women left the room. Friedman settled wearily in his chair and passed the bottle to Hod, who judiciously poured himself half another glass.

"Let's get down to business, Mr. Israeli —"

"Itzhak."

"Anyway, how do you plan to take care of my daughter? A jewelry salesman. Hah!"

Hod began quietly. "Even with three shops you remain a salesman. In America I guess if you had three shops, that makes you a corporation, huh, and chairman of the board?"

"Three shops?" Friedman said. "I didn't —"

Hod leaned forward and said patiently, "Mr. Friedman. If your daughter loves a salesman, shouldn't she love more a man with three shops? If I told her first there were three shops — Eilat, Tel Aviv and Jerusalem, how could I be sure that it was me she loved? Now I am sure." He smiled somewhat sadly. "When you're getting to be an old man, you have to use wisdom, Mr. Friedman."

"You could leave the business for so long? How long you been here, about six months? Mickey said about six months."

Nodding reassuringly, Hod said, "I have good people working for me. Besides, they know I'm here raising capital to expand. It's to their benefit, you see, to be honest. The monthly reports are all right, so I'm not worried."

"And no relatives to watch out for you." Friedman shook his head. "But what's this expansion?"

Hod put on a serious expression. "New roads mean new hotels. We put up more new hotels and guest houses in a year than France has put up in thirty years. Look, people fly to Israel. When they get there, they don't want to fly to Eilat, or helicopter to Nablus. They want to be in touch with the ground, see the people, see the factories and farms. Along all the new roads there must be hotels to accommodate the traveler, and I'm going into some of the new hotels. Nothing big; a display case or two, a pretty girl, maybe a Yemenite, to take charge of them in each place. This is all small by your standards, but a pretty good business by ours."

"So with all this," Friedman said, "how much do you make a year?"

As he floundered for a figure, Hod said, "Mr. Friedman, you know Israeli money isn't like American money.

We won't be living there the way you do here, but let me tell you, we won't be starving, either —"

"Forget I asked you," Friedman said. "Me and my wife want to give you a wedding gift. Yes, you can marry her, with my blessings. I always felt that Mickey needed a man older than her. Wipe all these social ideas out of her head. But the gift. You're a businessman and a businessman doesn't need fancy gifts. Just plain old money." Friedman chewed his lower lip. "Ten thousand dollars," he said hopefully, as if he had considered a gift of a higher figure.

Cautiously Hod asked, "Is it to be a gift or an investment?" But his mind was racing. Thirty thousand Israeli lira!

"A gift. When I want to invest in a thing I say I want to invest."

"Mr. Friedman," Hod said. "We appreciate it, but you don't have to. We'll be all right."

"I know I don't have to," Friedman said indignantly, "but I want to do it. Me and my wife. We talked about it."

"Then I thank you. We both thank you."

"Just use it wisely, that's all we ask."

Hod nodded. Few things had been given to him in his life. Now here was this man, Mickey's father, who as he'd said had never laid eyes on Hod before, giving him ten thousand dollars. Of course he meant for his daughter never to starve, to live comfortably, but that meant, too, that Hod would not starve. This man and his wife, Hod thought, were they the same people Mickey often laughed at, who angered her?

But now Mrs. Friedman was calling and Hod and Friedman walked together to the table. After the details of the wedding were set, Hod announced that he had one more trip to make before the wedding took place.

"Oh, I didn't know," Mickey said.

"It'll be short," Hod said. "Two or three days. Chicago again."

"There's a lot of capital in Chicago," Friedman said. "Lots of it." To his daughter he said, "business is business. You can come help your mother with the plans while he's gone."

Mickey nodded. She guessed she owed her mother that. Quit the job and stay with her while Itzhak was gone. The last time, perhaps. Who cared if you quit a civil service job? Sure, she'd stay with her mother. "Plans," Mickey said. "Don't make it such a big thing. You promised small. I'll come."

Mrs. Friedman smiled. "Small, I promise."

On the way home, Mickey asked coyly, "What did you talk about?"

"Oh, about the three shops and expanding into the new hotels," Hod said.

"He was very impressed," Mickey said. "He told me."

"And we talked a little about ten thousand dollars. That's their wedding gift."

"Momma told me in the kitchen. Aren't you happy about it?"

"Mickey-Siona, I feel strange about it. I made a weak gesture of refusal. Inside it must have made your father laugh. But just what will we do with the money? We certainly won't be able to use it where we're going."

"We can always use money. It can stay in the bank, I don't care. He wanted you to have it. I think he really does like you and he's a little guilty, too, you know. What camp did he ever have to go to? What Arabs did he ever have to fight? What soil did he ever have to scratch into for a living?"

"All right," Hod said. "I didn't mean to upset you. I'm a little uneasy when people give me things."

"But you're so generous yourself."

They had stopped now at the entrance to Mickey's walk-up, and she said, "I won't have to ask you to come up, will I? Didn't you have enough slivowitz?"

"Don't worry," Hod said. "I am coming." And he walked up after her. His eyes sought the dim flash of her bare legs at each lighted landing and the soft twists of her buttocks under her skirt. He began to undress her and himself as soon as he'd closed her door behind them, and in a moment they were rolling on the cushions on the floor.

seventeen

Hod did not like Montgomery. This morning it lay under an overcast sky; he could tell from his bed. This motel was the one most near where Herman Mahler lived, in what Hod thought must be the ugliest of all the neighborhoods in the city. It was in transition; blacks lived only across a main thoroughfare from the whites. They used the same supermarket, gas station and liquor store.

This was a white motel. Negroes worked in it, but Hod had not seen any Negro guests. He supposed they would not come here, the way the white help talked about Negroes, anyway.

Birmingham had places for Negroes to stay, and that's where they went. The one Negro hotel in Montgomery was two blocks from the campus where the three girls had been killed. The small, dingy cheerless rooms were upstairs; the dining room and bar were combined in one large room downstairs.

Hod did not know this, nor did he care to. What he

cared to know, he already knew. Herman Mahler no longer was a construction worker with easy access to dynamite. Now he drove a United Parcel Service truck. His wife worked as a cashier in the neighborhood supermarket. Mahler reported to his garage at 7:30 in the morning and was loaded and on the road by 8:30. He drove home for lunch. He returned to work at one and was home by 4:30, two hours before his wife arrived. There were no children. It had taken Hod three days to gather this information; now it was Thursday morning.

He had come to know the sounds of morning in this part of the city. There was the wheeze of the buses, the clatter of the few remaining streetcars, the loud exhausts of the old cars the factory workers drove, skirting on their way to work the conglomeration of Confederate statuary. Hod had come to know the difference in the timbre of the voices of the white and black workers as they entered the motel grounds to go to their respective jobs; the blacks talked in curves and swirls; the whites in up and down valleys and peaks, and rapidly.

Hod rose from bed at precisely seven o'clock and saw Mahler walking in his short, bowlegged stride toward the bus stop. A very ordinary looking and acting man, he thought, but the American woman who wrote about Eichmann, what did she say? Evil *is* ordinary. Maybe that was the difference between Israel and America. The Israelis had kicked him out. Political expediency or not, they'd done it. Mahler had been treated as a hero by whites, and the blacks had allowed him to live. Even the Arabs, Hod knew, had had his own name high on a list to be killed. What was the matter with the blacks? Regardless of what happened after, they should have seen to it that Mahler never polluted another street with his footsteps; they couldn't depend on the whites to do it.

At 8:45 Mahler's wife, big in the shoulders and hips, skinny in the legs and with a round face that was overly made up, walked down the street toward the supermarket. Hod wondered what she was like in bed, how they made love together. Perhaps what Mahler had done had made it better for both of them in bed. Sex was a crazy thing. He found her, however, totally unattractive.

Hod showered and dressed and went for breakfast. He had not known what grits were on his first day there, so he had not asked for them. Today, his last in the motel, he asked for them. Today, since he was leaving, he could have a real Southern breakfast.

By now the motel help believed he was a German salesman. A young waitress, noticing his accent the first day had asked where he was from.

"Germany," Hod had said. "Munich." He had noticed that Americans liked Germans. Why, he did not really know, but he suspected that the Americans with their cravings for gadgets and machinery were drawn to the Germans because they were even better with machines. And that was only part of it. The Germans and Americans were cousins and what had been deeply imbedded in the German culture that had led to the camps and ovens could be buried somewhere in the American psyche, too. There was the *sense* of that sickness; Hod could see it in the person of a man like Mahler.

But the young waitress had said, "Oh, Germany? My brother was over there. In occupation, you know?" Her eyes went over him, trying to fathom what he had seen and experienced in his travels. "How long you goin' t' be in Montgom'ry?"

Hod knew the type. Young, very young, too much makeup. Extremely friendly to strangers from the great outside. He had encountered girls like this in many places and all asked in their special ways to be taken away from the lunch counters, the five-and-dimes and department stores for a little while. They wished to touch what was not ordinary in their lives.

"Bet you been to France, too," she said. "My brother says you can't hardly get to Germany without goin' through France."

"Yes," Hod had said. "I've been to France."

"Paris, France, too?"

Hod had smiled. "Yes, Paris, too."

"London, England?"

"Yes."

"How 'bout Madrid, Spain?"

"Yes," Hod said, noticing the girl's eyes dancing. She left him for another customer and hurried back.

"I'll bet you're what they call a sophisticated continental, aren't you?" the girl asked. "One day, I'm going to travel to all those places. I'd look you up, because I sure wouldn't know nobody."

"I'd be honored," Hod said.

"My name's Jeanie, Jeanie Dobbs." Her voice rose as if she had asked a question.

"And mine's Bruno Schmidt." Hod had signed that name in the register.

"I'll call you Bruno. How long you goin' t' be with us again?"

"Just a very few days," Hod said, "and working very hard."

"Sure. You goin' t' be around this evenin'? I'd admire t' sit around and have a Tom Collins with a continental."

"I'd like to do that," Hod had said. Already he had sized up the thin, pitifully thin body, the tiny breasts, and he could not tell whether what he smelled was her or the food she worked with. "I'd like to do that," he had said again. "But I'm going to be busy tonight."

This morning she sullenly banged the plates as she set them before him, and managed not to look at him but at a point somewhere just over his head. "Well," Hod said when he had finished. The grits had not been bad. "I'll say goodbye to you, Jeanie. I have to leave this morning."

She stopped and looked at him, shocked, and he saw disappointment rise quickly in the eyes that were already flecked with too much of it.

"You're leavin' t'day. I thought you'd be around another day at least."

"No, no," Hod said. "I have to get back to Chicago before I take off for Germany."

"Well," she said sadly. "Enjoyed talking with you. You speak English real nice. Now you come back soon, y' hear?"

Hod turned on his heel and started for his room. He passed the Negro maids, who had strange knowing smiles on their faces which they kept turned directly into their linen carts. There was little to pack. He placed his bag in the trunk of the rented car and eased the automobile into the street and turned toward the airport. In fact, he went a goodly distance in that direction until he came to a phone booth. He called Mahler's garage. Told that Mahler was working the east end route today, Hod hung up satisfied; it was the same route he'd worked Tuesday. More important, Mahler had not gotten sick suddenly. Then Hod called the supermarket for Mrs. Mahler and while she was on the way to the telephone, he hung up. She, too, was right where she was supposed to be. It was eleven o'clock when he drove toward Mahler's house.

Working-class neighborhoods the world over are afflicted with men in shabby suits who roam the streets, briefcases or notebooks under their arms. They are detectives, bill collectors, welfare investigators, insurance men, door-to-door salesmen. They are forever in a race with the worker to get a piece of his money or to know what he has done with his money and why and where. The residents get used to the look of them; they are very much like the worn houses pretending to look respectable under tarpaper siding.

But then Hod was almost unrecognizable when he left his car two blocks from Mahler's. He wore a crumpled, large brim hat, the kind the men here wore against the sun; steel-rimmed glasses; a fake scraggly moustache that fell wanly over the ends of his mouth. He walked slowly through the empty streets, pausing to flip open a notebook and touch a stubby pencil wonderingly to his mouth as he looked around. With his elbow he pressed his thin display case hard against his body to keep it from falling; it was just barely thick enough to conceal a .32 revolver with a silencer attached. Hod swore by .32s; not too big but powerful enough to do a more than adequate job — especially if you'd taken the time to carve four deep lines in the deadly part of your bullets. Hod passed unnoticed through the streets and alleys he now knew by heart.

At the Mahlers' side door, he pored over his notebook,

then knocked. Without waiting for an answer — or lack of an answer — he opened the screen door and stepped into the hallway. He held the notebook and pencil poised, but his eyes roamed the windows of the next house. The shades were pulled halfway down. The curtains remained still in the muggy air. He focused on listening. Nothing. He tried the second door and found it open. Everyone poor, what's to steal? He stepped quickly inside and closed the door quietly behind him. At the same time he was stuffing the notebook and pencil into a pocket and opening his display case; the gun almost leaped into his hand. Hod weaved slowly on the balls of his feet, his eyes racing around the room. It smelled clean. He waited another moment, trying to determine what the smell was, and then he had it; a disinfectant. He took a couple of steps and murmured in the accent of the region, "Ha'mon? Ha'mon?"

The linoleum floors, he noticed, were spotless, and the windows unusually transparent, as though they'd just had a cleaning. They had. Hod saw the bucket, mop and squeegee neatly placed in a corner. He glanced at his watch: 11:45. A man with an hour for lunch — he had to leave the route at twelve, but it wasn't that far away, and leave the house before one — would make right for the kitchen. Hod tiptoed warily through the rooms until the kitchen opened up before him. He paused. Something was bothering him, something, but what? He thought, but it wouldn't come. He forgot it.

On the table, which was still strewn with the Sunday comics, he saw a can of soup, half a loaf of bread and a jar of instant coffee. The bologna was in the refrigerator, Hod imagined. There were two doors off the kitchen. One was partly opened and he could see that that was the bathroom. He moved to the other door and pulled it open. A closet.

Darkness greeted him and the smell of old clothes. Something else . . . the disinfectant! But of course, perhaps she kept it in here someplace. Now he turned his back to the closet and surveyed the kitchen. He could see every corner of it. Perfect. He turned to enter the closet, or had almost turned to enter it when he felt, nestling suddenly and viciously under his ear, cold unresisting metal and then he knew what had been bothering him; he should have felt that mop; should have judged how wet it still was. How many times had he been at the other end of the gun? How many times had he come out of silence shattering completely someone else's reverie? And now in a strange and hostile city, in a small dreary house, he found himself with the gun under *his* ear, and for a second it was too much and the fear rolled down upon him and he cursed in Polish, going back, way back to his youth. He had not spoken Polish ever except to curse the Poles who beat up Jews. In the next minute, he had leaned his weight on the end of the gun to give the man on the other end of it confidence that he would not attempt to grapple with him, which was precisely what Hod moved to do. But the gun jabbed, meeting his skull with a heavy, threatening motion and Hod stopped. He held his head steady, but his eyes rolled over and stared at the bare arm, followed it to the tattered shirtsleeve, to the body that was now emerging from the closet. Hod felt his own gun being taken from his hand. He didn't quite know why he was relieved when he saw that the other man, rather tall and thin, was black.

For a week Leonard Trotman had been going through the neighborhood, putting on a nigger accent, a nigger walk, a nigger shuffle, asking if he could mop floors and clean windows (motioning to the bucket on his arm) all for a dollar. He wore dark glasses and a bopper's straw skimmer and he became a familiar sight. He sang as he walked, usually one of Ray Charles's songs, pausing now and again to do a mournful little dance. He had become a nigger of the old school and white folks didn't see too many of his kind any more; they were all smart and uppity now. Perhaps that was why they liked Trotman well enough to have him clean for them. Here was a nigger who knew how to act like a nigger! Also, that was a lot of work for so little money. Like the old days.

Retha Mae Mahler had been unable to get her husband to clean the floors, and the windows hadn't been touched in a solid year. So she had called in the Negro. Everyone said he was good. She told him her husband didn't like niggers, and had in fact killed three, but he could clean up for her if he was sure he could finish up by noon. Trotman had bucked his eyes and yass-ma'amed and appeared this morning a half hour after Mahler had left. He'd gotten crisp instructions from Mrs. Mahler, who dogged his heels until it was time for her to leave for work. She told him to stop by the supermarket for his money, and if the place wasn't done to her liking, he'd never get any more work from the white people around there; she'd see to that. Trotman had done a modified buck-and-wing, promising that everything would be sparkling like new, yass, ma'am.

The first thing he did was check his gun, thinking, Here it is, 1973, and they still go for that Sam okey-doke. Like they just can't get *out* of it!

He started working, watching his watch move slowly, checking it every few minutes to make sure it was still working. Time crawled. He made himself work just in case she decided to run home and check on him. He knew where she worked; knew where her husband worked. His information, in fact, was as thorough as Hod's.

At 11:30, just in case Mahler decided to make an early run home, Trotman emptied his bucket, wrung out his mop, and set them in a corner together with the squeegee he'd used on the windows. He did not plan for Mahler to see them when he came in. The rubber gloves he wore he peeled off and jammed them into his pocket. It was 11:40 when he got into the closet.

He'd heard someone come in and he tensed, but Mahler didn't walk right through. Someone heavier than Mahler, he realized, was standing still for long stretches of time. Now the footsteps came again, heavy and cautious and a voice called softly, "Ha'mon? Ha'mon?" Now the man was in the kitchen. Who in the hell was it, one of Mahler's Klan buddies? Someone out to rob the cracker? Someone used to sneaking around and banging Mahler's old lady? Whoever it was opened the closet door. Trotman had his gun pointed right at his midsection; he couldn't see anything but a silhouette and it was a big one, but a dead one if it came at him. The man could not see the interior, Trotman realized, and he almost smiled. Nigger in the woodpile, baby. The man turned his back to the closet now, studying the kitchen, and for the first time Trotman saw the gun with the silencer on the end. *He wants Mahler too!*

Ah, no! They're on to *me*, he decided, his finger tightening on his trigger. Now the man turned back, almost turned back to enter the closet and Trotman thrust his gun under his ear, felt the man stiffen, and Trotman jabbed the gun hard now and reached forward and took the gun from the white hand. Then he heard the curses in the strange language as he backed the man out of the closet to get a look at him.

"Wait," the white man said. "Wait."

Trotman was inwardly shaken when he observed the bulk of the man.

"I'm a friend," the white man said.

Every inch of the white man cried power and Trotman didn't want to be too close to him. "Back up," he ordered. "What do you want?" He glanced nervously at his watch and saw that the white man did the same thing.

"Mahler, I want Mahler," Hod said, but he spoke with confidence now.

"Where you from with that accent?" Trotman hissed. "What's this all about?"

"The three girls," Hod said quickly. Time did not stand still. Mahler could come up that sidewalk any moment now.

"Who sent you?"

"No one," Hod hissed back. "Who are you? Why do you look at your watch, too, like you know Mahler will be here at any moment —"

"Shut up —"

"I want to help. I came here to help."

They were both straining toward the windows now, hissing at each other.

"Don't want your help. Don't need your help."

Hod heard him first. "He's coming. Give me my gun." He saw that the Negro was hesitating. Mahler came up the walk whistling; he was walking fast.

Trotman held the gun away.

"All right, then, you use it," Hod said fiercely. "It's got a silencer on it."

"I've got my own —"

Instinctively they were both moving toward the closet.

"Yes! To bring in the whole neighborhood. Can't you do anything right?"

Trotman would have hit him then, but he was sure it would have had no effect on him. The fact that they both had sought the cover of the closet was not lost on either of them. They huddled together and Hod could feel the Negro tremble from time to time, but he did not know if it was because of anger or fear. Men sometimes trembled for strange reasons. Excitement. Hod put his mouth close to the Negro's ear. "There is a bullet already in the chamber."

This was like a Marx Brothers comedy, Hod thought. Funny, ho, ho, ho. Yes, he'd come to revenge himself for what Greene had done and to give the black people a hand. (They were, some of them, like the Irgun these days, but somehow he kept thinking of them as the Arabs, too!) He'd come and found the blacks already here in the person of this one. He was as clever, obviously, as he, Hod, was. The man had got in; they'd selected the same hiding place. But his gun. No silencer. The silencer gave you extra time to leave the scene. It was a necessary piece of equipment. Hod hoped the Negro would use his, Hod's, gun.

"Be damned," they heard Mahler mumble. "Place is cleaned back to hell and gone."

They heard him open the refrigerator, heard the slap of a knife in a jar. Hod tugged at the Negro's arm for the gun; the Negro resisted. They both relaxed. They heard the water in the kettle whistling; Mahler was ready for the instant coffee and Hod knew that when he turned the kettle off, his back would be to the closet. He nudged the black, but he was already in motion and Hod, aware for the first time how much he was sweating, felt the man beside him uncoil, a long, soft sigh escaping from him. The Negro pushed open the closet door at the exact same time the whistle died in the kettle and Mahler stood, a black silhouette before the stove, framed in the light of two windows behind and beside him.

Hod saw him turn, thought he saw the cup falling, then it did fall and bounce on the floor (plastic) spewing a small cloud of powdered coffee. Like a shadow the Negro had moved across the floor to within inches of Mahler and Hod heard his gun spit. Again, and Mahler was slammed back against the stove. The Negro stepped back as though he'd thrown a knockout punch and wanted to give his man room to fall down. But in the falling, the Negro fired again, catching Mahler in the head. The gun spit three times more while Mahler lay unmoving on the floor.

God, that is how I used to kill, Hod thought as he moved out of the closet toward the Negro. He heard the Negro say: "That's for my sister, you white motherfucker. Trash. Garbage."

"Get out of here," Hod said, wresting his gun from the Negro's hand and putting it into its case. The Negro had gone rigid, staring down at Mahler's blood. Hod shook his wrist. He breathed easier now; he had been afraid the Negro would turn on him, but all the shells had gone into Mahler. Hod looked at the Negro's eyes and understood. Once he himself had stood like the Negro — at Deir Yassin, it was — so intent on slaughtering that nothing else mattered. Hod found himself shuddering.

Quickly he reached over and slapped the Negro on the back, but his eyes remained glassy. Then he slapped him just as hard in the face and the glassy stare was replaced by a grimace of anger. Hod gripped both the Negro's wrists, thinking, Not a killer, but everyone has to get a start some-where. "Are you all right, now?" he asked.

The Negro shook loose his grip and nodded.

"Then get out the way you came in. Don't forget your bucket." Hod patted his moustache, glasses and hat and left the house. He walked unhurriedly, wetting the point of his pencil and making random lines in his notebook. After a few paces he heard the jangle of the Negro's bucket, but he did not look around. The jangle faded in the opposite direc-tion. Hod gained his car and turned again for the airport. Along the way he broke and discarded his glasses, ripped off the moustache and shredded it in one hand. Then he placed his hat under his free foot and tore it up and tossed it into the wind. He settled back and took a deep breath, but found that he had started to shake. Aftereffects, he told himself. But he hadn't had aftereffects in years. But what had happened in Mahler's house had never happened before. So he, the Negro, had been a brother of one of the girls. That was fair, but that kind of killing was always filled with emotion. Had he, Hod, not been there, perhaps right at this moment the Negro would be dead, killed by the mob that surely would have been summoned by the reports from his gun. Just didn't care about that part of it, Hod thought. Revenge, only revenge. Pulling the trigger was the smallest part of being a professional; the very smallest part of it.

At the airport he returned the car, mailed his note to the Montgomery chief of police and boarded the 12:45 plane to New York. Greene, he thought. Do me a favor, Mr. Greene. Don't get caught in New York before the chief gets my note. Please?

Leonard Trotman, his shakes lessening, shuffled quickly down the street to the supermarket. Reason had returned. He had to stop by for the money, had to talk to Mrs. Mahler in order to gain time. Otherwise she might rush home to see if he'd robbed her. Oh, he knew these crackers.

"Where you been, boy?" she snapped when he walked in and stood humbly beside her cash register. The Negroes on line glanced slowly from her to him and back to her again.

Trotman picked at his hat and went into his shuffle. "Ma'am, it was plenty lot of work —"

"Is it clean now? That's all I want to know. Boy, you was beggin' for work. I guess you got out 'fore my husband came, otherwise you wouldn't be here right now." She wanted to say that he'd already killed three lazy niggers, but a glance at the line of Negroes quenched the desire.

"Yes'm. And it's all cleaned up."

She snatched her purse from beneath her register, took out a dollar and stabbed it at him.

Trotman decided to play out a string. He looked at it. "No tip? That was an awful lot of work. Now, I don't mind workin', but I *do* mind slavin'."

Retha Mae Mahler, scowling, a part of her vision taking in that sullen black line of people holding their smoked hocks and navy beans, bunches of greens and boxes of grits, snatched at her bag again, gave him a quarter and turned her back on him. Trotman tossed it in the air, caught it and smiled. "Thank y'all," and shuffled out of the store.

In a rooming house that stood within view of the college where his sister had died, Trotman changed clothes and called a Negro cab. He had replaced the mop, squeegee and bucket on the back porch. Now, *now*, he thought, if my luck holds out, I'll be back in New York this afternoon.

eighteen

The morning papers were cautious. They noted only that throughout the nation the evening before, the Negro sections of upwards of fifty cities were invaded by gangs of white toughs. Negroes had been beaten; 15 were reported killed and 62 in critical condition in hospitals.

The papers suggested that there was more than coincidence here and that the "paramilitary" operations appeared to be in retaliation for the police murders that had taken place in these same ghettos. While the invaders were not yet known, their tactics smacked of the Ku Klux Klan.

While the mayors of the afflicted cities called for immediate crackdowns on all kinds of violence and went into conferences with their police commissioners or safety directors, the sullen Negroes retreated to their tenements and talked.

The idea of the invasion of black neighborhoods began in the locker room of the precinct house where Carrigan had worked. The officer who voiced it was both weary and frightened. He could admit to being weary, but not to being frightened, and so he spoke with the vehemence which, had he been on his beat, would have been translated into what was called "violent force." He spoke in a room overflowing with men coming off or going on duty. He said: "What we really need to do is to go into those goddamn ratholes where they've been killing off our buddies one at a time, go in at night in plain clothes and work over those goddamn niggers block by block until a cop can work his beat without getting shot in the back."

There had come a grunt and a ragged chorus of approval and the idea seemed lost in the confines of the stuffy locker room. But within two days there were enough officers interested in the idea for someone to have run off a mimeographed sheet with instructions pertaining to Operation Black Out. Police groups in other cities had already been contacted; all agreed to the operation and to commence their activities at the same time for the greatest effectiveness. Thus the same machinery that manages to equip all police vehicles with little American flags and God Bless America stickers was put into motion; the reciprocal deals that allow a cop from New York to commit traffic violations and more and escape punishment in Boston, Baltimore or Binghamton were now cast up to a higher, more meaningful level.

The raids began at midnight; cops, clad in slacks and shirts that hung out to conceal their holstered guns and blackjacks, drove to the ghettos in groups of cars. On-duty cops, forewarned, used their passkeys to slip into establishments they usually cooped in anyhow, or in which they received their payoffs or took the neighborhood whores.

In New York the cops gathered in Bedford-Stuyvesant

and Harlem; the private cars were double-parked in a single line and the cops proceeded to walk from block to block, sapping, punching and kicking anything black within their reach. They moved silently; they might have been on parade, so lined were their ranks; they spoke no words. They fired into several bars sending some patrons diving for the floor. Others were not so lucky. They tossed trash cans through the windows of the few shops owned by Negroes and then withdrew.

As they did, the Negroes in city after city, who had recognized the invaders as cops, not only from sight but by their tools and tactics, reacted as any people would who were faced with the reality of the degree of their repression, now equally balanced with living death, and chose the one avenue open to them. In the shambles of their littered and broken streets, in the secretly laughing wailings of the ambulances and police cars, now suddenly too numerous to count, they prepared to retaliate and to take on the next assault that would follow.

By noon the following day across the country, more than twenty-five on-duty policemen had been killed or wounded in the areas where, the night before, off-duty cops had invaded. A number of other cops reported having been shot at.

The cops came back the second night, their numbers doubled; the word not to had not come down and it was clear that the police brass was as paralyzed as City Hall. The battle plan was the same: a line of men walking up the street so close together that a rat couldn't get through. They started walking from the place where they'd parked their cars, not really noticing how empty the streets were, or perhaps deciding that this was what they had expected.

They walked down the silent street one block; then the firebombs rained down upon their cars from a hundred tenement windows. This rattled the cops; the cars were their own, not the property of the cities they worked for. The damages would have to be explained to the insurance companies and police influence counted for very little with them.

Angered and nervous, the cops broke ranks to get back to their cars, but now the firebombs began to land among them and in the flames they became easy targets for the rifle and pistol fire which now assailed them. The blacks had not registered their weapons; why make it so easy for Whitey? Whitey want gun registration? Let Whitey register. It had become clear to the owners of these weapons this was the time to use them.

Old men and old women, children, youths, adults of middle age. Zip guns, rifles, shotguns, automatics, revolvers. Lye rained down along with pots, pans, pieces of furniture, dishes, glasses, lengths of iron, lead and zinc pipe; bricks from tottering chimneys, pots of boiling hot water, pans of cold water, knives, ice picks, broken lamps; more than one number-10 cast iron skillet sung down from the darkened windows and into the milling cops. The Negroes fought in silence too this time, and they shot out as many streetlights as the cops who were trying to return fire. The police shot blindly upwards at the shapes of buildings.

The on-duty cops in their darkened hideaways puzzled: what was going on? Last night it was all over in half the time. Now, distantly, they heard sirens. They sauntered out on the streets, guns drawn; something was amiss.

One gray-haired police lieutenant sat in his car and

gazed around the streets. Shoes, furniture — God, everything known to man had been thrown down upon them. He
had known about the raids, but pretended not to; *someone*
had to pretend not to. The smell of burning metal and
rubber hung stubbornly in the air; the ambulances, winking
red, pulled before the dead and wounded and began to load.
Tonight, this very night, the lieutenant knew, he would have
to start asking for resignations effective immediately; you
couldn't prosecute an ex-cop too well. He shook his head
and thought: "And now what? God, what now?"

Morris Greene had welcomed the news of the first raid
in which the "white toughs" had been recognized as cops.
Harlem and Bedford-Stuyvesant had reacted quickly and
bitterly and with the finality of people with their backs to
the wall. How many stories had he heard of plastic-wrapped
guns coming out of sugar and flour jars; of rifles coming up
from the floorboards where rats had built nests around
them? Greene had not wanted his people aroused, but cool;
now they were aroused and there was little he could do
about it except use it to his (and their ultimate) advantage.
This was shoot-out time, the nitty-gritty, the end of the trail.
The chitlins were gone, the greens froze; this was it.
Greene had welcomed the news because now he had
the diversion he'd been seeking. Even if no raid occurred on
the second night (but the citizens were already shooting
cops) the city would be busy, too busy to think about
someone wiring charges to bridges and tunnels. Early the
morning after the first raid, Greene had called his teams
together — the black guards and toll collectors, the engineers with their various specialties; they had been brought
together by the violent force of the American policeman

during a decade of rebellions that had gone nowhere; the cops hadn't looked at status symbols, only black faces, and therefore, pounding down the streets clubbing anything black, murdering anything black, had welded together the ghetto and middle-class Negro. The engineers still worked for the firms that had gone out to "hustle niggers" in the Sixties, or rather, bided their time with them.

Now they huddled together going over plans and time schedules; tonight the charges would be placed and wired in at points on the designated structures where they would do the greatest amount of damage with the fewest explosives. The points had been established months ago on plans taken from the Bridge and Tunnel Authority by a black janitor who also happened to be an unemployed structural engineer.

They might have been a group of deacons, so somber were they in speech and manner. When all was finished, Greene spoke to them:

"What can I tell you? Nothing. You know what the score is, you know why you're here; and if you've had moments of doubt, look what happened last night. We've got to get this Man off our backs or we aren't going to have any backs left for him to get off of. If they catch you, you know what they'll do; step on your balls, run five hundred pounds of pressure from a water hose up your ass. We've gone over the record; we know the Man can't stay away from your privates. They'll make you talk; that's Whitey's stick. He's been making niggers talk for half a thousand years. So listen, if they got your prick in a vise, just go on and talk." He smiled broadly. "The chickens won't even be here for them to find. But these cats here" — he gestured toward the collectors and guards — "if they can't get you in and out all right, nobody can."

They went out as quietly as they'd come in. Greene walked carefully around the room, the basement game room of a Brooklyn brownstone, and seeing nothing that had to be removed or destroyed, left it and drove to Manhattan. It was seven, three hours before the second raid on Harlem; he'd been with the engineers, guards and collectors since morning.

In Manhattan he was joined by Trotman; they greeted each other joyously and with warm embraces. It was on the eleven o'clock news that they heard that Greene was being sought in connection with the murder of Herman Mahler. The announcer said the Montgomery chief of police had received a note indicating Greene's involvement.

"Well, we'd better talk about it, Len. What's going on?"

"Wait a minute, Morry, I don't know anything about a note —"

"You got Mahler, right? I mean I didn't ask you when you came in, but that's why you went and I assumed everything was cool."

This was the first time one had ever had to ask the other for explanations and now it was dawning on Trotman that the white man in Montgomery who'd come to kill Mahler, too, might have been the same man who killed Carrigan. "Yes, I got him, Morry, but long story, and maybe I can explain that note, too."

Greene hoped so; important things were riding high at the moment. There could be no misunderstanding or betrayal. Trotman had become like a brother, more than a racial brother; it was as if they'd come from the same womb, twins, one right after the other. Still, he had to know.

Trotman launched his story, remembering as he did sights, sounds and smells, but as he went on, he found himself looking deep into Greene's eyes for some sign of understanding, of affirmation of the truth he was telling.

"Tell me about the big white guy again," Greene said.

"What's to tell? He was about yay wide, wore a wide-brimmed hat, steel-rimmed glasses and had a moustache. When I surprised him he spoke in a language that was strange, and when he spoke English he had an accent. We didn't have time to get into the where-are-you-from bag."

"That silencer he had bothers me," Greene said.

"I'm glad he had it; he made me use his gun, which was a good thing. He must have been some kind of pro —"

Greene cut in. "You know the cops think the guy who killed Carrigan — and that's supposed to be me, now — used a silencer because no one heard that shot in the elevator."

"The way I figure it," Trotman said slowly, "is that he was pissed-off at you for claiming you did in Carrigan. That's why he sent the note."

"And the markings on the bullets will be the same as the marks on the bullet that killed Carrigan."

"If he's a pro," Trotman said dryly, "he wouldn't have used the same gun."

"Yeah, yeah," Greene said impatiently. "But what I don't understand is, how in the hell did a goddamn paddy get in on all this in the first place? Why Carrigan at that particular time, after he killed the kid? Why Mahler, who'd killed three black kids?" Greene tried to mute the look of accusation he shot at Trotman. He paced the floor in stiff, short strides. "Could *Jessup* have some of those right-wing nuts dirtying things up —"

He broke off abruptly and went to the window and opened it up. "You heard about the raid last night, well, they're at it again." He closed the window and sat down. "Let's do it again, Len; let me take it from the top: "Carrigan kills a black kid. Carrigan gets killed — maybe by this strange guy you're talking about, but maybe, too, by some of Jessup's people. *We don't know for sure.* Nobody's admitting anything, so I figure it's a good chance to jump into the gap and let the brother know someone's looking out for him. The brother starts getting bold then, and he begins popping off the nastiest cops and the other cops start getting nervous and mad. You cut out to take care of Mahler, blood revenge, cool, although I could've used you here, but I dig, baby; something you had to do. You run into this guy, maybe Carrigan's killer, or again, one of Jessup's people. You assume he mailed the cops a note implicating me out of revenge for my claiming to have killed Carrigan. Off-duty cops are in the streets right now getting even for what the brothers did to the on-duty cops today, and Labor Day weekend really only a matter of hours away." Greene pressed his lips firmly together as if making a decision. He reached in his pocket, his fingers slid past the pack of cigarettes and closed heavily on the .32 snub-nosed revolver. He pointed it at Trotman and Trotman slowly raised his hands halfway. "Mine is in my righthand pocket," he said. Greene reached over and took it and placed it in his own pocket. He forced himself to sound angry and positive. "Len, the guys are out right now placing the charges and wiring them. The demands are ready for delivery as soon as the first ones're detonated. This is like where we are *now.*

"You came in here with a mighty strange story and maybe it's the truth; it's crazy enough to be the truth, but baby, I can't take the chance that it *ain't*. I just can't, and that note business makes it even harder. We got a day and a half until the charges are blown and you're going to spend that time in that closet over there. Now, let me tell you something else. Nobody knows where I am. Just you. One guy's got this phone number. That means that if the wrong people come through that door before those things are blown up, I'm coming to the closet for the same reason they're coming for me."

Incredulous, Trotman began, "Aw, man —" Then he snapped shut his mouth and when he opened it again he said harshly, "Okay, okay, brother. I understand." He turned and walked quickly into the closet, pulling the door closed behind him.

Greene locked it then placed his mouth close to the door and said, "Len? I hope you do understand."

"Forget it, man, just forget it, okay?"

Greene moved back from the door as though he had been stung. He sat down. What in the hell was it all for if it soured you on brothers? Or soured them on you? What kind of insanity lurked behind the attempts to alter an already insane society that had indicated that insanity was at its very core? He wanted to rush to the closet, throw open the door and take Trotman into his arms once again; tell him that black people were not going to have the same kind of revolutions that white people had had, where at some point, always, white turned against white as the revolutions progressed. He wanted to apologize to Trotman for behaving like a white man, and tell him that the *essence* of their revolution was that, *yes!* black people *were* going to be better than whites; were *not* going to make the same mistakes as white people; white *brothers* were going to be made, not white *enemies,* and by force which had proved to be mandatory. That's what this revolution is all about, to forge the opening to be better.

Yet here he was, like any old-line revolutionary, gun in hand, forcing a brother, a *true* brother into the closet. There was a margin of improvement in that; the old-timers would have just shot to kill. Greene hoped he would not be forced to do that. He whispered, "Please, God."

Throughout the night he listened to the sounds of distant firing, the sirens of fire engines, police cars and ambulances. He sat, sweated and smoked with the early September heat. Out there, he thought, the people were already in battle with the police, that thinning blue line white society had placed around and throughout black society. The demand having to do with the police restrictions and limitations was sure to have meaning now.

The first lightening of the sky appeared out over the East River. Greene was glancing at his watch every few moments. The guards and engineers should be out by now. Dawn had been listed by the weather bureau at 5:05; where in the hell were they, why hadn't he heard anything? He looked at the closet and his stomach turned into a knot. The minutes crawled by. He studied his gun.

The phone rang.

He picked it up and listened briefly and hung up with a sigh of relief. The sigh, he realized, was as much for the men in the tunnels and on the bridges as it had been for himself and Trotman. He walked heavily toward the closet.

Trotman called out, hearing his steps, and said, "Everything all right?"

Greene, unlocking the door, knew that he, too, had heard the phone. Maybe he was just as relieved as Greene. "It's okay, Len. Listen. I'm going to let you out to go to the crapper. Then we'll eat and after that you go back in. I'm sorry."

"All right, brother." Trotman's voice was heavy and sad.

They ate mostly in silence, although from time to time Greene would speak. "Try to understand, Len, we've just got too much going."

Trotman said, "Oh, I understand, man. But you've got to understand something, too." He paused and looked across the table at Greene's gun which rested near his elbow. "What we had, we've got no more."

Greene did not respond.

Trotman continued. "I'll go back to the closet when we finish. I'll stay there until the bridges and tunnels go. After that, I don't know what you'll do; maybe do me in? In any case, Morry, it's over. I mean, you can't really expect us to have what we had, not after you've held me with that gun. All right. The story was wild, but that *is* the story. We've been through some things, man, I mean *things,* and we always trusted each other. Later."

"Yeah," Greene said. "I thought about all that last night. Look, man, I didn't want to do it, but I had to. I have to protect those men. Okay, we're not a team, that's all there is to it."

"We've got the same kind of revolution everyone else has had, haven't we?" Trotman said. "Well, shit, it figured."

"You finished?" Greene asked, pushing back from the table. He didn't want to hear any more; didn't need to hear any more.

"Finished," Trotman said, also pushing back his chair. He watched Greene pick up the gun.

"Got to go back to the crapper?"

"Naw. I'll get in my closet and go to sleep."

They stood for a moment and watched a golden rectangle of bright sunlight press against the floor. Greene sighed. "Len, what would you have done?"

Gingerly, Trotman slipped his foot into the rectangle. "What would I have done? I thought about that in the closet, of course. Just to change the goddamn pattern, man; just to make it a different bag altogether, to break the continuum of revolutionary history, to take the fork in the road from the white cats — I'd have trusted you. If you'd told me that God came out of that closet down there and killed Mahler, I'd have believed you, or at least, never let you know that I didn't."

Greene nodded and gave a gentle wave with his gun toward the closet and Trotman went in. Greene closed and locked the door. He walked slowly to the couch and lay down, placing the gun on his chest. He went to sleep.

nineteen

"I tell you, you're worrying too much." The Don had worked himself into a frenzy and had gone outside to the terrace. He was shouting inside.

The reason for his frenzy was that Carlo and his nephew Peter were packing, packing feverishly. They heard his shout and paused to look meaningfully at each other; they shook their heads. Peter finally stepped outside.

"Uncle, maybe we are worrying too much, but better safe than sorry. I tell you they're all upset about what's going on here, not to mention the rest of the country. Aw, c'mon, Uncle. You know these guys and what they can be like. You *told* me, remember? Nobody, but nobody comes to the clubs or restaurants any more; the whole damn city is like a ghost town, and the guys say they're dropping three hundred grand every day and they don't like it. Rizzo and the others are tracing it all back to Carrigan's getting killed; they're asking questions and paying for the answers —"

"I don't care what they've been asking," the Don said.

"Do you think I'm afraid of those butter-soft punks with their stinking white shirts and crumby suburban houses? Christ, people like me cleared the brush for them and they know it."

Peter looked out over the park, which seemed unusually quiet. "You know they couldn't care less, Uncle. You told me that, too. Look, it was all my fault. I never should have listened to Gene, but I figured it couldn't hurt. Jesus, I didn't think it would snowball like this."

He hunched his shoulders determinedly and smacked his open hands together. "Anyway, Uncle, Carlo and I decided that it's time we took that long fishing trip to New England."

The Don was mollified and perhaps it was because he saw his nephew's determination to take charge of things. About time. "All right, all right," he said. "I said I would go. I'm ready when you are, just don't give me that business about what they'll do if they find out who put the bee on Carrigan."

"Sorry," Peter said. They understood each other. They'd leave his uncle alone, but they'd sure do a job on *him*, the only relative, and that, in its own way, would slowly kill the old man. Peter knew he couldn't beg for himself, which was exactly what he was doing; he had to make it look as though all the concern was for his uncle, and indeed, much of it was. "There's a kind of madness on the loose, Uncle. We'll be better off in the woods, fishing and sleeping."

"And your girl?"

Peter hadn't forgot about that. He said, "Ah — a girl. I thought about it, but —"

"No sluts, Peter. I can't stand sluts; I've had enough of them in my life. Christ, no sluts."

"She's not a slut. But I don't know how well she'd take to the woods. Maybe she'd get restless for the bright lights, the Village scene, you know."

"Sounds like a slut."

Peter shrugged. "Even a slut's got to have a chance not to be a slut."

The Don looked at him curiously. "What's that you're saying?"

"A chance." Peter smiled. "An equal opportunity."

Now Carlo hovered behind them. "Suppose," Peter said, "when you got off the boat, you and my father and grandma — suppose no one laughed at or hated Italians and Sicilians; suppose this had really turned out to be a country where a guy had a free choice: do you think we'd be what we are now?"

The Don scoffed. "*I* told you that a hundred times!" He looked at Carlo as if seeking support for his amazement at his nephew's statement. "You think *I* don't know what this great big democracy does to a lot of white people who are too damned blind to realize it, *too?* Those cops running around in Harlem and Brooklyn now, they ain't sick and crazy?"

"Everything's ready," Carlo said. "And I've locked up."

"What, are you kidding?" the Don asked. "You've gotta have the car checked, what're you talking about?"

Carlo and Peter exchanged glances and Peter said, "We had the car done two days ago, Uncle. If Carlo says we're ready, then we're ready."

"Not so fast," he said. "Carlo, cigars?"

"Yes."

"Fishing rods?"

"They're up there."

The Don stroked his chin. "But Peter's gotta go get his girl."

Peter said, "She's downstairs in the car."

The Don sat back and stared at both of them. "So you let me sit around here on my fat ass and you two got everything ready to run away, is that it?"

Carlo winked at Peter. "That's it, Don." All of this, Carlo thought, and the Don was dying to get north; now he had the best of reasons: Peter wanted to go, too.

The Don placed his hands firmly on the arms of his chair, ready to hoist himself. "I wonder," he said, "about that fellow, Browning. Nice man, nice man. But I worry about him a little." Now he stood up and stretched. "I'll slip into something comfortable for the ride. And listen, Carlo, let's stop at that little place in Mystic, you know, where they have that oyster stew. You'll like it, Peter."

When they arrived downstairs, the Don peered inside the car and looked at the girl. She was pretty: black hair, blue eyes. She would put on a few pounds later, but she wouldn't get to look like a bag.

"I'm Angela," she said.

"Well, Angela, you sit back here with me. Those two can sit up front." He saw her glance at Peter who smiled and nodded. Good girl, the Don thought.

When the bags were all loaded, the Don said, "Carlo, let's take the West Side Drive and go over the Cross County. We don't need to go through Harlem, not during these times."

Ah, the Don thought as they moved north, look at it.

Dirty, filthy, and they keep putting new buildings right on top of it. Where in the hell do all the people come from and how do they live in this heat and dirt? They're at each other's throats, and I guess that helps. The last days of Pompeii, the fall of Rome.

"Move, stupids," Carlo was muttering. Traffic was not moving. They were a little north of 125th Street and the highway glistened with the cars lined up before them and after them; there was no southbound traffic.

"C'mon, c'mon," Peter Vigianni muttered.

Almost at his bidding, the cars began to inch forward again. Up ahead a column of thick black smoke speared skyward; horns began to blow and traffic halted once again.

Carlo suddenly pointed ahead. "Look!"

The Don strained forward. There was more smoke now. He saw cars maneuvering for room to get out of the northbound lane; some had made it and were careening back south, leaning at dangerous angles on the riverbank or trying to force paths through the cars to get into the southbound lane. "Carlo," the Don said. "Turn around. Turn around somehow and head back south. Do just like those other guys —"

"Something's happening up there," Peter said.

"C'mon, Carlo, get going," the Don said.

"What the hell is it, Carlo?" Peter asked.

Carlo backed and pulled forward, backed and angled once again and finally pulled in a sharp turn back south, kissing the bumper of the car in front of him. The tires screamed and he was glad they were not at a place where there was a divider. Carlo bumped up on the lawn and drove on the grass. Now panic seemed to have touched the drivers of all the cars; like ants they turned this way and that seeking room to get off the road and turn around.

"Now what?" Carlo asked, sweating, although the car was air-conditioned.

"Take the 59th Street bridge." The Don closed his eyes. "It seemed to me that the jigs got to the highway, finally. All that ruckus spilled over. Turn on the radio."

While they gained the streets the radio told them that the highway had been blocked with benches by Negroes who were tossing firebombs at the passing cars. Five cars had burned and were still on the roadway. Rock-throwing and firebombing continued.

"After the bridge?" Carlo asked. They were approaching it now through streets that were all but empty on this Labor Day weekend.

"We go out to the North Shore on the Island and take the ferry to Connecticut. That's the safe way."

"I never would have thought of that, Uncle," Peter said, grinning.

"No," the Don agreed.

They had cleared the bridge; were, in fact, a block from it when they heard the explosions. The Don spun around, almost bumping heads with Angela; Carlo strained to see in the rearview mirror. None of them saw completely the shuddering bridge, but they saw spans crumple with terrible, slow dignity and plummet into the East River below.

They drove on in silence for several moments. "I wonder," the Don said, finally, "if they did that, too. Busy as hell these days, Peter. You ought to be proud of your friend Browning."

Peter, ashen, was pondering the possibility of other

structures they might have to cross; there were none. He said, "Uncle, it is time to fish; it's a good time to take a vacation —"

Dryly, Carlo remarked, "Listen, it may even be time to go back to Italy. They've got fish there, too, you know. Like where I come from, Belluno, the trout are something special —"

"C'mon, Carlo," the Don complained. "Let's make some time before something else happens, and if it does we won't even get a taste of New England trout, let alone those goddamn Belluno trout you're always talking about."

Carlo pressed down on the gas and made one more comment. "What a country, what a country!"

twenty

The broken glass was underfoot; they were married, it was done. Hod accepted Peretz's hand and steadied himself under the man's back-thumping congratulations. Hod led his bride from under the canopy and a happy murmur filled the room as the guests crowded forward, all eager to offer more congratulations.

Hod's eyes were drawn to the elderly Negro couple who, with fixed smiles on their faces, pushed in from the rear of the crowd. The woman worked for the Friedmans, he had discovered. Her husband did not. Hod listened to the strains of a record, *Jerusalem, City of Gold*. Yes, he would have to show Mickey-Siona how the city became golden at sunset. Somehow he lost Mickey and found himself surrounded by men. The drinks came — served by another, younger Negro in black pants, white jacket and black tie. The *l'chaims* were repeated endlessly.

Another Israeli record was played, a haunting, Semitic tune that wailed of love down through the centuries, and then the records became more lively. Hod set down his drink and went to his bride.

"Watch," he said. "This is a dance of joy."

He knew the record; it had begun slowly and he moved with it, thumping and clumping. He reached in his pocket and pulled out a handkerchief and flailed the air with it. The beat became faster, and without losing time he seized Peretz's hand and drew him into the circle that had formed. Then there were two handkerchief-waving men thumping ponderously around.

"We're not Chasidim," Peretz panted, "but the handkerchiefs, they look good, hah?"

Before his bride, Hod turned in a proud little circle and winked at her. The record was over and someone started to play American music.

"I didn't know you were such a good dancer," Mickey said, marveling as they moved to the music.

"That's because we've never danced before," he said. "I felt there should be a few surprises left for you."

"And you have surprised me."

She watched him lead her mother in a waltz. How careful he was; he made her appear to be a wonderful dancer, so beautifully did he lead her. Mickey's father would never dance with her, she was so awkward, and now he looked on in surprise until he realized that it was his son-in-law who was good, not his wife.

Hod danced and drank, drank and danced. And why shouldn't I kick up my heels? Who should I put on the dog for, these people I'll never see again, except, maybe, Mickey's folks? Tomorrow night, 11:30, and *foof*, off to Eretz Yisrael, not by boat, but plane. Direct, nonstop. Toledo some other time.

Mr. Friedman had insisted. "Look what's going on

here," he had said. "The schvartzes and the cops, two days and no one knows what's happening next. The city is in for a blood bath. No, you don't wait for the fifteenth; you go the day after the wedding; yes, Sunday night; who knows what's going to happen on Labor Day. Zim, El Al, they're Israeli government, no? Then you make a deal, everything is deals with travel these days anyway, no? Better still, get the money back; I'll pay the fare. First-class on Friedman, how about that, Mr. Israeli? You ever had a father-in-law like me before? Well, listen, I never had a son-in-law like *you* before, neither!"

Hod had agreed. Why not, what remained here? They had no fear of what might happen in the city, but they felt their new life should begin as soon as possible. Yes, Toledo some other time.

Now Peretz was pulling him aside. Hod followed his eyes as he surveyed the guests with cold self-satisfaction. "Do you know, everyone's talking about a trip somewhere, to Israel, maybe?" A smile touched his lips. "You know, Hod, it just might be that a big race war would be the thing that could bring us some American Jews, what do you think?"

Hod knew Peretz was not expecting an answer. In a different tone, Peretz said, "So how's the jewelry business in Israel with expansion all over the place, eh?" He smiled slyly. "How did you manage to get past such a sharp American cookie?"

Uncomfortable, Hod said, "Well, you have to work on these things, you know." He had come to like Friedman in just the few days he'd known him.

"The girl, your wife, does she know?"

"She knows I'm not going into the jewelry business. The other things, Peretz, she does not know about. Do you understand, *she does not know.* You and me, we've made our deal. We're going to the settlement —"

Peretz wagged a finger. "Tut-tut, Hod. You're now a man of capital, I'm told, and do you know, your father-in-law is thinking of combinations: his fabrics and your jewelry and perhaps even a special line of Israeli fabrics to go with your jewelry. So! What this means is that it might be possible after a short stay at the settlement for you to get out and put that capital and these plans to use."

"I don't know anything about business," Hod protested.

Peretz waved the finger again. "Don't despair; your wife, she might know."

"Well," Hod began. "You know I didn't want the money. I guess I did and I do now, but —"

"Relax, Hod. It's only money," Peretz said. "Now don't hold me to it, but I think some things are possible. We're assuming that you've reformed, that the sight or smell of an Arab doesn't send you into killing rages. We have to assume that . . ." Peretz paused as though he was considering something else to say, then said, "We'll see," and walked away.

Hod felt Mickey's hand on his arm; he knew the touch and feel of it so perfectly that he didn't have to look. "Why so pensive?" she asked. "Why so deep in thought?"

He patted her hand. "Maybe because I've never been married before."

She said, "It's too late to think about it, much too late."

The next evening they crowded into the small El Al waiting room at Kennedy. Here were the Chasidim, the tour groups, the harassed-looking hostesses and stewards; here were the movie cameras gripped tightly, the handbags looped securely over the shoulders.

The hostesses led them down a back stair and on to the 707. Cries of goodbye filled the air and were barely heard above the whine of the engines.

When they were airborne and had craned their necks until the lights of New York faded behind them, Hod and Mickey tilted their chairs and went to sleep.

Dawn came rushing up, too soon, midway over the Atlantic and the stewards and hostesses began to thump and pound up and down the aisles which were filling with people too restless to stay in their seats.

"Please, everyone, take your seats," the stewards asked, but no one moved. Only the lox and bagels sent them to their seats, and as soon as the trays were collected they were in the aisles again, their humor growing as the plane drew nearer, passing over the Alps, Florence, Athens, and then homing in on Tel Aviv. Now lines stretched from the rest rooms forward and when they ended and everyone was strapped in once again, they entered Israeli air space.

Hod said to Mickey with a motion of his hand as they approached Lydda, "Look. Tel Aviv. We're home."

She clutched his hand and stared out the window. Streets, cars, palm trees; houses, apartments, buildings. Home. Throughout the plane she heard voices raised in exclamations. Here it was, a little piece of sand, rock and very little plain — home; and it had taken over two thousand years to get it. But it was there and there was someplace in it for every Jew that walked the earth; all he had to do was come get it.

Now the pilot was putting on power. They felt the

plane lunge slightly ahead and suddenly the runway was beneath them. So smooth was the landing that they did not feel the first bump; then the craft seemed to settle gently on its haunches. The passengers broke into applause that could not be deafened by the engines being reversed.

twenty-one

The morning before the first police raids, Gene Browning had stalked deliberately into Barton's office. He had planted himself squarely in front of his desk. "Bill, I have got to get away for a few days. Now, let me tell you just how it is before you answer. I'm taking off, whether it means the job or not, because I don't really care about it any more."

Barton had been glaring at him, but now, like a balloon being slowly deflated, he relaxed. "Yeah, man. Okay, sit down. Don't stand there like you'll be at my throat in the next second. Sit the hell down."

When Browning had sat, Barton said, "Take the time, Gene. You've more than earned it. I needed someone to lean on here. IRJ has gone the way of so many organizations I've worked for, so I've got to get my hat again, too. I tell you that in case you want to, one, get yours as well, or two, take over my position and try to get this thing back on its feet." He pounded a huge fist into his opened hand. "God-damn it, if I could just get a lead on Greene—" He looked bleakly at Browning and said, "Yeah, I'm still for that. I'd make the trade, Greene for a chance to continue on a full budget and help hundreds. I see it as a fair trade," he said belligerently.

"Maybe I'll never know how it's supposed to work," Browning said. "The government will give us money to keep going if we find Greene, but it doesn't give a damn about our intervening for the militants — which we can't really do anyway because we haven't got the bread. Beats me. When are you planning to leave?"

Barton threw out his hands. "Just as soon as I can get me a gig, that's when."

"I'm leaving too," Browning heard himself saying. "I can't cut it any more."

Barton closed his eyes and nodded. "I could see it coming."

"Maybe Dunbar or Tate could replace you," Browning said.

Barton nodded even more vigorously. "Where in the hell did it all go, Gene? That's what I don't understand."

"Maybe working from within instead of outside the system. Can't be done, just can't be done; if you're working inside the system then you're not working at all." Browning felt an immense relief.

Barton said, "You going back to teaching?"

Browning shrugged. "It's all I know, that and this, but I won't teach the way I taught before. I'm going to teach down this system, if I can, but I know teaching's a part of it. It's late, but I suppose I'll be able to scare up some part-time lecture work in the schools around town."

Barton spoke as if he hadn't been listening. "You

know when all our troubles started? When that goddamn cop shot that goddamn kid —"

"Yes, but we should've been ready; we should've had our little nest egg together and not been caught short that way. It's the system, man, the goddamn system and we ought to know by now just how it works."

"But you keep hoping," Barton said. "Haven't you ever heard of it?"

"Sometimes I think I invented it," Browning said.

"How long you planning on being away?"

He sneaked that one in, Browning thought. "Starting this afternoon, right through the Labor Day weekend, ten days, maybe a couple more."

"Then you'll come back and help me clean up things here? Will you, man? I'm going to need help. Who would you recommend to take my place, Tate or Dunbar?"

Browning studied him for a long second. "Do you really think it makes a difference, now?"

Barton had already arrived at that conclusion and now he grimaced at the sharpness of Browning's comment.

Browning rose. "Okay, I'm gone."

"Tell the family hello, will you?"

Browning had reached the door when he heard Barton say: "Oh! Got a note from Braithwaite this morning. Says to tell you hello."

Browning had not turned around and his breath caught in him, held him motionless waiting for the blow, which did not fall. He heard himself saying, "He's a nice guy."

"Wish we had his money. See you, man."

Browning passed through the door and closed it behind him, his stomach churning. In a daze he made his way to his own office, gathered a few things and walked down the stairs; he felt he had to move to fight off the shock. Had he taken the elevator he would have shaken all the way down.

Unthinking, he rushed into the street and hailed a taxi, and was not even surprised when it came to a stop for him. He rode to the nearest car rental, checked out a car and drove home. He parked quickly and rushed into his building. He had to get away from the Bartons, the Braithwaites (whom he'd almost forgotten), the Mantinis — the hurricane of threats that seemed to have gathered overhead all of a sudden.

He hurriedly typed a few notes to people he knew in the political science departments of the local colleges, stamped the envelopes and wandered through the apartment thinking of things to take to the country. He paused before the window that gave the view of the Harlem rooftops. Dun-colored dynamite. With Greene on the loose.

When he had changed clothes he went back downstairs, got into the car and drove uptown, toward the Triboro Bridge. He would surprise the family; he'd just drive up and the week or so of vacation would commence. He had to hurry to beat the outward-bound traffic that soon would be filling the Expressway.

The additional lanes of the Triboro swept in a great concrete and steel curve almost over Randall's Island. They'd needed the new lanes for years. Now they were already obsolete. Idling cars stood in endless lines before each booth from which toll collectors, most of them black, leaned in and out taking coins and passing change.

Once past the booths, he pressed the accelerator and managed to maintain a high, steady speed all the way out. He longed to feel the ocean on his shoulders, eat corn cooked in its shucks, littlenecks filled with butter, and to drink cold beer. That was going to be nice. Great. He could feel himself relaxing already. He called up images of driving up to the house, and amid laughter, being greeted by his girls.

It was about dinnertime when he pulled into the driveway, surprised to see the car gone. Oh, hell, he thought. Suppose they'd all gone to a movie or something, what was he supposed to do, cool his heels on the doorstep until they came back? Make a bonfire on the beach? Hell, he was hungry. He didn't give a damn whether he'd called or not; he wanted to be with his family, eat with them, especially right now.

But now Nora came out of the house, a shocked look rapidly being replaced by a bright smile; and then Chris, looking somewhat apprehensive. Both were in halters and ragged dungaree shorts, no shoes.

"Surprise," he said. "Where's your mother?"

Chris said, "Oh, she went into town, said she might take in a movie or something."

Nora bounced down the stairs to take his bag. "But we're still here, won't we do?"

Browning thought he saw strain in her face, but he kissed her and Chris and said, "Everything going all right? How's Woody? How's your love life, Chris? Hear you got yourself a cute little fella. Anyway, I'm hungry as hell and I sure wish your mother were here."

"How long this time, Daddy?" Chris asked. They had climbed the stairs now and entered the house.

"How about ten, twelve days, how's that grab you?"

"That's great," Nora said. "Glad you finally got that

nasty Billy Barton to give you the time off. How about some franks, beans and beer?"

"Kid, if that's the best you got, I'll take it. Tomorrow, though, we're going to have a feast. I may even barbecue some ribs."

He left the girls to prepare his dinner and stepped inside the bedroom he and Val used. He stopped, stunned for a moment. Sure it was a small, haphazardly put-together summer house with too little closet space, but Val had always been neat about things no matter what. The bed was unmade and clothes were scattered on it, the backs of chairs or on the floor. Puzzled and feeling as though he were on the verge of some new knowledge, Browning walked slowly around the room, picking up her things and hanging them up. A frown creased his forehead. Val had never been like this; a stranger seemed to have been sleeping in their room.

Back in the kitchen, crouched over his plate, he said irritably, "It's not like your mother to go off at dinnertime." He glared at Nora, who moved her shoulders helplessly. She said, "Daddy, I know you just got here and you're upset because Mother's not here, so I hate to ask you . . ."

"Hell, go ahead and ask."

"Daddy, can I borrow your car so we can go to a movie over in East Hampton? This is the last night and I promised Chris we'd have like a girls' night."

Almost absentmindedly Browning nodded. "You're playing mother now. Good. What time you be home?"

"About half past eleven."

Browning looked up. "Just how long's your mother been gone?" He saw the glance that Chris gave her sister, but Nora said, "Actually, just a little while before you came; a few minutes before you came." She had not ac-

knowledged her sister's look. Then again, he was not at all
sure he had really seen the looks.

"The car's yours," he said. "Got some money?"

"We got," Nora said.

They whisked into their room and in minutes were
back in skirts and blouses. They kissed him goodbye and he
stood in the door and watched them back out. "Have fun,"
he said, but he was not sure they'd heard him.

For a long moment he listened to the sea grinding
softly against the beach not far away. And the crickets were
picking up volume. It was going to be a clear night with a
three-quarter moon. Now, he thought, if Val were only here;
we could have a couple of drinks and make it as wild as we
wanted to with the kids gone a few hours. The house carried
every sound, but with them away — *wow!* Then he had an
idea. He peeled off his shirt and trousers. When she came
in, he was going to be ready for action, and she'd better be
getting back soon.

In the bedroom he came out of his underwear and,
whistling, decided to place her diaphragm on her pillow, so
she'd get the idea in case he fell asleep. Once, with some
embarrassment, he bought a gadget called a Panic Button.
You pushed the button and a little flag came up. On the flag
it said, "Let's." He didn't know what happened to it, but he
had worn it on his pajama tops for a while. Val didn't take
the pills; too much trouble with weight fluctuations. Where
in the hell is it? he wondered, going through her pantie
drawer where she kept it. He found the case and, grinning,
carried it to her pillow and opened it. The diaphragm was
gone.

He felt as if his stomach had fallen away. He stared at
the empty case, touched its emptiness with a finger, then

snapped it shut and returned it to her drawer. No, he thought, taking it out again. He studied it for a moment and then hurled it as hard as he could against the wall. The effort drained him; the effort, the diaphragm, his secrets, and he fell on the bed, nude, and drifted into a troubled sleep.

He awoke when he heard the car door slam and at once his heart commenced to race. Was it the kids or Val?

He heard the high heels striking the steps and then Val's voice: "Hey, where are you kids?"

Browning heard their room door bang against the wall and his wife saying to herself, thickly, "Where can they be? Oh, maybe down on the beach."

By this time she had entered the room where Browning lay tight against himself. She flicked on the switch and the room filled with light. Browning had propped himself up on one arm, a thoroughly theatrical pose, he knew, but it seemed to still his anger.

"Oh, Gene!" she said. Emotions chased one after the other over her face and one of brightness finally settled on it. "You frightened me." She giggled. "Where are your clothes, man? Why didn't you call? When did you come? Where are the kids? Oh, I'm so glad you're here." She came forward to kiss him and he slipped his mouth past hers.

She drew back, subduing panic in her eyes. "No kiss, eh?" she said evenly. "Feeling evil, I guess."

Browning was surprised to discover that his voice was level and steady. "I drove out. The kids took the car to go to a movie in East Hampton. Maybe they didn't want to see the same movie you saw. I got here" — he glanced at his watch — "three and a half hours ago. The kids said you'd left only a few minutes before." He watched her as she began to undress, her back to him. "You've got quite a load on you, haven't you, baby?" he said.

"I had a couple," she said. "I stopped afterward and had a couple."

"I thought maybe they'd started serving it in the movies out here."

"It gets pretty lonely around here, you know, Gene. Listen, I'm sorry I wasn't home. I didn't know you were coming."

"Since when did you start leaving the kids to get their own dinner? You always insisted on the family eating together. You used to get real salty at me if I couldn't make it to dinner."

"I needed to get out, Gene."

"You sure got out while you were getting," Browning bitterly.

"I'm going to take a shower," Val said.

"I guess maybe you'd better."

"What do you mean?" she said cautiously, her voice unsteady.

"Look, Val, see that diaphragm case over there on the floor?"

She cast a wild look at him and then turned around and in the turning stiffened and a moan escaped from her.

Browning said, "Just get on with your shower and everything's going to be real cool, I mean real cool. We aren't going to have any things in front of the kids —"

She started to cry.

"— What the hell are *you* crying for? Because you got caught? That's the only reason you got to cry, Val. I came out because I wanted to be with you and the girls. There're a lot of things going on and I was tired of the office, tired of that empty apartment, tired of the city. The girls went off. I might as well have been back in Manhattan, but I think they left because they knew. Then I thought when you came back, we'd hop right in the sack and really do it up. I wanted you to wake me up if I fell asleep; I wanted you to know that I wanted you. So I got your diaphragm, only it was gone. I assume you're wearing it."

Her face seemed to crumble and she fell to her knees with a thump and her body came forward until her face touched the floor. He dressed hurriedly and went out to the car and drove to the beach. He sat smoking, watching a fire and kids sitting around it, passing a bottle of something they were drinking. Kids. Old enough to get hard-ons, they weren't really kids any more. The waves washed in, boiling white, to crash against the shore and hiss back out to sea. He thought of and resolved many things sitting there until the kids extinguished the bonfire and drove away, leaving him, he felt, almost alone in the world, pressed somewhere between sea and sky now emptying itself of the bright moon. He could almost feel the hours pushing heavily past him. He searched his pack for a final cigarette, and finding none, decided to return home.

The kitchen light was on and Nora was waiting up. "Hi," she said, studying his face carefully.

Browning frowned at the cigarette she was smoking. There was a wan, exhausted air about the house. "How was the movie?"

"Chuck got the chick in the end, you know, but in between there was some good stuff. Want a drink? Coffee, Daddy?"

"Oh, I guess a little Scotch and water. Why don't you have one with me?"

She rose to fix them and with her back turned she said, "Mother's sleeping. The doctor's been here."

"What?" Browning looked up, startled. "What for?"

"When we came home she was in hysterics. Babbling to herself, crying, scratching herself up, so weak she couldn't get off the floor. At first I thought she was just —"

"Drunk?" Browning said, already on his way to the bedroom.

"He gave her something to calm her down . . ." Nora said, placing the drinks on the table.

Browning pushed open the door and saw Val lying flat on her back, her arms thrown above her head as if awaiting a sacrificial knife. He went closer and looked down at her in the subdued light. Her breathing was steady and deep, her face crisscrossed with scratches. Browning returned to the kitchen and took the drink Nora handed to him. "Give me the doctor's number."

As he dialed he studied Nora. How much did she know? Something, something. "Woody okay?" He realized that it was a ridiculous time to ask about Woody, but he was reaching for balance and he thought she understood that as soon as he asked.

"Doctor," he said into the phone. "I'm sorry to call so late, or early, but this is Mr. Browning. You were here earlier to see my wife. Tell me something about what's going on . . ."

Val would be out all night, no need to worry. The doctor would be around the first thing in the morning. Just try to keep it quiet if she woke up early. The problem? She was just terribly upset and anxious; hysterics.

When he hung up Nora said, "You two had a fight, didn't you?"

Browning clung tiredly to the phone. "We didn't have a fight; we had a few words. Have you ever known me to fight with your mother?"

"It's the same thing," Nora said. "I wouldn't expect you to fight with your *hands*. What happened, can I ask?"

"Sure you can ask, but that don't mean you're getting an answer. You ain't that grown," he growled. He took a large swallow of his drink and rested his head on his arms. "Why do women think they're the only ones who ever get lonely and scared? The whole damned human race is like that."

"I'll get you another drink, Daddy."

"No you won't. I'll get it. You go on to bed. Chris all right?"

"She was a little shook up, but she's okay now. How about you?"

"I'm all right. I'll just sit up; hang around in case your mother needs me. Go to bed, baby."

"Daddy, you ought to go to bed, too. You don't look so good."

Browning lowered his head to his arms once more and said, "Go on, girl. I'm probably the best-looking thing you'll ever see in life. Put your little rusty-dusty in bed. I don't want to have to tell you again."

"Okay, g'night."

"See you, baby."

When the door had closed, he glanced at his watch; half-past three, what was the use of going to sleep now? He rose and felt the weariness attack his legs. He fixed himself another drink and went to the sun porch from where he could see two forlorn lights down along the road; they seemed to sway back and forth, but he knew that it was the branches of trees moving back and forth in the wind that caused such a saddening effect. He turned the radio on and sat down; it had been a long time since he listened to the late jazz shows. He swung the dial back and forth until he located what sounded like a soul station. And there was jazz, the old jazz that strained against the formal restrictions until they appeared to burst. Chuck had managed to kill jazz too, almost, with his rock groups and their superficial, adolescent scores. But here it was pouring softly out of the box, real jazz with the great instrumentalists from another time. Yet they had been within *his* time, too. Then I've lived a thousand years, a thousand, thousand years.

The music was faded under the announcer's voice. Gangs of white men in Harlem, Bedford-Stuyvesant and in over fifty cities. Negro death toll reported at 15; 62 critically wounded. The attacks were thought to have been for the purpose of avenging the deaths of white policemen in recent weeks.

Browning had come upright with the news. He waited for more. There came the rustle of paper and the announcer spoke again. Morris Greene was being sought now by the Montgomery, Alabama, police in connection with the slaying of Herman Mahler, the man convicted of killing three Negro coeds in a dynamiting two years ago. Greene? Aw, no. Couldn't be, Browning thought. Maybe Trotman? It was Trotman's sister who'd been killed. How did Greene get mixed up in it? What in the hell was going on? Had Greene and Trotman fallen out?

So, he thought. The simple, selective violent act, calculated to deliver a message, had become magnified. All the black populace he had been trying to save from slaughter looked like it was being slaughtered after all. If only they hadn't started killing those cops! Then Mahler's death could have had the same meaning Carrigan's should have had. What would Mantini know about Mahler's death?

Aw, man, he thought. It's too much, just too much, and he pulled up a nearby blanket and turned the radio even lower and began turning the dial again. This he had to follow. The *Times* would be in at ten. Somewhere between the listening and dialing he fell asleep.

He knew it was still very early when he awoke because the morning still held the quality of suspension that the night had held. Val was sitting before him, holding a cup of hot black coffee.

"Hi," she said in a whisper. "How do you feel?"

"Hi, yourself," he said. "I feel kind of woozy. How do you feel?" He took the cup. Now he could see that her scratches had been daubed with Merthiolate. He took one of her arms and looked at the deep scratches on it. Her eyes were puffed. "You ought to be in bed, Val. The doctor's coming back this morning."

"I'm going back. Whatever he gave me has still got me, but I just wanted to know you were here. I came out of it and didn't find you in bed and" — the tears started to come again — "I got frightened again, Gene, and I could feel that stinking old loneliness clear down to my toes. I looked at the kids' room and you weren't there. So I came out here . . ."

"Where in the world did you think I'd be?"

She shrugged. "I thought you might be going somewhere; isn't that the way this thing goes?"

He sipped the coffee that was so hot it made him jump. He looked around for a cigarette. "Gimme a cigarette, baby."

She fumbled in the pocket of her robe and passed them to him. He lit up and said, "Phaww. Jesus, why don't they start doing something about nicotine addiction?"

"Gene, you didn't answer my question."

Browning lifted his head sharply and darted his cigarette toward her. "Woman, go on back to bed. I'm not going anywhere; nowhere at all." He lowered his head and his voice and said bitterly, "Shit, I've been lonely myself."

She pulled the robe up to her face to conceal the tears; she tried to speak, but her convulsing body would not let the words through. She was a fortyish mass of quivering, flowered robe and Browning reached over and stroked her arm and she went, head still bent, into the house and back to bed.

The news was covered more fully now that it was morning, and Browning followed each detail until Chris came to get him for breakfast. He put his arm around her as they went in. Things must be coming pretty thick and fast for her, Browning thought. True, she liked the truth of things straight out, no fooling around, but too much of it at fifteen . . .

"How's mother?" they asked at breakfast. They ate quietly.

"She was up already," Browning said, noticing that his tone had carried a hint of pride. "She had a little coffee and went on back to bed. We'll just try to keep it a little bit quiet until the doctor comes."

Nora said, "Will she be up for the barbecue?"

Browning frowned. This was not like Nora. "No barbecue, I'm afraid, until your mother feels up to it. It'll keep a day or two, won't it?"

Nora nodded.

Minutes later when Chris left the table to carry in orange juice and coffee to her mother, Browning said to Nora: "You knew, didn't you, hotshot?"

Nora's eyes widened. Yes, Browning decided. Her eyes are too wide, like an unseasoned actor trying to convey something to the balcony. "Knew what, Daddy?" *

He turned away from her, but turning back said, "Good. Let's just keep it right at that."

He returned to the radio after breakfast and stayed with it until the doctor came. Val could get up later, in the afternoon, and sit on the porch or in the yard. Take it easy a couple of days. No problem. As soon as the doctor left, Browning got into his car and drove to town, the radio going, his mind sifting this information, checking it with what he already knew or thought and deciding then on the accuracy of the news. Now reports were coming in about organized sniping in Los Angeles; the snipers were black. Jessup, maybe, Browning thought. Going while the going's good.

He picked up the *Times* and started to read it while standing in the street, then he caught himself. This ain't very cool, he thought, returned to his car and drove home. He planted himself in front of the radio and opened the paper. There had been no report so far of cops or "white toughs" invading the Watts section of Los Angeles. Too big, Browning thought, too dangerous. But now his eye caught a box: "An apparently well-disciplined group of snipers, reported to be black, have thrown the Crenshaw shopping area into panic. . . ."

Jessup. Browning set his lips firmly; yes, Jessup. Five police officers killed in the Crenshaw area. Ah, Jessup trying to draw the cops out there into Watts, perhaps, and then the people would do just as the people are doing elsewhere. Round robin: killaniggerkillacrackerkillaniggerkillacracker. By midafternoon when Val joined him on the porch, Browning was nearly exhausted with listening. There had been no call from Barton and that was the surest sign that his ties with IRJ were at an end. Browning and his wife were like two patients in a sanitarium; both lay on couches and gazed listlessly through the tree branches and leaves to the calm blue sea. The girls were already on the beach. What were they talking about, thinking about?

"It sounds like the end of the world," Val said. "It's out of a nightmare."

"It's both," Browning said, getting up to get himself a beer.

Inside, he looked at the telephone. What, no call, Mantini? Aren't you going to bug me just a little bit about what's happening? Oh, come on, now. Ring, you bastard. Then he thought, Okay, *don't* ring.

He saw the sports car pull slowly into the driveway. A young man, maybe twenty, was at the wheel. He drove in with the assurance of one who had been in the driveway before. Woody Chance. He was tall and well tanned; his hair was between brown and blond from the sun. His regular face was composed, his eyes keen. Browning smiled at the nub of a beard beginning to fret on the youth's chin, the stretching sideburns.

He clutched a tightly rolled towel. Browning went to the porch to meet him. The youth came steadily up the stairs. "Hello, Mr. Browning." He glanced at Val, wrapped tightly in her robe, her eyes masked by sunglasses. "Mrs. Browning."

"Hi, Woody," Browning said. They shook hands.

Browning glanced at Val. She leaned forward and gave the boy her hand and he said, "Mrs. Browning, that's the first time we've ever shaken hands."

"Yes," she said. "I'm sorry."

Now Woody smiled. "So am I," he said softly.

"Want a beer to hold you until you get to the beach where Nora is?"

"Sure, thank you, sir."

Browning walked into the kitchen, the boy loping behind him.

"Mr. Browning," he said, once they were alone, "I really wanted to see you."

Browning opened a bottle and handed it to him and leaned against the sink. "C'mon, now. You're not asking for her hand or some such dated crap, are you?"

"Well, no, sir. Not yet, anyway. Here." Hastily he put down his towel and unrolled it. Two handguns, an automatic and a revolver, and two boxes of ammunition.

Browning remained still. "What's this?"

"Well —" Woody was red in the face. He started again. "I've been listening to the news, too. And you know some of those guys over in East Hampton — the Sea Scape guys; well, they're trying to get together and shoot up the black neighborhood there and maybe come over here, so —"

"How long have you had those things, man?"

The boy sighed and said firmly, "Three years."

"Jesus," Browning said. "Jesus."

"I thought I'd hang around, Mr. Browning. I can sleep on the porch or something —"

"Wrap those things up, Woody."

Slowly, looking questioningly at Browning, the boy did as he was told. "Now what?" he said.

"Give them to me." Browning reached and took the towel. He looked at Woody a long time, then opened the cupboard door, placed the towel in it and said, "We'll keep them up here. Ever use them?"

"No, sir."

Browning forced a grin. "A helluva lot of help you're going to be — if your boys decide to come."

The boy shrugged. "What's to know? You load them, point them and pull the trigger."

Browning touched the youth on the shoulder. "A final thing before you go to the beach: do your parents know where you are?"

"Yes, sir. I gave them your number."

"Okay, man. Go ahead and look after my girl. Her sister's with her."

Val's eyes followed Woody away from the house toward the beach, then she said, "Good news or bad?"

"Good. He's going to stay with us for a while."

"That's good news?"

"Said some of those Sea Scape nuts in East Hampton were going to have a shoot-out with the brothers over there and maybe here. Brought something over to make the whole thing a little more equal, if it happens." He looked anxiously at his wife.

"We'd better pull the cars behind the house, down the hill," she said. "And there's a loose wallboard in our closet. You'll find a .22 rifle there. I bought it a few years ago from a farmer out here. Never did like being in the country without something to put my hand on."

Without a word, Browning got up and one by one drove the cars carefully to the rear of the house. Then he got the .22. The magazine was full. "Are there any more shells around?" he asked.

"Same place. A box."

When he had thoroughly checked the .22, he returned to the porch.

"What do you think?" Val asked.

"Maybe, maybe not. What do you think of the Chance boy now?"

Val gave a half-smile behind her glasses. "Maybe I made a mistake, maybe I did."

"Feeling better?"

Val said, "In some ways all cured, in others, sick as hell. Gene, I'm really and truly sorry —"

"We've got to start talking again, Val, about all kinds of things, dreams, fears, failures. That used to keep us going when we were young, eighteen, even twenty-five and thirty, running like hell from lower-middle-class backgrounds and not knowing it; gossiping about people on the faculties where we were. We don't even talk about money worries any more, Val, do you know that?

"Remember when we began to discover Negro history — twenty-five years old and *blam!* there it was, and it was sort of like peeling an onion, one thing leading to another, translucent, slippery, thin. Remember when we started to feed it to the kids and Nora's reaction: 'But that means slavery had existed for two hundred fifty years when Jefferson wrote the Declaration of Independence and all those people signed it!' And Chris's reaction: 'Daddy, why do people tell lies like that?' "

"Darling," Val said. "I know, I remember, but you started to go inside yourself at Weston when you got so deeply involved in things; your manner was that we ought to have known that you had to put everything, *everything* into the Movement. We made love in a hurry; your mind was always somewhere else, and if not that, you were always *going* somewhere, and there we were, waiting, always waiting for you to come back to us . . ."

He said, "Val, you're a woman, I'm a man. I mean a man. So, one morning, I don't even know when it was, one morning I woke up and the enormity of what's been done to us was resting like a ball of badly digested lead in my stomach, but it had got down; it went down, and I couldn't pretend any more that it had no meaning for me. Not only for me but for all the Negroes out there. And I knew I had a family, too, that needed care and love, and I hoped they understood."

"We did, but —"

"The buts are something I've been learning all summer."

The girls with Woody remained in the house all evening. The family gathered on the porch in the darkness and listened to the radio and watched the headlights of cars rush past on the highway; none slowed or stopped. It was Woody who said, his voice rising with excitement, "They're fighting back!"

One by one the family peeled off in the early hours of the morning to go to bed until Browning remained alone at the radio. Woody snored softly on the couch Val had used. Dawn caught Browning still up, groggily listening to scattered reports and trying, with an uncooperative mind, to sort them out again.

He remained up during the day and when the reports came of the destruction of the bridges and tunnels and the announcement of Greene's demands, he retired to bed for a few hours. Hours later, he woke and stumbled red-eyed to the porch. The house was strangely silent. The bright sunshine blinded him for a moment, then he saw his wife.

"Baby, where's everybody?"

"Down on the beach," she said. "They insisted. 'Life's got to go on,' said Woody, and they went with Chris."

"Why are you all dressed?"

"I thought I'd feel better," Val said.

"You do," Browning said. "Say, how long have they been gone?"

"About ten minutes. Are you going, too?"

He did not answer. Instead he took her hand and said gently, "C'mon." He led her into their bedroom and without a word he began to undress her. When she stood before him, naked, the shyest of small happy smiles on her face, he too undressed. He was already hard, and as he lay her down, he thought of the second time they'd ever made love; not in a closet filled with musty clothes, but in a borrowed room. She curled her legs around him as he entered her, touched her deeply, and she found that her eyes were wet. She thought this would take a long, long time to do again, but they began to move together, to rock, and her hands were on his hips pulling him closer and deeper and they arrived at the same point together and then he led her to points still higher until she felt that one more would start her trembling so much that she would not be able to stop for hours; it used to be this way. And now, as if leisurely approaching the crest of a steeply inclined hill, she felt his movements quicken again just slightly, and he hesitated, delaying the moment, then let himself go, and she received him firmly and she began to babble: "I want to talk, I want to talk," she said, and without waiting, "I'm sorry, I'm sorry, I'm sorry."

She stroked his back and he said, "Better. It's going to be better."

She did not know exactly what he was talking about, but she reached for him with both hands and gently kneaded him until he was hard again and then, hands held around him as if in supplication, guided him back into her. That was the way with things.